CASUALTIES

CASUALTIES

TERRENCE HEATH

COTEAU
BOOKS

Edited by Edna Alford.
Book and cover design by Duncan Campbell.
Cover image, *Loyalist Offensive along the Rio Segre, near Fraga (Aragon front). November 7, 1938.* © Robert Kapa / Magnum.

Printed and bound at Gauvin Press.

Library and Archives Canada Cataloguing in Publication

Heath, Terrence, 1936-
Casualties / Terrence Heath.

ISBN 1-55050-318-9

I. Title.

PS8565.E18C39 2005   C813'.54   C2005-904906-5

1   2   3   4   5   6   7   8   9   10

2517 Victoria Ave.
Regina, Saskatchewan
Canada S4P 0T2

Available in Canada & the US from
Fitzhenry & Whiteside
195 Allstate Parkway
Markham, on, Canada, L3R 4T8

The publisher gratefully acknowledges the financial assistance of the Saskatchewan Arts Board; the Canada Council for the Arts; the Government of Canada through the Book Publishing Industry Development Program (BPIDP); and the City of Regina Arts Commission, for its publishing program.

  Canadä

This novel is dedicated to my dear sister,

Anne Moulding,

*who lived through many of the events
described here and who related to me many
of the family stories that are background
to the tale I tell*

CHAPTER ONE

It was now two o'clock in the morning. The house was still. From the distance came the sporadic sound of cars passing on the throughway. "What did it mean?" Clara held the piece of paper almost warily, its creased sections hanging from each other. In the past three hours, she had read the letter many times. "Why would he have kept it, hidden?"

To see her, you wouldn't think she was in her sixties. Her hair was greying, well, whitening now, but with a good deal of assistance from her hairdresser, was a pale, straw blonde. She combed it back in a faultless sweep and kept it in place with a Spanish-style comb. There were a few lines around her eyes and mouth, but not many, and her skin had the soft, cared-for look of the wealthy. She sat in the middle of the couch in front of the fireplace and stared into the flames. Her chair and Chuck's chair were at either end of the couch and stood empty. The funeral and wake had been over by five o'clock. The last friend had gone home, wishing her well, caressing her with good advice and trying to be as up as possible in the situation. They had tried to keep their minds on the occasion and her loss, but she could hear conversation drift back to their everyday concerns, had even caught a bit of laughter over something said.

Afterwards she had just wandered around the house, putting things away, shifting chairs to their proper places, picking up glasses. She threw out the remaining sandwiches and left the dishes for Mary to do in the morning. Then she had decided to get a grip on matters and had gone upstairs and started to sort through his desk and closet. The sooner she got on with her life the better, she had thought. But, after she took his clothes out of the closet, she had broken down in tears on the bed and sobbed until she could cry no more. It was after that she had found the letter.

She lifted the paper and began again to read the lines she had read so often since she had found the letter folded up in the inside pocket of his tuxedo. A secret place certainly. She never looked in his pockets in any case – Chuck didn't like her prying, as he called it, into his things – and, it had been quite a few years now since they had gone regularly to "black tie" events. Why had she gone to that suit, to that pocket, today of all days? The funeral was over, the wake had ended, and she had suddenly been alone. Alone in her black dress. Perhaps she had unconsciously remembered that she had last worn this dress when they had gone to the Sapphire Ball. Perhaps she had wanted to reach him again, just once more, to touch and smell the fabric of his clothes. Or to remember his arm around her as they danced to the old music, what she still called "underwater music."

The letter was not dated but she could tell from the brittle paper that it must predate the Second World War for it was the kind of paper they had used for airmail letters in the thirties. So long ago – another life. It had been in a sealed, unaddressed envelope, as if ready for a now undiscoverable addressee. No stamps. Had he ever meant to post it? For a friend? To whom?

How easily she might have packed up all the clothes, including the tuxedo, and sent them to the Sally Ann without looking in the pockets. She hadn't wanted to know what was in the pockets of his suits, if anything. Nevertheless, when she had cried herself out, she had set his other suits aside and gone straight to his tuxedo. In going through the pockets, she had found business cards, a handkerchief, faded instructions for tying a bow tie, and this letter.

She reread the cryptically short message:

I killed Margaret. I had to do it. She would have died anyway, perhaps even more horribly. Her body lies in a shallow cave on the road near the railway building on the east side of the mountain. It is about three kilometres from Teruel. There is no forgiveness.
Thomas Pennan

It was typed on some old typewriter that filled in the *o*'s and had wonky letters in other places. After the typed name, someone had scrawled a large letter that looked like a *T*. She turned the paper over and felt the indentations of the letters on the other side. Some of the letters had almost broken through the paper as if they had been hit harder than

3

necessary. And that was all. No address, no explanation, no instructions.

How long had Chuck carried it in his tuxedo pocket? Why would Chuck have been carrying such a letter in his pocket? Who was Thomas Pennan? Where was Teruel? Ought she to tell someone about it? But, who? She and Chuck had celebrated their forty-fourth anniversary last summer – over forty years married, and she was sure she had never heard him mention a Thomas Pennan. Nor did they know any other Pennans. She had even looked through his "little black book," as he liked to call it, for a Pennan, but nothing. Perhaps tomorrow she would look through the telephone directory. But not now.

But there had been a Margaret. Before they met. A neighbour, maybe a girlfriend when he was younger? Was this that Margaret? Chuck had never said anything about her death. But he had told her a story once about her mother's death. No, it was her father. He had hanged himself in the shed at the bottom of the yard, near the outdoor privies. Later, Chuck said, he had sat many times in the outhouse and thought he heard the creaking of the rope in the next yard. He'd been almost afraid to come out and had imagined his mother having to come down to the privy to bring him back to the house. Even horror can be funny. Dear, dear Chuck. He was so awkward socially. He must have had a few drinks to have told her that story. He was always reluctant to talk about his early life. She had read somewhere that men, well, women, too, probably, who had risen in society or in work but who did not really have the background for their position often thought of themselves as imposters. Perhaps that was how he had felt, why he didn't talk about his background. She really didn't know all that much about the man she had lived with, shared a bed with, loved.

So long ago now. And so unimportant. But still. If it was the same Margaret and if this Thomas Pennan had killed her and buried her body, she really should tell someone or do something with the letter. It was a confession to murder. She should...Not tonight. Not tonight.

She got to her feet and checked the fireplace. She slowly walked over to the stairs and started up to their bedroom. She grasped the handrail tightly with her right hand and held the letter in her left. The staircase seemed to go on forever. Suddenly she felt very tired and very much her age. It would all have to wait until morning.

At the top she walked into the large bedroom and bent over the clothes, still lying on the bed. She carefully replaced the letter first in its envelope and then in the inside pocket of the tuxedo. Better to leave things the way they were. Her hand caressed the fabric one more time. Then she took down her nightgown and walked across the hall to the spare bedroom. She didn't want to sleep alone in their marriage bed.

CHAPTER TWO

"We get your type here. Boys who think the church is a political pawn for one ragtag socialist party or another. It won't wash, my lad, not with me. Our Lord said, The poor will be always with you. And sit up straight when I am talking to you." The principal's face was red and horribly swollen over his clerical collar. He grasped a yellow pencil so tightly in his left hand the eraser seemed to be squeezing out of its core. The Reverend Jeremiah Keele did not look very Christian at that moment, but then he liked to preach on the wrath of Jehovah and the retribution that was to come to those not of the elect. The United Church may have officially joined Methodist, Presbyterian, and Congregationalist, but its preachers still manifested the characteristics of their original strain of Protestantism.

Thomas could feel his own face flush and begin to sweat. His throat had seized up, he was so angry. He had wanted to scream obscenities at this stupid man. But he had just sat there, reddening, unable to defend himself or the causes he had thought he held so close to his heart. The thought of letting himself be dressed down in this way, without his saying a word, rose like a betrayal in his mind. He had even straightened up.

"Furthermore, this is the third such offence and you have only been with us for one month. You know our rules. You either follow them or leave. And I suggest that you made up your mind when you first left the grounds without permission. Had you even gone to some worthwhile charity event. That might have been excusable, *might* have, but to go to some bolshevik gathering in the North End..." He began to drum the point of the pencil on the top of the blotter on his desk.

"It was not Bolshevik. It was a soup..."

"Bolshevik meeting. I have no choice but to advise you that you will have to leave. Your behaviour not only sets a bad example for your fellow seminarians, but I cannot imagine that you will ever be capable of taking up the work of the Lord. Your sponsor will have to be told that tuition cannot be refunded. You know that, don't you? Don't you?"

"Yes sir."

Yes sir. Is that all he could think to say to the fat bastard? Yes, sir.

Thomas looked out of the train window at the fields lying yellow and parched in the hot autumn sun. The sun glared angrily, it seemed, through the clouds of dirt blowing up from a summerfallow field west of the cropland. The sky was a dirty white. Thomas placed his arm on the window ledge and his sleeve came up covered with a fine layer of dust. Exasperated, he slapped at it with his Bible, sending up a cloud of powdery dust.

"Is that any way to treat the Good Book?" The voice broke into his self-absorbed thoughts almost like an extension of his own thinking. When he realized it was coming from across the aisle, he turned abruptly, self-consciously, to see who had spoken. A young man about his own age, maybe a little older, sat comfortably in the wood-slat seat across the aisle from him. He was dressed in clean, but simple work-man's clothes, bib overalls over a grey shirt, buttoned to the neck. His neck and face were sunburnt. His hair was red – a rich true red, not just a pale copper like Thomas's. His hands were large and he held a cap on his lap.

"Something in there made you angry?"

"No. No, not in the Bible. Something, someone else."

"Not God then?"

Thomas smiled almost in spite of himself and turned back to the speaker. "No, not God. Just someone who thought he was god almighty."

"Ah, there are lots of those. Men who think they are gods and act like devils."

Thomas heard an accent behind the voice. He thought at first it was Irish, like his own slight childhood one, but it was a bit too abrupt, or something. It was comforting though, a confiding sort of voice with perhaps a bit of strangeness to it that made him both attracted to and wary of it.

"It's the Ukrainian you hear. What your people, if I judge you rightly, might call Galician or just plain Bohunk."

Thomas began to protest, but stopped, both because the man was right about his "people" – damn bohunks are causing all this trouble. You mark my words. They should all be sent back to where they came from – and because he had so instinctively and accurately known what Thomas was thinking.

"Peter's my name. Peter Stemichuk. But they call me Chuck."

"Glad to meet you – uh, Chuck." Thomas half got up and leaned over to shake hands. "I'm Thomas. Thomas Pennan."

"Pennan? Now, that would be what? Irish?"

"Well, North Irish. Least my father. He's Protestant and mother's, well, used to be Catholic. My mother's Irish too, but from London. But I'm Canadian."

"So am I." Chuck said it a bit belligerently, perhaps: Thomas later thought he may have been trying to see what his reaction would be.

"Of course. How stupid of me."

"No. It wasn't you that said I was a bohunk. I said that, but I meant a bohunk Canadian, not a bohunk bohunk. So, you can't send me back to where I came from, 'cause I come from here."

"Here? Manitoba?"

"No, Saskatchewan. On the ABC line."

"Oh." Thomas tried to think what the ABC line was, feeling he should know.

"You know, the CN that's got all the towns alphabetically arranged – Hubbard, Ituna, Jasmine, Kerrobert, Lanigan... Don't know if they actually start with *A* before that but when they get close to Saskatoon, they reach *Z*, that's Zelma, and then begin again, Allen, Bradwell, Clavet. You would have thought they could have been a little more imaginative, wouldn't you? Perhaps, named them after a homesteader or maybe even given them some Indian name. Even a bohunk name would have served. Like Stemichuk, perhaps. Well, the railroads are not known for their imagination."

"I come from Regina."

"Ah, a city lad."

It sounded to Thomas like criticism and he, as usual, leaped into a defensive position.

"I grew up on the edge of the city though."

Chuck looked at him closely and then broke into a huge smile that ended in a sort of free, barking laugh.

"I mean, on the outskirts, out by the Mountie barracks."

Chuck stopped laughing and grew suddenly attentive and serious. "Out by the Mountie Barracks, you say?"

"Yeah. When I was a boy, we used to play out there all the time. Watch the Mounties riding and things like that. A neighbour of ours, down the street, wanted to be a Mountie."

"What happened?" Chuck's sudden interest was apparent.

"There were a lot on the list, what with everyone unemployed and all. Then, one day he got a letter saying they wanted to interview him and it was just a week after he'd got married and so he was disqualified. You know, you got to be unmarried for the first five years."

"Yeah, so I've heard." Chuck stood up and crossed the aisle, "Mind if I sit over here?" He tossed his hat into the corner and sat across from Thomas. "Go on."

Once started, Thomas told him everything: That his father was out of work; that his mother had to bake and try to sell bread and scones to make ends meet; that his sister was train-ing as a teacher while she worked part-time at a department store, but didn't get paid much; that he had a cat; that they'd only lived in the house for a year, before that they had lived next door in a nicer house, but it was too expensive; that his father had finally gone on relief, but hated having to pick up his money. Chuck listened, nodded, asked a few questions.

"And where is your house exactly?"

Thomas told him and Chuck nodded thoughtfully.

"You wouldn't want to take in a boarder, would you?"

"A boarder? You mean you? I don't know. We don't have much room. They're really small bedrooms. My father and mother have one. Nell, that's my sister, has the other. And I have what used to be the living room. Course, Nell is moving out soon."

"Well, I'll be looking for a place in Regina."

"What do you do? For a living, I mean?"

"A living? Thomas. What does it look like I do?"

"A workman, I guess."

"A workman. Yes, I'm of the working class all right. I work for an organization called the Unity League. Ever heard of it?"

"I don't think so. What do you do?"

"I guess you could say I organize the organization."

"Oh."

"But, back to the room. Do you think there might be a place for me? I'll pay, of course, either just for the room or for room and board."

"Well, you'd have to share with me. At least for awhile. It's a big room, well, fairly big."

"Are there a lot of houses around there?"

"No, just a few on Seventh and some more down by the streetcar tracks on Dewdney Avenue. Why do you want to know?"

"Just wondering. I like somewhere quiet, no traffic. You know."

"There's sure no traffic out there. No one's got a car and the streetcar is two blocks away. Only noise is the cows in the morning."

"Cows?"

"Yeah, the dairy farmer pastures his cows around there. It's all prairie around our house, so he just keeps them there during the day."

"I like cows." Chuck smiled again. "So, is it a deal?"

"Deal? You'll have to talk to my mother."

"Your mother makes the decisions, does she?"

"Mother and father. But mother makes most of the decisions."

"I see. Let's shake on it anyway. I have a feeling we are going to be good friends." Chuck's grip was strong and his huge hand calloused. He clapped Thomas on the shoulder with his other hand.

Thomas felt a sudden warmth flood his body. He felt like crying. His brief stay in Winnipeg had been his first time away from home. And now, he was returning in disgrace. The clap on the shoulder was the first friendly gesture he had received, it seemed, in a long, long time.

"But first we've got to sort out your problems. You have been having problems I think. I watched you for nearly two hours after we left Winnipeg. You are angry and hurt, I think. What's the problem?"

And as willingly as he had told Chuck everything about his family, he now told him about his month at Bible college, training to be a minister. Chuck listened intently, nodding his head, sympathetically it seemed. Thomas felt his eyes watering. He rubbed them and looked out the window at the baked fields.

"Thomas... Can I call you Tommy? Tommy, you are a right fool, that's for sure."

CHAPTER THREE

"Since you are the only beneficiary, Mrs. Stemichuk, there will probably be no need to probate the will. My secretary will prepare the certified documents for the bank. The house title is already in your name and the car can be transferred by presenting this certified copy of the will at the licence bureau. There should be no problem and little expense." Mr. Strathcona sat, fat and happy, across the table from Clara and smiled a huge, jolly smile. If he was this happy over a will, who knows how happy he might be over a real estate deal.

Clara smiled slightly in response. She actually did not like Mr. Strathcona even though he had been one of Chuck's buddies. They had bought and developed several strip malls in the Niagara region. Chuck had been the silent partner. Wouldn't be good if the bank knew about it. The malls were the usual sort of thing – doughnut shop, pizza parlour, confectionery, all anchored by a bank at one end and some sort of "local" pub at the other. Operated under a numbered company. And, apparently, Mr. Strathcona had advised Chuck, when he was diagnosed with cancer, that they should sell, "divest themselves of their joint assets." They had, at a considerable profit. She shouldn't be cynical. Mr. Strathcona's timing had been right. Chuck liquidated everything and put the proceeds into a joint bank account. That way, Clara had access to a considerable amount of money and did not have to arrange any formal transfer. So, in a way, she really should be grateful to the horrid little man.

She uncrossed her legs and caught Mr. Strathcona glancing appreciatively. Horrid little man. "Thank you, Mr. Strathcona."

"Oh, come, Clara, after all these years you can surely call me Cecil." He actually rubbed his moist little hands together as if he savoured the idea.

"Thank you, er, Cecil." She turned to go.

"I do understand what you are going through. Ever since my Betty died five years ago, I have often felt lonely, yes, very lonely indeed." He patted his belly or at least his bulging waistcoat. "We all need companionship, don't we?" He waited for an answer.

"When did you say your secretary would have the papers ready?" She opened the door and stood there a moment, poised it seemed for flight.

"Yes, well, yes, tomorrow afternoon. Yes, well perhaps I could bring them over to the King Edward and we could discuss them over a drinkie."

"I'll be in this area tomorrow. Can I not just as easily pick them up?"

"Yes, well, yes. Yes, of course you can."

Before he could say anything more or even smile once more, she walked out into the secretary's office, closing the door definitely behind her. She let her shoulders sag for a moment, recovering from her annoyance. Four days since Chuck's funeral and his partner was already hitting on her. Goddamn little eunuch! Clara smiled at her own imitation of Chuck's language. He swore, had sworn a lot. But it had never seemed to come naturally. It was as if the words were something he had learnt and never quite felt comfortable with. Dear Chuck. He had been a bit of a swaggerer, around her at least, but she had liked that about him.

She walked to the parking lot and got into their car. It was a dark blue Mercedes. Chuck liked big cars and they really had never needed a second car. He had a chauffeur-driven car for getting to and from work. She understood his need for a big car. It had to do with his status that he had worked so hard to achieve. From a Ukrainian farm boy to a vice-president of a bank had not been an easy path. And he had done it all on his own – night classes after the War, long hours, attention to detail – and luck. He had always said you would think he was Irish, he was so lucky. All his peers had got to where they were in part by friendships and old family ties and in part, of course, by good degrees from the most expensive and exclusive universities. How had he done it? Work, work and more work. And good judgement, careful planning, even manipulation, yes, that too. Clara, who came from a wealthy family and had gone to expensive schools, knew the toll it had taken on his health. The furies had always been at his heels. And he had never been able to settle back and enjoy his successes. There was always something eating away

at him, making him restless even on a Sunday. Hounding
him, sometimes, through sleepless nights. Clara sighed
before she started the car. She had loved him because he was
self-made and independent and maybe, she had to admit,
because he was so, so...The word didn't come. Perhaps
predictable. The corners hadn't been knocked off by glossy
schools and ready money. Her bit of rough, as her snotty
sister had said. Yes, by God, he was her bit of rough all right.
Her sister seemed to forget that their grandfather had been a
hell of a lot rougher. She pulled the gear lever into drive and
manoeuvred the big car past a tree at the side of the angled
parking places of the law office.

She drove a bit too fast up the driveway beside the office
building and out to the street. It was an escape. The oncom-
ing cars came in their usual wave of traffic-light-monitored
clumps and she entered the stream of vehicles at the first
opportunity. The interior of the big car seemed empty and
she did not even want to turn on the radio. She turned at the
first corner and headed out Mount Pleasant Road. It was
habitual; she had done it every day since the funeral. Out
Mount Pleasant Road, then right and into the cemetery. She
would park the car and walk over to the newly turfed plot
with the marker, Peter Russell Stemichuk, 1914 – 1999. The
granite headstone was still not finished. She'd stand at the end
of the plot and make the sign of the cross. Thirty years since
she had regularly attended Mass and now she was standing
under the trees in the cemetery making the sign of the cross.
Where was Chuck now? A stupid question – unknowable.

Don't ask any question you don't know the answer to, was
what Chuck had always said. If you do, some bastard will be

sure to put you down. But that was just macho talk. Chuck asked all sorts of questions to which he had no answers. Like why did she love a guy like him. He had had low self-confidence, was either too boastful or, even worse, self-deprecating, and played the game of macho modesty whenever he thought it suited him. Maybe he initially thought she was a little rich girl who would like a good fuck. She smiled when the word came to her mind. Actually, she knew he was quite shy under his bravado, and his feelings were easily hurt. Was that why she loved him? All she knew was that even as his body wasted away with the disease, she still loved and caressed him. If he asked himself that question, she doubted he came up with an answer. Nor did she have an answer for that matter.

It was frustrating to think of him down there. He would have hated it. He liked to be doing something. Usually, staying late at the office, or down in the basement working on accounts. Sometimes, he would barbecue, or drive around looking at land or buildings. On Saturday evening he liked to sit on the patio and have a glass of wine with her. Well, one thing he wouldn't hate about that miserable coffin and the cement chamber down there. At last, he was alone. He would like that. He had always been a loner. And, she had to admit, as the letter came to mind again, secretive. He wouldn't talk much about himself or what he thought. He wouldn't talk about death, not even when he was so ill. Except that once when he had drunk too much and blubbered on a bit about friends dying in the War. Usually, he simply said he had seen too much. After serving in the War, he had the right not to talk, she supposed. Lots of men didn't want to talk about what they had seen.

Clara fingered the letter in her pocket, which she had taken out of his tuxedo again and reread many times. Chuck must have killed too. He could not have fought in a war over a period of almost six years without killing. He must have understood what it was to kill. But why did he save a letter from someone confessing to killing a woman named Margaret? Perhaps he had thought, One more death, and shrugged as he had done whenever he didn't like something. Why send the letter? Why add to the unhappiness in the world? But who was Thomas Pennan? A friend? Or was Margaret the friend? That might explain why she had never heard of Thomas Pennan.

And, now, she had another puzzle. A man had phoned yesterday evening. He had read the obituary in the paper and wondered if Chuck was the Peter Stemichuk who had served with the Mac-Paps in Spain. Clara had said, No, Chuck had served with the Winnipeg Rifles in the Second World War, but she didn't know about any war in Spain. And who were the Mac-Paps? Apparently they were the volunteer regiment from Canada in the International Brigade which had fought for republican Spain in the late 1930s. The man had been a little testy about her not knowing anything about the war. Chuck was their Commissar, the man said. A great leader, dedicated to the cause but a real leader, not just an apparatchik. An apparatchik? Yeah, an apparatchik, like the bozos sent out from Russia. Chuck was working class, not some petit bourgeois pouf from Oxford or Cambridge who thought they could lead men because they had read a bit of Karl Marx. He was a true party man, but he was a leader too, the man had said. And you're saying, this Chuck was a communist? Clara thought of her

Chuck and smiled. Yeah, a communist, a bolshie as they used to call us, but we were all fighting for the same cause; we were all loyalists fighting against the Fascist pigs. We – She broke in, I think you must have the wrong person. Chuck was a banker, he worked in a bank. The man dismissed the idea, No. Nope. Peter Stemichuk, called Chuck, from Saskatchewan? Fought in the Mac-Paps? Got to be the same person. Haven't heard that name since I was with him in the Retreats. The man had started to tell the story, but Clara cut him short. Then it occurred to her to ask about Thomas Pennan. Tommy? Oh, yeah, he was in the machine gun unit. They were wiped out at Teruel.

It was too much of a coincidence. Clara stared down at the grave plot, almost willing Chuck to explain it to her. There was some simple explanation, she was sure. She had known Chuck and even if he didn't talk about that time in his life, she would have known if he had been communist. He wasn't even political. Voted Conservative, just as she did, when he voted. She realized she didn't actually know if he had ever voted. Anyway, he certainly was not a communist. And, she had had to face it finally, he was not really a leader either. A sort of second-in-command. It was true he worked hard and knew the banking business probably better than anyone there. Very good at his job, as the president of the bank had said to her at the wake. But not one to take the lead or to have people follow him. A good and natural vice-president, even though he had complained when he was past over for the presidency of the bank. A loner. But she would see this man and listen to what he had to say. He had said he didn't know Chuck very well – he was just one of the rank and file, so to speak – but he'd bring someone around who did.

CHAPTER FOUR

When Chuck and Tommy got to the house, Tommy's mother and a neighbour, Mrs. Ryan, were sitting over a cup of tea in the low, back kitchen. Weak tea with lots of milk. Mrs. Ryan liked a bit of whiskey in hers, but in Mrs. Pennan's house she was always on her best behaviour and suffered just milk.

Tommy's mother was a pleasant-looking woman with the typical "peaches and cream" complexion of the old country and the beginnings of a streak of grey hair. Next to her, Mrs. Ryan looked positively wrung out and hung up to dry. A tall gangly woman, her face brown and lined, Mrs. Ryan stood out in any crowd. Oddly enough though, it was Tommy's short, dumpy mother who carried the authority. In her quiet way, she seemed to be judge and jury of whoever was around, and no one in Tommy's experience had ever gainsaid that authority.

But she didn't daunt Chuck. He burst into a grin and, bowing slightly, said in an almost impudent but boyish way: "Well, Mother, I've brought your little boy home safe and sound."

"Thomas! What has happened? What's the trouble?"

"Nothing, Mom. Nothing." Tommy looked as if he would go over to her but stopped. "I'll tell you all about it. Later. It's okay." He turned to Chuck. "This is Chuck, Mom."

"How do you do, ma'am." He bowed again and then, to everyone's surprise, gave her a hug. And she just stood there looking a bit taken aback, but not displeased. Then he reached out his hand to Mrs. Ryan. "Name's Peter, but everyone calls me Chuck."

Mrs. Ryan, who ran a café downtown and had learned to size up people pretty quickly, asked: "And what's your last name, if I may ask?"

"Stemichuk."

"Well, it's not exactly Irish, I'll say that. And my late hubby wouldn't have thought much of it, if I can be blunt. But, well, it suits you. A big blocky name with a bit of a lilt to it." She smiled. While Chuck was turned to Mrs. Ryan, Mrs. Pennan gave him a careful scrutiny from head to toe. Then, she shifted her attention back to Thomas.

"Thomas, what are you doing home?"

Thomas told the whole story again. His mother's expression showed concern, but was noncommittal. Mrs. Ryan, however, reacted.

"The bastard – oh, excuse me Mrs. Pennan. It just makes me so mad. All the good boys that are out on the street looking for work and men like him, Christians they call themselves, putting them down, calling them bolsheviks and worse. It just makes me so mad. And scabs getting the work, not our boys." She plucked at Chuck's sleeve. "I'm old Irish, working Irish, you understand?"

Peter held out his huge hands. "And I'm working bohunk. Your secret's safe with me."

Mrs. Ryan laughed hugely. "I like your friend, Tommy." It was obvious.

"Sit down, Peter." Thomas's mother motioned to a chair at the end of the table, a mark of special favour. "Some tea?" If she didn't like someone she would sit them on a chair in the other room and make them balance their teacups on their laps. That's as far as Mr. Fines and Mr. Williams, who came by to preach the virtues of the new Co-operative Commonwealth Federation, had got so far. And then there were the few who could sit comfortably at her kitchen table with cups resting on the clean oilcloth.

And, so, Chuck, or Peter, as Mrs. Pennan always called him, was accepted into the Pennan household.

That night, lying on the couch in the living room, Tommy thought about Chuck. He was going over the day's events. Why had Chuck seemed so anxious to befriend him and come home with him? They surely didn't have much in common. He was annoyed at himself for being suspicious about Chuck's motives. He had said nothing out of line, had asked for nothing except if he might rent a room. He was ready to pay whatever Tommy's mother asked. But why would he want to live way out here, three miles from downtown? What could he gain from living in the Pennan household? They were neither wealthy nor influential. Perhaps the spying and suspicion Thomas had encountered at the Bible college had rubbed off on him. And yet, when he thought about Chuck he wasn't even sure he liked him. Too smooth in his bohunk way? He had to learn not to trust people so quickly. Well, he'd find out tomorrow, when Chuck came back with his "gear." Thomas turned over and, after punching the pillow several times, drifted into sleep.

In the morning he rose early, although not earlier than his mother, of course, who always seemed to be the last to go to bed and the first to rise. She was at the stove pouring boiling water into the brown Betty teapot. On the table she had set out two slices of toast and some marmite. Tommy grunted a good morning and sat down to his breakfast.

"Well, Tommy, what are you going to do now?"

"Try to find work."

"Your father goes out every day to do that. There's no work."

"He's old." Tommy regretted saying it as soon as the words came out. "I mean, most of the jobs want someone young." His mother said nothing. She had work to do. He finished the toast, drank some tea and headed for the door.

"Don't slam it."

Yesterday afternoon Chuck had walked to the streetcar, a couple of blocks away. So, he had the money for that. The people around here walked downtown. The streetcars went back and forth mostly empty, except for the occasional gaggle of Mounties coming from or going to the barracks out on the edge of the city. Well-fed, young, hair short and shaved up to above their ears, hard to miss them. Tommy always felt a little more secure because they were there. As a small boy he had spent hours out at the barracks watching them riding horses and exercising. They had been his heroes, and his friends and he had played at being Mounties chasing down crooks in the northern wilderness (which of course he had never actually seen). But his mother dismissed them with a wave of her hand. "Police are always on the side they want to be on and that's not usually the side of the poor," was all she would say.

He walked diagonally across the field toward the tracks and Dewdney Avenue, past Crawfords' dilapidated two-storey house on York Street, past Metcalfe's place next door, past old man Shafer's outbuildings where he housed the crow he had taught to talk by splitting its tongue and coaching it all day. He was much more aware now of how rundown these houses were than he had been as a boy. Well, perhaps they were less rundown then. There was no money now for paint and repairs in this neighbourhood.

The dust from the path coated his shoes and the lower part of his trousers. The trail had been worn into a shortcut across the prairie by the few people who lived out in this end of town walking back and forth to the city centre, looking for work, going to the hospital, and, recently, going to pick up their relief cheques, those hated relief cheques. It flagrantly denied the careful grid planning of the city administration that laid out blocks of land bounded by poorly kept roads. Boardwalks stretched along those streets deemed more important than their neighbours, but they were only used if it was wet, and that had not been very often during the past years of drought.

Tommy kicked an empty cigarette package out of his way. Why was he angry? He had gone off to Winnipeg with so much hope and, he admitted it, happy to see the last of

Regina with its sad pretensions to being a city. He had heard Winnipeg had two rivers meeting in its centre and tall buildings. He had longed to see them and to find out what a real city was like. And it had been exciting. He'd made friends quickly with some young Winnipeg men and they had tramped the streets savouring its sights even though they couldn't afford to buy them. He had seen more poor than he thought could exist and had volunteered to work in the soup kitchen on Main Street. Evenings, he had gone back to the College and prayed for them.

At Alexander Street he stepped up onto the boardwalk and continued south toward Dewdney Avenue, his footsteps echoing on the slivery fir planks. The number of houses per block increased and, just before Dewdney, he hesitated and then stopped. He knew he had to face the Reverend Evans sometime. But, not now, he decided. As he started to walk on, he heard his name. "Thomas." The voice brooked no opposition but was kindly and certainly clear. It said, come in and explain yourself. Tommy looked down the street as if determined to go on and then sighed and turned into the front yard he knew so well. The Reverend Evans was not a man to be ignored.

He stood, filling the doorway of the tiny clapboard house. "Well, Thomas, it is you then? I've been hearing that you might return." Tommy fleetingly wondered how he could have possibly heard anything about him, but knew from experience that both God and Reverend Evans moved in mysterious ways. The Rev, as he was called familiarly in his poor parish, seemed to be everywhere and to know everyone and everything. He made it his business to know. When he had first arrived in the huge sprawling parish on the edge of the prairie city, he visited every household, Protestant, Catholic, or in between. And he came back regularly. When there was trouble he was the first on the scene; he married them, buried them and, sometimes, birthed them as well. If they had trouble getting a bed in the Catholic hospital down the road, one of the family would appear at his door and he'd go down and talk the sisters into making room for just one more, even if it was in the hallway. But, in Tommy's eyes, at least, his main claim to fame was that Tommy's mother trusted him and she was not an easy truster.

He was also a mesmerizing preacher. Twice every Sunday, at eleven in the morning and seven in the evening, he poured out a mighty, roaring flood of words that swept away everything in front of it. His passion was directed against injustice, mistreatment of the poor, police brutality, political corruption, and what he called the larceny of the capitalist system. His favourite prophet was Isaiah and he rolled out the words of the prophet as if they were spoken directly to the people of Regina in the midst of their troubles and afflictions: "And he shall feed his flock like a shepherd: he shall gather the lambs in his arms, and carry them in his bosom, and shall gently lead those that are with young." Some called him the Red Reverend: "Why should ye be stricken any more? Ye will revolt more and more: for the whole head is sick, and the whole heart faint. From the sole of the foot even unto the head there is no soundness in it....Your country is desolate, your cities are burned with fire: your land, strangers devour it in your presence, and it is desolate, overthrown by strangers." But he was not a communist. True, he often spoke at their rallies and supported many of their causes. He was seen at their office and he shared the podiums with them, but he was not a party member. He was what would later be called a social gospeller, but even that designation didn't cover his political activity which, even if not communist, skirted very close to it. As the economic situation in the city, and especially in his parish, worsened in the early 1930s, there was standing room only on Sundays in the little United Church at the corner of Arthur Street and Eighth Avenue.

"Come in, son, come in." He didn't mean to bellow but his invitation could have been, and probably was, heard all the way down the street. As Tommy stepped into the house, the Rev put his arm around his shoulder and guided him into the sitting room. The room was so familiar to Tommy. When he had decided he might go into the Church, he had sat there in the threadbare armchair tracing the patterns in the cheap velour brocade and trying to sound as if he really believed God was calling him. The Reverend had perhaps seen through Thomas's "calling." "It doesn't matter, Thomas, if God wants you or not. God doesn't always take the lead, you know. Look at John crying in the wilderness. What was he crying about? He didn't know exactly what was what, did he? He just went out there and sort of made up what he thought God might want to do. That's the way I see it." And the Rev's red-haired, overworked wife would bring them tea. Some said they weren't even married. That she'd been beaten by her husband out on a farm somewhere further north and he'd been found slightly chewed up in the threshing machine a couple of weeks later. Meanwhile, the Reverend had given her shelter and she'd just stayed.

"So you jumped ship, did you?"

And Tommy told his story again, this time a bit more embroidered with his own justifications and the principal's villainy. "Well, well, well." said the Rev, "So old Keele is still spreading the word of the Lord." Tommy tried to protest, but Reverend Evans was quickly in full spate. "He didn't like it when I helped the union men in the General Strike either, but I explained it all to him at the time, so he knows better. Jesus didn't come for the rich, I said, even if they do give more to the College. Well, well, well. Course he never listened to me. He always did speak directly with the Lord and not with His creatures. When the police banged me on the head, the church quickly sent me out to a rural parish in Saskatchewan and, you know, I think that also came about because the Lord spoke privately to the Reverend Keele and showed him a way out his dilemma. Ah, Jeremiah, who can suppress you or dampen your ardour?" The Reverend Evans spoke lightheartedly enough, but perhaps a keen ear might have heard a note of anger under the bantering tone.

"What are you going to do now?"

"I'm going to find work, I guess, somewhere. Seeing as the church doesn't want me...."

"Oh, don't jump to that conclusion, Thomas. There have been a few like St. Paul and even St. Peter that must have thought the church didn't want them at one time."

"I'm no St. Peter or Paul."

"Nor am I, Thomas. Well, well, well. Let's see: First there's some good works that have got to be done in the parish – food, clothes to distribute. And then..."

"I've got to find a paying job. I've been thinking I might find some work as a baker. I hear there are some that take on apprentices. Doesn't pay much but everybody needs bread."

"Now, I don't want to distract you from your good intentions, but the breadmaking's being taken over by the corporations. Conveyor belts, thousand loaves at a time."

"I can't live off Mom and Dad and I owe you the tuition money. Look, I've figured out exactly how much I owe you and, if we add the interest..."

"And now I'm a usurer as well. Is that it?"

"No. I didn't mean..."

"Well, we'll see about all this. I can't say I don't need the money, but there's time."

He walked to the door with Tommy and put a hand on his shoulder. "Aye, there's a time for sowing and a time for reaping. Well, I'll send up some smoke signals. Meanwhile, if you're on the way into town you can drop this bunch of books off at the hospital. Just a moment." He ducked back into the house and emerged with a bag. The books all had the Rosemont Church stamp on them. "No one comes to the church to read books, now do they?"

CHAPTER FIVE

Clara parked her car on the street beside the café where she had agreed to meet the mysterious caller and his friend. This area of the city was unknown to her and made her uneasy. It lay close to the mouth of the Don River, or what had been the mouth. The Don was the largest of the small rivers which at three- or four-mile intervals divided the city. The ravines, cut by innumerable creeks flowing into these rivers, provided the secluded residential areas which pushed far into the commercial and industrial sections of the city and made the downtown inhabitable. Across the road from her, industrial buildings, most of them abandoned it seemed, stood along the concrete walls that some engineer had built to join up the river and the lake. Dilapidated barges hung by their cables to the walls. Behind the café building stretched a field of concrete slabs which had been laid out over a huge space, probably as a truckyard or parking area, and which now were heaved up here and there by weeds, grass, and neglect.

The building the café was located in and the one next to it were the only structures on that side of the street in that block. They were old buildings with the fake, insulating brick siding put on shortly after the War. The sign, Docklands Café, was also from the fifties. Its letters were now partially faded and obliterated. Clara's was the only car on the street. She pulled down the visor and straightened her hair in the tiny mirror. She had put on a blue businesslike suit, a silk patterned scarf at her neck, no jewellery and, for some instinctual reason, high heels. Whatever impression she might make, she was certainly not going to look like anyone's fool. The thought, however, had crossed her mind that she was being foolish even coming to this meeting. There were all sorts that read the obituaries and preyed on the grieving.

She climbed the four wooden steps to the café and pushed open the door. The inside of the café was everything the outside had promised but, if it was worn and tired looking, it was nevertheless clean. The smells coming from the kitchen were the usual frying odours, but the oil smelled as if it had been fresh that morning. The glass counter under the cash register was filled with what had to be homemade pies, and the plump woman in a white apron standing behind them looked as if she could well have just made them. Clara looked around and then over to the wall of booths. Sure enough, two-thirds of the way down sat two men, one of whom wore a bright green, peaked cap as he had promised. He motioned to her, and she walked elegantly down the linoleumed aisle to the booth where he sat.

"Mrs. Stemichuk?"

"Yes, and your name is?"

"Walter Chapman and this here is Bill, Bill Kroker. He's the one I was telling you about. Knew Chuck in the old days. Sit down, won't you." Bill moved away, over against the wall, and nodded. He seemed permanently bent over and had a few days' growth of grey stubble. Clara sat carefully down near the end of the booth across from the men.

"Coffee?"

"Please." Clara looked at the man called Walter, who wore his jaunty bright green hat and a sort of leather sports jacket with a crest on the chest.

"Oh that, that's my grandkid's hockey team. Won the city league last year, they did."

The plump woman in white set a cup of coffee in front of Clara and thudded off to her place behind the counter.

"Now Mr. Chapman..."

"Walt, call me Walt. We don't need to stand on convention, do we?"

"Well, Walt, I'd be interested in hearing your story and why you think you may have known my late husband."

"Like I told you, Mrs. Stemichuk, I didn't know him so well but Bill here, he knew him, didn't you Bill?"

For the first time Bill spoke up, almost, it seemed, woke up, reluctantly. "Yeah. I knowed him. I would, wouldn't I? We fought together for two years in Spain. He was our Commissar. You know what that is? It's the ideological leader, like he taught us why we was fighting for the loyalist cause and why the Fascists had to be beat. He was right too, later events proved that, didn't they now? And he'd cheer us up like, give us encouragement, make sure the boys down the line got food and ammunition up to us, that sort of thing. But Chuck, he was even more than that. He was always right there beside us in the front line and he didn't take extra blankets or nothing just because he was leader neither. He was one of the best men I ever had anything to do something with."

"It's very gratifying to hear so many complimentary things about this, ah, Peter Stemichuk you knew, but..."

"But nothing. He was called Chuck 'cause of his last name like and he was from Saskatchewan, from one of those towns on the CNR railway. Ituna, that's it. He was from Ituna."

"Well, it is true Chuck was born in Saskatchewan. But there could have been another Peter Stemichuk from there." But he was from Ituna. She'd tried to talk him into taking a trip back there, when he first got sick. But he wouldn't even discuss it.

"Chuck never mentioned no other family. Said his father had been killed, murdered like, and they never found who did it, and his mother, well, she died too. I forget how, but he didn't have no brothers and sisters. I know that. He used to say, 'If I don't get married and have kids, there'll be no more Stemichuks. So, I can't afford to die, so stay with me and you won't get killed either.' Things like that. To keep up our morale, you know. We talked a lot of baloney, but it was the right thing to do, go to Spain, I mean, the best thing I ever done. Shit...Oh, pardon me, ma'am. Anyway he always said he was the only Peter Stemichuk he knowed of, unique like." Bill took a slightly belligerent gulp of coffee. "It's got to be him, all right."

"It's true, he didn't have any parents. Not when I...They'd died a long time before I met him." Clara looked down and fingered the lipstick stain on her coffee mug. She realized that Chuck could have gone to Spain in the thirties, long before she met him. After all, she had been only twenty and he already forty-one, almost forty-two, when they met and married. She tried to calculate his age in the thirties.

"When was the war? The Spanish one, I mean?"

"1936 it started. We was sent home in '38."

"My Chuck would have been twenty-four then."

"Well, there you go then. You can be right proud of Chuck, Mrs. Stemichuk, right proud. He done the cause proud, he did. He was a hero. He might've been a Bolshie, but he didn't get into any of them interparty rows. No sir, he was a straight shooter, Chuck was."

Clara reached into her handbag and withdrew a photograph of Chuck taken at a bank dinner. "Is this the man you knew?"

Bill looked at the photograph and handed it to Walter. "Hard to tell, like he was only twentysomething when I knowed him. Like you said. And we never saw him in a suit and tie. He didn't have no moustache them days either. He was a redhead – he was red through and through. He looked sort of like that I guess. Sort of familiar. But I wouldn't have recognized him from that picture. Anyway," he hesitated and took another swallow of coffee, "there's one thing troubles me about all this."

"There a number of things about what you say trouble me, Mr. Kroker, but what troubles you?"

"Well, Mrs. Stemichuk, you see, Chuck was killed in Spain, on The Retreats."

Clara gasped. She got abruptly to her feet and covered her mouth with one hand. No one spoke for a full minute.

"Lots of the boys died in Spain. Lots." Walter reached out a hand to comfort her, but Clara pulled back.

"You stupid man. I was married to him for forty-four years. Forty-four happy years. I buried him. I..." She started to cry.

"Please, ma'am. Please. Don't cry. Sure. Sure. Bill here may 'a been mistaken. It was such a mess. Cold. They poisoned water holes. Maybe..."

"I weren't mistaken. No way. I found him. He was dead. Knifed. I tried to carry him, but he was too heavy. And the planes were...It was, everybody was dead. Everywhere. Blood. Planes. Killing us. Oh, Christ, Christ." Kroker dropped his head onto his hands on the booth table and shook.

Walter turned and put his arm around Kroker's shoulders. Clara looked down on them for a moment and then turned and hurried out of the café.

She drove absent-mindedly up the driveway to their large, three-storey brick house on Highland Avenue. Of all the stupid things. It was just silly. But there was no reason for him to lie. Still, Kroker was an old man. Probably confused. War's so horrible. Maybe he just imagined it was his Chuck that had been killed on The Retreats, as he called them. He said he'd seen him, dead. Knifed. Or, maybe he wasn't dead. They were on the run. Perhaps he was picked up or somehow got to safety. Kroker said it was chaos, men shot, dying of cold, the water poisoned. Chuck had had various scars on his body. What he had called his appendix scar flashed into her memory. Chuck had simply lived through all that. Somehow. War was so awful, no wonder Chuck wouldn't talk about it.

The house was empty. Of course it was empty; she lived alone now. But it was empty now in a different way; it was as if it had been abandoned. Clara tossed her hat onto the sofa, realizing again that she had become messy, inattentive to how things looked. The TV guide from last evening was on the floor near the sofa, the newspaper lay in scattered sections in front of the fireplace, three fingermarked glasses with varying amounts of liquid stood on the coffee table. She'd told Mary to take a month off. What was the point? You picked up things for other people, not for yourself.

She rewound the telephone answering machine and listened: "Clara, Cecil here. I was wondering if you signed the letter for the bank yet. I could come by and pick it up, if you like. Or maybe you would like to meet me someplace. Do get in touch. Bye." In a pig's arse she'd get in touch. For a moment she wondered what he would look like without his immaculate clothes. It defied her imagination. Chuck's body had been in pretty good trim until the disease wasted it away. A little heavy, and he didn't like it being mentioned. Well, she was a little heavy too. She could feel the snugness of her skirt waist as she plunked herself down inelegantly on the couch. What the hell was the use of keeping up appearances?

She kicked off her shoes and put her stockinged feet up on the glass top of the coffee table. It didn't seem possible that Chuck could have ever been a Communist, but who knows? He may have been a different person before the War, before two wars, if Kroker's story was right. She remembered her father saying, if hadn't been for the War, the communists would have taken over the country, overthrown the government.

Now what? She didn't know. Why anything? She felt suddenly very tired and leaned her head back against the couch cushions and, eventually, slept.

CHAPTER SIX

In the autumn of 1934 Chuck moved into the small bedroom which Tommy's sister Nell had vacated for an uncomfortable cot in a teacherage near Eyebrow, Saskatchewan. When Chuck heard the name of the town, he wagged his finger at Tommy and winked. "A code, Tommy, mark my words. There's also Elbow downriver from there and I wouldn't be surprised if we didn't find other parts of the body scattered around here and there. It's a bolshevik plot. I think. To dismember the country." He chuckled. Chuck often made remarks like this one, ridiculing the fears of a communist plot to destroy the country that the newspapers were trying to whip up.

Meanwhile he had found Tommy a job with a cartage company. It was night work, loading and unloading freight from railway cars. The work was heavy sometimes and paid very little, but it meant the household had a small, regular income from that and from the rent Chuck paid. Tommy also started paying off the amount he owed the Reverend Evans for tuition. Tommy was to remember it as a happy time in spite of the poverty, the constant news of farms closing and businesses going bankrupt – and the wind that blew dust into every crack, coated every shelf and lined the inside of nostrils and mouth like a black scum. Chuck loved to tease and laugh and, much to the surprise of Tommy and even more of his father, Tommy's mother joined in and gave as much as she got. When Nell came home on weekends, it was obvious that she and Chuck were developing a special relationship. Only Tommy's father still suffered from his inability to get work, to be the man in the house; every so often he would disappear into the cellar ostensibly to stoke up the furnace, but really to sit, ashamed, on the bottom step and weep internally.

It was that autumn that their neighbour, Mr. Long, went out to the shed at the end of the yard and hanged himself. His daughter Margaret found him. She had taken over running the house since her mother had disappeared with an out-of-work cowboy who had sauntered past one morning. Her father seemed to have decided to run off too and then changed his mind. He had appeared at the Pennan household's back door the night before, a turkey made out of a teatowel over his shoulder containing his clothes and some food.

"I'm going," was all he said and turned and walked off down the road. He must have come back later, because the next morning Margaret went out to the back shed and found him hanging from a bit of rope that had been left in the shed from the days when a horse had been stabled there. His turkey lay neatly on a plank. His clothes had fallen out of it onto the dirt floor and there were bread crumbs lying around where he had sat and eaten his last meal.

Chuck heard her cry of agony and rushed out to her. She fell into his arms and sobbed uncontrollably. "The bugger. The cowardly bugger." She said it over and over. "The bugger." Chuck held her and stroked her hair, waiting for her sobbing to calm.

"It's not him that's the bugger, Margaret. The real bastards are the ones who drove him to it. The filth that live in luxury while others starve. Those are the real buggers." Chuck said the words gently and confidently as if he was simply explaining something to a child who had got hurt and needed comfort. The three of them, Mrs. Pennan, Nell, and Thomas, watched from the kitchen door not knowing whether to go to them or to wait. Then, Margaret turned her face up to Chuck's and pulled him down to her and kissed him long and hard on the mouth. Nell gasped.

In the autumn of 1933, the Reverend Evans emerged as the leader of the left-leaning part of the Ministerial Association of the city. The Association had been established as a grouping of Regina's clergy. Its chief work was to coordinate the social work of the churches throughout the city. It was not political in any overt sense, but it depended on donations from those with money and so tended to side with the authorities. The lefties, as they were dismissively called, could rant and rave all they liked but the majority of the ministers leaned to the powers that be. The Red Rev was, as he liked to pronounce every so often, a voice crying in the wilderness. He would then add, the wilderness of God's chosen people. However, he could garner enough support to be included on the governing board as a sort of token member.

For months, all through the winter of 1934, he had sat on the governing board and railed against the system that let people starve. Perhaps he was tolerated because his voice both stirred and salved consciences, but, since he was a minority, didn't require any action. As the Depression deepened, his tirades and predictions, which had been dismissed as too radical and farfetched, seemed to be pretty accurate descriptions of what was happening. As farms closed and businesses went bankrupt, Reverend Evans gradually moved in people's minds from a marginal fanatic to a prescient prophet who saw the world as it really was. The newspapers, the newscasts, what the ministers saw every day happening even in the more well-to-do parishes began to reflect the Rev's concerns. When the Association met, the men of the cloth began to listen to his warnings even though they did not yet heed his advice.

In the late Spring of 1934, the Association's tri-annual election for president came up. It was usually a pretty humdrum affair. The Reverend Bullock, minister of the largest and wealthiest of the churches of the city, had held the position now for nine years. He was, or had been, a shoo-in. All that changed in 1934. The actual election became a pitched battle between Reverend Evans and the conservative incumbent, the Reverend Bullock. Twice the Association vote was tied. Passions ran high. The Reverend Bullock called for a week's respite to let everyone reconsider their votes.

That week became a story to be told and retold: ministers suddenly learned that there might be a chance that their church would get a new organ or a paint job done or some repairs made to the roof. Meetings took place night after night in church basements and tales of Reverend Evans's affiliations with the Communist Party abounded in the city. Fistfights after church services were reported in confidential whispers. People refused to go to their local parish church and would walk across the city to attend service at some other church whose pastor was sympathetic to the side they supported. The little church at Eighth Avenue and Arthur Street was packed on Sunday.

"Are you telling me a man of the cloth is not to meddle in politics? Christ said, Render unto Caesar what is Caesar's.... That's true, but does that mean no one is going to speak up for the poor and the starving? I don't think that is what Jesus meant. He fed and clothed and comforted the poor. And that's what I think we ministers should be doing, not dining on silver on the southside of the city, not going to Winnipeg to order our suits, not telling you that the poor will be always with you. Do you want to leave the care of the poor to the Communists? They do care. You don't see them driving around in cars and strutting up and down Wascana Park on Sunday afternoons to walk off a roast beef dinner. They live and work with the downtrodden. And I tell you, the clenched fist and the cross of Christ are not so far apart." A gasp went through the congregation; some walked out; but most trembled with the excitement of his words. "I tell you the revolution is not some far-off event; it is a process and that process has already begun to unfold right here in this city. The Philistines are once more oppressing the people of God." And he raised his fist in a gesture of defiance that could have been mistaken for, and was reported as, a communist salute.

A fternoons Tommy sat in the small office at the back of the church and organized the Reverend's correspondence, drafted up replies and speeches, and tried to keep some order in his affairs. They, the Rev and he, were a good team. The Rev was a notoriously messy person, always mislaying his sermons or dashing off in the middle of something to attend to someone. Thomas would come in and straighten out his papers and answer his correspondence.

"Well, Thomas, it is too bad we didn't put something away when the cows were fat, eh? Although there are still fatted cows to be had. There are indeed." He sat down in the only other chair in the cramped office, looking somehow like a petitioner rather than the rising star in a political arena. "How's the straw vote going?"

"Bullie should never have given the Association a week's respite. Your support is growing."

"Well, the Lord's will be done. Specially if it's going our way, eh?"

The Reverend leaned his elbows on the desk, suddenly looking tired. He wore a black suit and had a white beard and quite long hair. He looked from the distance a bit like an Edwardian dandy. Up close, though, you could see the coat was old, so old it had the slightly brown-green gloss that seems to form like a subsurface patina on old black cloth.

The cuffs and elbows had been mended and the mends mended again. His black boots were shiny but had holes in the soles and his black hat was not in much better condition than the ones the Irish navvies wore on the railroad gangs. He was what was called "proud poor," that is, down at the heel but clean and erect.

"And what's the news in the parish, Thomas? I haven't been making my rounds as regularly as I used to. I've got out of touch. How's that young woman next door doing? Margaret?"

Thomas reddened and looked down. "She's...ah, she's fine. She's doing just fine."

The Reverend looked amused. "So, she's doing just fine — even though her mother's run off with a cowboy and her father's committed suicide?"

"Yes, well, no. She's...She's grateful for your burying him just as if he hadn't taken..."

"You seem to be a bit at a loss for words this afternoon, Thomas. She's a pretty girl, don't you think?"

"Yes. Yes." Thomas busied himself with the papers on the desk.

The Reverend got up and made to go. "Maybe I'll just drop around and have a chat with her and your mother this afternoon."

"Ah, she's not home. She's working for Chuck. Volunteering. Down at the office."

"Ah. Party work?"

"I suppose so." Tommy glanced up but the Reverend had already turned and was going out the door. His voice came back from the hall, "See you in Victoria Park this evening."

It was foolish of him to be jealous. Especially since he had not dared to say more than the usual trite things to her. Chuck had taken her under his wing and sent someone there to be with her and help with the funeral arrangements and so on. He had even paid for the funeral when he found out Mr. Long had left nothing for Margaret's upkeep. She volunteered at Party headquarters but Chuck made sure she had pocket money and gave Tommy's mother a bit extra so she could take over some soup once in awhile. You couldn't fault him, but the image of the two of them kissing was burned in Tommy's memory. Even that wasn't Chuck's doing. Still.

Tommy felt an anger. It was so stupid of him. Chuck went out of his way to be a good friend, not only to Tommy but to the whole family. To Margaret. And, he had to face it, he himself had done nothing for her. Too embarrassed. He dreamt, sort of wide-awake dreaming, of coming to her rescue, perhaps even moving in with her and using his income to support them both. Her house was right next door. He dreamt of other things, too, that made him feel guilty. Chuck was right, he looked to heaven for answers he could only find on earth. He got up and kicked the desk.

That afternoon in Victoria Park people began to gather near the cenotaph to witness what was anticipated as being the most sensational confrontation of the forces of Reverend Bullock and the forces of Reverend Evans. Not that both sides were going to present their case. The speaker of the day was to be Mr. McKenzie and his talk was entitled, "Good-bye to Bad Times." But everyone knew that he was a strong supporter of the Reverend Bullock and they also knew that the Reverend Evans would be there.

The sun had beaten down all day and now, in the late afternoon, there was not so much cooler air, as a feeling of respite from the relentless glare from the cloudless sky. People had brought blankets and sat in groups on the grass under the trees. It was a respite from their troubles.

The speakers' platform was decked out in red, white and blue bunting and Union Jacks. McKenzie, it was made clear, embraced law, order and the Empire. The theme of the speech suited Mr. McKenzie. He was a plump, congenial-looking man, the sort of Englishman, although he boasted of his patriotism and Canadianism, who is almost Dickensian – rotund belly, white side whiskers, jovial, not too intelligent, but clever. His cleverness on this afternoon seemed to be aimed at linking the work of the Reverend Bullock and that of the Premier of the province, and taking a sideswipe at all "this leftwing nonsense and bolshie talk." Perhaps Mr. McKenzie was anticipating a political career for himself and wanted to establish both a strong economic and ethical plat-form.

It was a seemingly endless and repetitive speech. The children had long escaped their parents' grasp and were running around the bushes, shouting and playing tag. Mr. McKenzie droned on, but finally drew to a close with a raised voice proclaiming that the Premier of the Province was like Moses leading the tribes of Israel through the desert to the new land of milk and honey. And around him stood the pillars of society, the men of the cloth, read the Reverend Bullock, the businessmen and, yes, the workers, who would follow him to the Promised Land. There was silence after he finished, and then cheers from a group surrounding the Reverend Bullock and desultory claps here and there among the rest of the audience.

The Reverend Evans was sitting a bit to Mr. McKenzie's left, obscured by a shrub. He now stood up and the crowd hushed in anticipation, giving him all the attention Mr. McKenzie had not been able to command.

"Mr. McKenzie, I have listened to your remarks with a great deal of interest. Now, did I hear you rightly that you are comparing the present leader of the government with the leader of the Hebrew people during their wanderings in the desert? For forty years, if I remember rightly?"

Mr. McKenzie gave a noncommittal gesture which Reverend Evans seemed to take as agreement. He looked down thoughtfully at the ground.

"And that we men of the cloth, as you call us, are sort of elders whose job is to support this new Moses?"

Mr. McKenzie tried to answer but Reverend Evans hushed him with a movement of his hand.

"Then you and the Premier perhaps also see many of the demands and complaints of the people here in Saskatchewan to be like those of the Hebrews when they lost confidence in their leader and demanded that he show them this land he kept promising them? Perhaps you even feel that if we do not follow the Premier and his elders, or at least some of his elders, and yourself of course, we are worshipping strange gods, even idols?"

Again, Mr. McKenzie looked as if he wanted to speak, but he just nodded somewhat hesitantly.

"Perhaps you also see the government relief programs as something like the manna from Heaven that appeared at Moses' request? The only difference being, as I see it, that the ancient Israelites, we are told, ate their fill, for it says, does it not, 'and they gathered every man according to his eating.' Would that be approximately what you are trying to tell us?"

The Reverend Evans moved to a position directly in front of the podium. Mr. McKenzie seemed to back away a bit. He no longer gestured agreement, but seemed not to know what to do. The crowd by this time was hanging on every word of Reverend Evans.

"How far can we carry this comparison, Mr. McKenzie? It occurs to me that you may see the dust storms as similar to the pillars of cloud by day and fire by night that led the Israelites out of Egypt."

Now, Mr. McKenzie was shaking his head. No, that wasn't what he had meant at all.

"Well, I shall not go on then. I see that you are now uncomfortable with this comparison you have made between Moses and the Premier, backed up of course by men of the cloth, businessmen, and even workers, although God knows there are now more unemployed than employed. There is, however, one last question I would like to put to you, just to clear up the comparison for us simpler folks. Would you say that, like Moses, the Premier will pine for the Promised Land but in the end God will not let him lead the people across the river to take possession of its fertile valleys and cool meandering streams?"

The crowd started to titter, then laugh. Mr. McKenzie drew himself up to his full 5'4" height and made a blustery exit, but not quickly enough. He must have heard the Reverend Evans's last speculation, "Then, perhaps, Mr. McKenzie, you see yourself as Joshua."

After that, McKenzie was called Joshua or simply Josh and hecklers would shout out, "Surely, you're joshing us," amid much speculation about his blowing horns and bringing down the walls of Jericho/Regina. Since Joshua lived on to conquer and rule, it is unlikely the Reverend Evans would have pushed the comparison that far.

CHAPTER SEVEN

His face changed from a smiling young man to something frightening. It was as if the bones themselves melted and the features spread into an amorphous mass. Then out of the featureless glob another face began to form, this one rough and stubbly, threatening in some way. There was nowhere to run. His face began to come toward her. He reached out suddenly to touch her...

Clara awoke with a start. At first she didn't know where she was; the house was dark with the only light coming in through the front windows from the street light. The dream seemed to be still there and she whirled her head around to face him. Nothing. She was alone. She sat up and wept.

The grave's a fine and private place
But none, I think, do there embrace.

As her sobbing petered out, the lines came back to her from some book or lecture room. Who wrote that, Donne? Marvell? How true it was! She had to get out of this house, out of this city, at least for awhile, see something else. The thought of travelling alone, however, depressed her and frightened her a little. She had always let Chuck make the arrangements, book the flights. Well, his secretary really did it. There would be no one to talk to or share with. There was no one here, either, for that matter. But there were friends here if she wanted to call them. They had stopped phoning every day to see how she was. Perhaps they were a little embarrassed or perhaps they were just getting on with their own lives. Chuck's death must have been just a distant event for them. They were her friends, not his, in any case, or, rather, he kept to himself and didn't open up enough to have true friends. So he sort of shared hers on occasion. She did still have a childhood friend in Vancouver. Patricia, who was on her own again after her disastrous affair with that Indian artist. Maybe she should go out to the Coast, someplace completely different. She could even visit her sister in Kelowna. She hadn't seen her in a long time. No. Best to leave that sleeping dog lie. The familiar phrase of Chuck's. Anyway, the family had just faded away for her after she left the Coast and came to Toronto. How long ago? Forty-five years. It couldn't be. But it was. She was an old woman even if she still felt young, well, younger than she actually was.

Another thought struck her: Maybe this Pennan, or his family, lived out at the Coast. Chuck mentioned once having been in Vancouver when he was younger. They might have known each other out there. Perhaps, Pennan had given Chuck the note to keep in case... Her thoughts dried up. Well, it could be. Of course he'd probably be dead by now. "I killed her."

Clara struggled to her feet and walked stiffly out to the kitchen. Her skirt was crumpled from lying on the couch and her mouth felt dry. She glanced at the time shining greenly out of the microwave oven: 4:45 a.m. "Morning has broken..." The Cat Stevens song drifted through her mind and she filled the kettle with water and put it on a burner. She'd have to go out and put some flowers on Chuck's grave before she went. Then...So, she was going, already planning out everything that had to be done. When the kettle whistled she poured the water over a teabag in a mug and left it to steep and cool a little. She went down the hall to the powder room, humming the rest of the Cat Stevens song under her breath. Yes, she'd go to Vancouver. Nothing holding her here. She'd try phoning Patricia after dinner.

As she walked through the long blue-carpeted hallway of Terminal 3, she realized how cocooned she had been for the past two months. Here were people, hundreds of people, all going about their business, carrying cases full of papers, talking on cellular phones, reading newspapers, telling their kids to be quiet, drinking coffee, looking out of the windows at the airplanes, staring off into space, working on their laptop computers – just as if Chuck had not died. As if her house did not echo emptily with her footsteps. And ninety percent of them probably had their own houses and spouses and kids. They drove cars bigger and smaller than Chuck's, well, hers. Clara went over to the bar, called The Oyster Bar, and ordered a large cappuccino. It was the first time she had splurged. She laughed to herself a little at the word "splurged" for a cappuccino purchase. A young woman standing next to her smiled back.

She felt good. This was the right decision. She'd get out into the world and meet people. The thought crossed her mind, meet a man, and she immediately pushed it back out of mental sight. She'd enjoy the trip, pretend it was a holiday rather than an escape. Patricia hadn't answered the phone. Perhaps she was away. It didn't matter. Clara stirred some sugar into her coffee and looked around. A man at the far end caught her eye and held it for a moment. Clara felt her cheeks burn a little. She hadn't expected it. She hurriedly drank her cappuccino and then went over to the waiting area at Gate 78.

Yesterday she had bought a small suitcase on wheels, one that slipped into the stainless steel contraption which measured it for fitting under the seat or in the overhead bin of the airplane. She pulled it behind her down the ramp and onto the airplane. She should have gone business class. She had the money, but it had seemed too much to spend just for a trip. So she found herself crowded in the narrow aisle of the economy section, trying to get her suitcase up and into the bin.

"Can I help?" It was the man from the end of the bar.

"Oh, thank you." Clara could not believe she would still use that old yes-you-wonderful-man tone. She almost thought she would see Chuck's disapproving face, glaring in the window. Well, most men had always been very helpful. Chuck teased her (he was a bit annoyed she knew) about "the nice gentleman" that always appeared to help her when she got into trouble.

He lifted her bag and secured it carefully in the bin. "There. Are you sitting here?" He motioned to the three seats and she smiled in affirmation and slid into the window seat. Clara still wore her wedding band and she turned it round and round on her finger as she looked out the window. The man sat in the aisle seat and took out his newspaper. They waited, each, Clara thought, very much aware of the other sitting one seat away. She was a foolish woman but it was fun to feel the feelings again. And this was a holiday!

All the rituals of flying gone through – safety mime show, drinks cart, plastic tray of food with cold cutlery in a plastic sheath, would you like a magazine, we're flying at 33,000 feet, arrival time – and conversation: the activities of travelling had started them talking. Excuse me, please, when she had squeezed past to go to the washroom, would you like the paper, if you're sure you're done with it, on a pleasure trip, no, business, and you? going to visit a friend, where does she live?, in Vancouver, ah, yes, a beautiful city, work for an ad company, used to write copy, now see that others do it, yes, long trip, and then, I've watched you turning your ring round and round on your finger, oh, that, well, I lost my husband recently (sounded to her as if she had misplaced him), that's hard, I'm sorry, my wife died last year, cancer, married thirty years, yes, well we were married over forty years, you don't look old enough, well, he was quite a bit older than me, so you're on your own, and you? why not join

55

me for dinner after we arrive, why not? why not? Clara looked fixedly out the window into the gathering darkness and saw her own face looking back, mildly surprised. My name is Sidney, Sidney Penner. Did you say, Pennan? No, Penner, a Mennonite name. Oh, oh. And your name? Clara. Why did you react to my last name, a friend, an enemy, don't like Mennonites? No. I mean...nothing. Well, it's just I, I would like to get in touch with a Thomas Pennan. Where does he live? I don't know. Where does he work, then? I don't know. I see. That may be a little difficult.

"I know it sounds daft but I ran across that name in my husband's papers and it's important that I get in touch with him. But there was no address and my husband hadn't seen him for quite awhile. And I never knew him. I just have the name. I'm almost positive though that he doesn't live in Toronto or anywhere in Central Canada, for that matter. Of course, he may be dead by now. He fought with Chuck, in, in the Second World War."

"Well, when we get off, why don't we look in the Vancouver telephone book and see if there is a, what was the name?"

"Thomas Pennan."

They sat at a corner table in the dining room of the Vancouver Hotel. They now had a subject for conversation and together they planned how to check for Thomas Pennan. First, the Vancouver telephone directory. Surely the waiter would bring them one; Sidney was a regular customer. Then, tomorrow, if that yielded no results, Sidney would have one of his staff go onto the Internet and see if the name could be found. But dinner first. Clara had not had any wine for almost a year and she felt it rise immediately to her head. She should have stopped with one glass, but she sat with the second glass half gone and her dinner only half eaten. What the hell, it was a holiday! Chuck for some reason or other had never liked holidays or travelling for fun. For that matter, he hadn't liked her drinking, either.

"Peter Pennan? I am trying to locate a Thomas Pennan. You wouldn't happen to know a Pennan by that name?" It was the seventh Pennan they had phoned. They had taken turns calling them. Sidney was on the cellphone for this one, the last Pennan in the directory. He looked across the table at Clara and held up his hand and leaned forward, listening. He explained, slowly and in an exaggerated way, that the name had come up in the private papers of a man in Toronto who had recently died.

"Who? Oh, you mean what was his name? Just a minute, his wife, er, widow is here with me. I'll let you talk to her." He put his hand over the phone and whispered, "Sounds a little drunk." He then handed the cellphone to Clara, making facial expressions to let her know he thought they were onto something.

"Hello?" Clara pursed her lips and wished she had not had the last two glasses of wine. She was feeling quite marvellous but a little reckless. In reaching for the phone, she knocked her purse off the table. Sidney scrambled to get it. "Just a minute," she said into the telephone. She took the purse and smiled at Sidney.

"There. Now, you know Thomas Pennan, do you?"

"Didn't say I did."

"But I thought you told Sidney, my, er, friend, that you knew him."

"Didn't say I didn't."

"Well, Mr. Pennan, perhaps I can explain." Clara realized she couldn't explain at all. She couldn't tell him she had a letter confessing that he had killed someone. Oh, why had she bothered to pursue this anyway? "He was a friend of my husband's, a long time ago, perhaps fifty, maybe sixty years ago. I don't know much more than that but the name came up in my husband's papers. I thought I had better try to get in touch."

"Who was your husband?" Did she hear a little interest in his voice? Hard to tell.

"Peter Stemichuk. Does that mean anything to you?"

"Might."

"Well, Mr. Pennan, if you could tell me anything about him, I would be very grateful." Clara heard her sob-story voice come into action, just a little. It had no effect on Peter Pennan.

"How grateful?"

"You mean you want money to tell me?"

"You sound rich."

Indeed, Clara did sound rich. She had that slightly clipped way of speaking that one heard wealthy women use on saleswomen in Holt Renfrew, the one the saleswomen in Holt Renfrew used on customers who were not wealthy. Sidney was leaning forward, obviously curious about where the conversation was going. When he realized that the man was demanding payment, he shook his head energetically to tell Clara not to give him any.

"How much would you want, Mr. Pennan? I have a little money that my husband left me. I couldn't give you very much, but I would try to help you out if you needed a little extra money. I know Christmas is coming and everything is so expensive. Do you have children, Mr. Pennan?"

"No. A hundred dollars."

"That's quite a bit for..."

"Give me the phone." Sidney took it from Clara's hands. "Now, look here, Pennan, you are talking to the widow of man who has just recently died. All she wants is the name of a friend of his to settle, well, to clear things up. What kind of game do you think you're playing?"

Sidney looked down at the telephone, as if trying to see the man's face. He glanced up at Clara, who simply sat waiting, showing no sign of anxiousness or excitement. "Okay, Pennan. We want it. How much? Fine, where do we meet you? Where's that? Okay, okay, got it. We'll be there at ten tomorrow morning then." Sidney flipped the phone closed and banged it down on the table. "Bastard."

Clara reached out her hand and gently rubbed the back of his hand. "Thank you, Sidney, for handling that for me." Sidney took hold of her hand and she softly withdrew it and put both hands on her lap.

"Clara..."

"No, Sidney. I'm tired now. I think I'll go to my room. Thank you for a very interesting evening."

Hiding his disappointment – but what had he expected? – Sidney summoned the waiter. When he had signed the chit for the meal, he looked appraisingly at Clara. "I enjoyed it very much. You probably won't believe me, but this is first time I have had dinner alone with a woman since my wife died."

Clara knew he was lying, but she liked him for trying to make her feel special. She rose from the table and gathered up her purse and papers.

"Well, until tomorrow morning, then."

CHAPTER EIGHT

It was late Spring, 1935, and after an early germination and growth, the crops were already shrivelling under the June sun. The heavy loam of the southern prairieland had developed a scablike crust, and deep rifts had appeared in the yards and fields. And the wind, the wind got up by midday and blew relentlessly, dropping to a breeze only for a few hours in the early morning. Tommy's mother had stuffed rags around the windows and doors to stop the dust coming in, but still, whenever a plate or glass was taken from a shelf, it left a round, clean spot in the midst of the surrounding grey film.

Tommy stood by the eastern side of the train station, watching the sun come up. The cartage trucks were loaded and the railway cars sat empty, their doors opening onto their cavernous interiors. The eastern sky was a wide swath of pink undercut with darker rose, red and green. The breeze was cool and fresh, smelling of sage and sweet grass. Tommy was tired. He turned and walked into the office to punch out for the day. It was pleasant to walk home in the early morning before the city was awake. Only the Grey Nuns Hospital showed lights and bustle at this time in the morning.

As he walked, he thought about the message he had received when he came onto work the previous evening. Why would the cartage company want several of the trucks delivered to the Mounted Police barracks immediately after the night shift on the weekend? He had just passed his licence for driving a truck, but he had thought he would have to wait a long time before an opening came to drive on the day shift. This was not that opening, but the foreman had said specifically that he wanted Tommy and a couple of other new men, who had just got their licences, to take the trucks out there. For extra money. Tommy shrugged his shoulders and dismissed the thoughts. Money's money.

When he arrived home, he usually had breakfast with Chuck before Chuck went to the Unity League office. He then went to bed. Chuck was preoccupied these days and didn't share much information. He would have breakfast, talk a bit about the weather, find out what Tommy was doing, and then go and knock on Margaret's door. The two of them would set off across the prairie into town. Tommy would watch them go and his mother would watch him. He still hadn't said anything to Margaret. He couldn't even ask her out, on his wages. But there was a church picnic coming up at Boggy Creek and he was planning to ask her to go with him.

This morning Chuck seemed very anxious to get going. When Tommy told him about the trucks though, he stopped and sat down again. "Tell me about this."

"That's really all there is to tell. The foreman said he wanted John, Eric, and me to deliver the trucks to the

Mounted Police barracks first thing Saturday morning. There aren't so many deliveries on the weekends, so I guess the trucks can be spared."

"What do they want them for?"

"How should I know?" Tommy bristled at Chuck's insistence.

"Surely he said something. Where at the Mounted Police barracks?"

"I don't know. We're just supposed to ask at the entrance where the booth is."

"At that time in the morning? There won't be anyone there."

"Well, apparently there will be, because that's what he said to do."

"Which trucks?"

"The usual ones, the two-ton cube trucks. The ones we use around the city."

Chuck fell silent, his eyes searching Tommy's for any hint that there was something he wasn't saying. He stared so long and fixedly that Tommy became uneasy.

"Something wrong?"

"No. No. I don't think so. Look, Tommy, can you see if you can find out anything more about this?"

"Is it important? I suppose they just want the trucks to move something around out there."

"Maybe. Maybe."

Late Thursday afternoon, Tommy returned from the church at around five. Chuck and Margaret were waiting for him. He walked into the yard past the privies and the shed where Margaret's father had decided enough is enough. The two sat on a bench outside the kitchen door, a bench where Tommy's mother sometimes sat to shell peas and peel potatoes. They were deep in conversation when Tommy came into the yard, their heads close together. He could feel the intensity of their discussion from across the yard. His mother was working at the sink in the kitchen. As Tommy approached the house, Chuck called to him to come over. As always, Tommy bristled at what he thought was a pre-emptory tone that Chuck used with him.

"What's up?" Tommy affected a deliberately casual stance, but as Margaret looked up at him, Hi Tommy, he felt awkward. She was wearing slacks, which bothered him. It was too far from his world of church meetings and church pews. He found himself tracing in his imagination the flesh beneath the cloth.

"We've been talking about your visit to the Mounties this Saturday."

We, we. Tommy made a face. "What about it?"

"Well, here's the plan."

The plan, for Christ's sake – Tommy bit his lip at his curse.

"Margaret is going to go with you. She can pretend she is helping out with the paperwork or whatever."

"I don't know. Mr. Williams won't be too keen about someone else in the truck. This is my first time. Driving, I mean. He's pretty keen about getting these trucks out there right away. Keeps fretting about the time and so on."

"You'll simply take the truck and head for the barracks as if you were going straight there, but you'll just make a couple of blocks detour past here and pick Margaret up."

"But why do you want Margaret to go? I mean, I don't mind, but it might look strange, that's all." Tommy ended his weak objection on a weak note, and felt he was being used. "What's it all about?"

"I just want Margaret to snoop around a bit, ask a few questions, find out what these trucks are being used for."

"I can do that."

"Oh, I think Margaret may be able to get more information out of them than you will." Chuck winked and Tommy reddened. Margaret smiled, then giggled a little. She obviously liked being attractive to men. She also knew how useful that could be for Chuck's cause. Her information, often garnered from young Mounties travelling on the streetcar, was fed continually into his office and then used in their attempts to organize the growing ranks of unemployed men who loitered around the city.

Saturday dawned grey and cloudy. An unexpected relief from the usual sun reddening the eastern sky. It might even rain. Tommy felt excited at driving the truck, proud of having been selected. The shabby old truck he was given had had a gallon of gas put into it for the trip. Apparently the Mounties were expected to supply whatever they might need. Tommy went around the truck and checked the tires. He didn't notice Mr. Williams smiling at his self-important trek from wheel to wheel. Okay, let's go. It was like a military operation. The three drivers climbed into the cabs and started the engines. Tommy let John and Eric move out of the yard first, then he followed more slowly. They were the only vehicles on the road. It was impossible for John and Eric not to notice him when he turned off. Tommy fretted and fumed at Chuck's insistence that he make the detour to pick up Margaret, even though he was anxious to show off his driving skills. She could have walked the two blocks up to Dewdney Avenue. But no, she mustn't be seen until they are safely in the grounds of the Mountie barracks, says Chuck, and Chuck is always right. Chuck is always in charge.

When he got to Alexander Avenue he abruptly turned right, hurried down to Seventh Avenue, turned left and came to a stop in front of Margaret's house. Margaret rushed out, this time dressed in a skirt and a freshly ironed white blouse. Her hair was up in a ribbon. Chuck stood by the house and raised a hand in what? greeting, goodbye, encouragement. Margaret quickly climbed up into the cab and Tommy started shifting through the gears. He turned left at Connaught and then back to Dewdney. The other two trucks were just barely in sight on Dewdney Avenue. He sped or at least went as quickly as the old truck could go to catch up with them. When they neared the barracks entrance, Margaret unbuttoned the two top buttons of her blouse.

As Tommy turned up the gravel road to the gate, he could see that John's truck had already been waved through and Eric's stood at the booth waiting for permission to enter. He pulled up behind and looked at Margaret. Don't worry, Tommy. She put out her hand and touched his arm lightly. She was beautiful.

"Name? Okay, right. Whose with you?"

"It's, ah, my sister."

The Mountie looked appreciatively at Margaret and smiled. She smiled back. "Okay. I guess it won't hurt. Out for the ride?" He was a young man, fully six feet tall, well-built and probably starved for female company.

"Oh, yes. My brother said I could come with him and see you, see what you do out here." She leaned forward.

"Well, we can certainly show you some things. If you wait a moment, I can take you around myself."

"Oh, would you? That would be nice."

Thomas silently fumed.

CHAPTER NINE

By the time Tommy had delivered the van back to the cartage company, Chuck and Margaret had had their talk and Chuck was sitting in the kitchen chatting with Tommy's mother. When he saw Tommy coming across the prairie, he came to the kitchen door and leaned against the frame.

"Well, Tommy, that was an outing, wasn't it?"

Tommy grunted and pushed past him into the house. His mother turned slightly to greet him but he was already in the other room. In a moment he reappeared in some clean clothes and stormed back out of the house, heading across the prairie in the other direction, toward the railway depot buildings.

"I'll go after him and see what's wrong, Mom." Chuck started after him. He went more slowly than Tommy, letting him get ahead, be on his own a bit. Eventually, Tommy sat down on the bank at the edge of the railway tracks, where they cut diagonally into the yards. Chuck waited and then went up to him.

"What's wrong, Tommy?"

"Everything."

Chuck sat down on his haunches a little distance away and stared with him across to the buildings the colour of dried blood. Neither spoke. Tommy looked on the verge of tears; Chuck was grim.

"You're feeling used. Right?"

Tommy nodded.

"I'm sorry. I should have kept you informed. There's so much to do now and we have to put our personal life aside and live for the future. That's just the way it is, Tommy. The Revolution is imminent and we have to be prepared. We have to know what the police are doing. We have to protect the people, prevent them getting hurt unnecessarily. When we are in the midst of the last turmoil, then it will be time for laying down our lives. Not now, not to a few tinpot Mounties. Do you understand?"

Silence.

"Tommy. Can't you see? We're being exploited. You working for slave's wages. Your father without work. Your mother trying to sell a few scones door-to-door. Your sister holed up in some godforsaken teacherage looking after some bedraggled kids. The system is rotten, Tommy. Rotten to the core. And all your Reverend Evanses and talk about what happened to the people of Israel is not going to help one goddamn little bit."

Silence.

"The capitalist system simply has to be overthrown and replaced with a society in which everyone is equal, in which everyone is paid according to their needs, not according to some businessman's charity. The CCF can jabber on about socialization, but it is not enough. We have to have a revolution. We have to destroy the old and build the new, not mess around trying to make the old corrupt system a little better. It's rotten, rotten to the core." Chuck's voice rose and took on the fanatical tone of his public speeches.

Silence.

"You don't trust me, do you Chuck?" The question was spoken tiredly to the air around him rather than directed at Chuck.

"No. No, I don't Tommy. You're not committed to anything. I only trust commitment."

"I'm committed to the church. What you mean is, I'm not committed to you." Tommy turned and confronted Chuck. Chuck looked down at the dry grass and then at Tommy.

"No, to the Revolution. But not because of me, but because of what I stand for."

"And what do you stand for? Some bedraggled bunch of loafers who couldn't get a job even if there was one. Communists! Yes, sir. No, sir. Yes, Mr. Stalin. We'll all do what you say, Mr. Stalin. Horseshit! That's what you are, Chuck, full of horseshit. You and your whole bunch are one steaming pile of horseshit." Tommy stood up, breathing heavily.

"Perhaps, Tommy. But let me tell you something. I'm not telling people that if they just let themselves be mistreated and abused in this life, then they will live off caviar in some heaven where the angels sing all the time. I'm not fucking around with their emotions. I'm giving them a chance to look at the situation rationally and make a rational decision. No pie in the sky stuff."

"Rational? Do you call blind adherence to an ideology, rational?"

Silence.

"Anyway, I don't want to be used any more." Tommy turned to Chuck, sticking out his chin in a perhaps unconscious gesture of hostility.

"Okay, Tommy." Chuck turned and started back toward the house.

"Wait. Wait, Chuck." Chuck stopped and turned. "I did that for Margaret. I, I love her." Again, Tommy looked as if he was on the verge of tears.

Chuck waited. Tommy took a few steps toward him, stopped.

"Good, Tommy. She's a wonderful girl."

Mrs. Pennan stood by the side of the house and watched the two figures coming across the prairie. She dried her hands on her apron and dried them again. Then, she turned and went back into the house.

CHAPTER TEN

When Clara awoke it was already nine o'clock and the sun was cutting a shaft across the room. She stretched, thought for a moment about the previous evening, then about Sidney, Sid, she thought it was by the end of the evening, and snuggled down into the covers again. Oh, Jesus, nine o'clock and they had to be somewhere by ten. She swung out of bed and into the bathroom. No, better phone Sid. She rang the number he had given her on a yellow Post-it Note before he let her go off to bed. No answer. Probably already down in the breakfast room. What should she wear? First the bathroom.

Clara walked into the breakfast room, dressed in the blue suit she had last worn to go to the lawyer's office. Sidney sat near a window where he could see everyone who came in, and he stood up when she entered and came over to escort her to the table. Ah, a gentleman. She supported equal opportunity but why couldn't men be gentlemen as well as equals? She smiled.

"This place he wants to meet isn't in a very good part of town, I'm afraid. It's down in the rubby area – drugs, homeless, that sort of thing. Maybe I'd better go alone."

"No, Sidney, Sid. This is, after all, my problem. I shouldn't have dragged you into it in the first place. Besides you have work to do, I'm sure. I'll just go on my own."

"I couldn't let you do that, Clara. I'll send a taxi and have him brought here, then."

"No, no, not here. I don't want...It would be better if we went there. He'll be more comfortable."

"I see what you mean. I think you should change your shoes then. Perhaps you have some low heels with you?"

The Railway Park was hardly a park – a patch of grass with three trees and a cement walk. And two benches, one of which had a prone figure under newspapers stretched out on it, and the other with two unshaven men passing a cigarette back and forth. Clara and Sidney walked quickly from their taxi to the bench occupied by the two men. Mr. Pennan? Grunt. Well, see you, Peter, after you talk with your posh friends here. Grunt. Mr. Pennan? That's me.

"Before we start you've got to understand, Mr. Pennan, that we're not paying good money for nothing. Your information better be good or no moolah. Understood?"

Grunt, this time with some overtone of affirmation.

"Okay, what do you know?"

"Where's the money?"

"After you tell us."

"Nope."

"Twenty up front?"

"Fifty."

"Okay, but it better be good." Sidney counted out two twenties and a ten. Pennan grabbed it, recounted it and stuffed it into his shirt pocket.

"Well."

"Thomas Pennan was my uncle." Pennan looked belligerently at Sidney as if daring him to contradict.

"Yes, Mr. Pennan. Is that all you have to say, or could you perhaps add just a bit of information to that?"

"Sure. What you want to know?"

Clara rushed in, "Who he was, where he lived, everything."

"Don't know everything. He was my uncle. Lived in Regina."

"Regina! When? How long ago?"

"Don't know. When I was a kid he wasn't there no more."

"Where was he?"

"At war."

"We know he was at war. Almost every man was at war those days. Can't you just tell us a bit more about, about, well, about the situation?" Sidney was getting impatient but realized that it would get him nowhere with Peter Pennan. Pennan was beyond responding to others' impatience.

"My mother was his sister."

"That figures, Mr. Pennan. What was your mother's name? Her first name, I mean."

Peter Pennan looked at them both suspiciously. "Her brother was Tommy. I was a baby when he went to war."

"The war, Mr. Pennan?" It occurred to Clara that he might not mean the Second World War.

"That war in Spain."

"The Spanish Civil War? How old are you Mr Pennan?"

"I'm sixty-four. Get my pension next year." For a moment he brightened and looked almost alert.

"You were born in 1935, then?"

"Yep."

"In Regina?"

"Yep."

"Why won't you tell us your mother's first name? The other fifty isn't coming to you until you tell us all you know."

"Her name is –was – Nell."

Clara and Sidney stood in the shade of the tree growing behind the bench and looked perplexedly at the scruffy old man sitting watching the pigeons pecking at nothing on the baked earth around his feet. Then, as if stirred by some long hidden emotion, Peter Pennan started to speak without prompting.

"He went to war and left my mother and my grandmom and granddad without no way of supporting themselves. Except my mom. She worked for peanuts. Then, my grandmom died and that left granddad and my mom and me by ourselves, like. Then after that my mom died."

"What about your father?"

"Didn't have one."

"Come, come, Mr. Pennan. You mean he wasn't there or did he go to war too?"

"Tommy, my uncle, died, you know."

"Where, how?"

"In that war there. He died. Maybe he was shot or something. He died, anyway." Pennan nodded his head.

"You're sure he died in the Spanish Civil War, not the Second World War?"

"I remember the Second World War, don't I? Granddad got a job cooking for the men. Tommy was dead. So was my mom. I'd remember that, wouldn't I?" His rheumy eyes filled.

"There, there, Mr. Pennan, we didn't mean to upset you." Clara reached out and touched his shoulder, much to Sidney's discomfort.

"Not upset. Nothing upsets me." He glared up at Clara and shook off her hand.

"Now, one more question and the fifty dollars is yours. Who was your father, Peter, and don't tell us you don't know."

"He died too. In Spain, like Uncle Tommy."

"His name, Mr. Pennan."

No answer.

"Do you want the rest of this money or not?"

"A bohunk named Peter, Peter Stemichuk."

"Oh, God!"

CHAPTER ELEVEN

Almost every weekend, some way or another, Nell managed to get home. Unless the snow and blizzards of that winter clogged all the roads. The teaching job was difficult and lonely. She lived in a two-room teacherage on the schoolgrounds about ten miles from town and a good two miles to the nearest neighbour. The salary had been cut in half the previous year, so she barely made enough to buy food and the few clothes she needed, even though she paid no rent. But the children responded to her and often brought her small presents from home – half a dozen eggs, a drawing, and once a newborn kitten, just to show her. She had thirteen children in six grades ranging from grade two to grade eight and practically no resources. Oddly enough, the children were all from two families and all had the same last name. But one family was relatively well-to-do and the other was dirt poor.

She and Chuck, or Peter as she always called him, had become very close over the winter. When she came home, he was noticeably more often around, and they spent time together doing schoolwork preparations, talking, going for walks. Nell at eighteen was a good-looking young woman, a bit gangly, but handsome in an outdoorsy way. Her eyes were her charm, brown with green specks near the pupils. And she was tall. She was just under five feet eleven, slightly taller than Chuck. He tended to stand up very straight when he was with her. They obviously loved being in one another's company, but their behaviour in public was always very proper. Nell's announcement in May of 1935, therefore, came as a surprise.

"Mom, Dad, I have something to tell you. I don't know how to say this, except straight out."

Her mother and father stood together near the kitchen door. Her mother had just taken a pot from the stove and still held it with a tea towel wrapped around the handle. Her father was trying to take the slop pail out from under the sink without spilling it. "Why don't you ever take that out when it's only half full?"

"I'm with child."

The quaint biblical phrase was not out of place in the Pennan household, but on Nell's lips it sounded as if she had memorized it for Sunday School. Neither her mother or father reacted at first. They stood there in the kitchen on the worn linoleum, frozen in their tasks, looking up at Nell, not able, it seemed, to say anything.

"It's Peter's child." The tone of Nell's statement seemed to suggest that this part of the announcement was meant to be reassuring. But, again, neither her mother nor father was able to respond. "I'm sorry to inflict this on you."

"A child's no infliction." Mrs. Pennan found her voice, reached out and placed her hand on Nell's shoulder. Simple, perhaps even stilted as this statement and bit of affection were, they broke the dam of Nell's tears and she wept. Her father put his hands in his pockets and looked out the window.

"I am so sorry. I know how much you have to put up with already. But I love Peter, and I want to have his child. Don't worry about the money. I'll get a job here in the city somehow. The department store manager said that if I ever wanted to work there again, he'd try to find me something."

"A job?"

Nell looked up and then turned away. "I don't think Peter and I can get married. Not yet."

"Not going to get married, eh?" Nell's father mumbled under his breath. He had fallen into the habit of muttering under his breath of late. He looked at his wife as if she could figure this all out. "Not married?"

"No. Peter has no money and he is so busy right now, with, well, with all these issues. You know, the unemployed. And he doesn't have any prospects for a job, well, not a regular job. The League pays him a bit and he earns some speaking. It wouldn't be right to saddle him with me and a child right now. Anyway, he actually doesn't know about it yet. I thought I would tell you first." Nell blurted out the words in starts and stops and then stopped abruptly. "He's waiting for me in the other room. I'm going to tell him now." She ran into the living room, leaving her parents standing motionless in the small back kitchen.

Ten minutes or so later, Chuck came into the kitchen slowly, somewhat hesitantly, and stood with his hands at his sides. Nell came and stood a bit behind him. Her mother and father were sitting at the table. Chuck addressed Mr. Pennan.

"Nell has told you, she is going to have our child, sir. We've talked about what we should do. As she has told you, I can't accept the day-to-day responsibility of a family right now, much as I would like to. I've got to continue with the work. It's at a critical stage right now. Everything depends on the next month or so. I'll of course give her and you whatever money..."

"Money!" The word exploded from Mr. Pennan's mouth. He pushed back his chair with a crash and walked belligerently toward Chuck. "Money, young man!" He stopped, seeming not to know what else to say. He shoved his hands in his pockets again and, visibly shaking, returned to his post at the window.

"To help, Daddy. Help with the extra costs." Nell moved between Chuck and her father.

"So that's the way it is, is it? That's our gratitude, is it?" Mr. Pennan looked down at the floor. "It doesn't matter how hard I try. It always goes wrong." Tears came to his eyes and he openly wept, the tears running down his nose and onto the floor. "That's the way it is, is it?"

"I'll take care of Nell, do anything I can for her and the baby. But I can't marry her. I have to serve the Revolution. Things are in motion."

Mr. Pennan stood up straight. "The revolution? That's what you have to serve, is it? That's all you have to say, is it?" He seemed to be willing Chuck to say something more, but Chuck kept his silence. "Well, if you have nothing more to say, then you will not be permitted to darken our door again."

"Daddy!"

"Go. Leave my house immediately."

Nell stepped forward. "Daddy, if Peter goes, I go too."

"Nell, I can't have you with me. You..." Chuck reached out and placed his hands on Nell's shoulders. She shook him off and stepped defiantly in front of her father.

"If Peter is banned from this house, then so am I. We'll find some other place to live."

"Nell, you can't come with me." Chuck tried to turn her around so he could speak to her, but she refused to move. "Nell, I can't take you with me. Not yet. You can't be of any use to the Revolution."

She turned on him, stunned by his words. Her hands grabbed at the air as if to grasp hold of something. Her face flushed with anger. "No use for the Revolution? I'm good enough for you to sleep with me, I'm good enough to have your baby, but I'm not good enough for the Revolution? Who is good enough? Tell me that. Who? Who have you got lined up for that job?" She was shaking with anger. "Margaret?" Suddenly, she looked as if she was on the verge of breaking down. She sat down heavily on a kitchen chair and turned away from him.

Chuck stood there, looking huge in the little room. His hands were trembling and he seemed to lean toward Nell as if his heart was physically pulling him there. Nell covered her face in her hands and began to sob. Her mother put her hand on her shoulder but said nothing.

"Get out! Get out of my house!" Mr. Pennan wrenched open the kitchen door and motioned Chuck out. Chuck looked at Nell, at her mother, then stepped past her father and left.

CHAPTER TWELVE

"What now?" Sidney leaned on his elbows, looking across the table at Clara. The remains of their lunch lay on the plates between them.

"Sidney, I don't think Peter Pennan was telling the truth."

"About your husband, you mean?"

"No. No, I think that part was true. I don't know how it can be true. I mean, how I could not have known...I would have thought Chuck would have told me. Or, we would have heard from one of the family. Something. No. I think Peter Pennan was telling the truth about that. He called him a bohunk and I don't think he would have said that if...Well, you know. And, Chuck was in Regina before the War. I do know that. He mentioned it a couple of times. I don't know what he did there. I don't think there was much work of any kind in the thirties. He said he used to work for a newspaper but I don't know when or where, or..." here she hesitated, "or even if that is true. It didn't seem important at the time." Clara was running her finger around and around the rim of her glass. Sidney reached out and took her hand.

"It's no use brooding, Clara. Lots of men in those days were just drifting..."

She withdrew her hand. "Chuck was no drifter. He wanted children. He would never have just left her. I couldn't have children, but he wanted them. He wouldn't have just left her. Not Chuck."

"I didn't mean that. It's just, well, the times were hard and lives were mixed up. He may have simply lost contact with them. It happened in those days."

"I suppose. Still."

"What don't you think was true then? You said you thought something Pennan said was not true."

"I didn't believe him about his mother, about her dying. Somehow I felt he was lying. Why he would lie about that, I don't know. He said she was dead, but he, well, he looked away when he said it. There was something else there, something he didn't want us to know or he didn't want to say."

"Maybe he just didn't want his mother contacted, bothered."

"He looked upset when he finally told us her name. It's just a feeling I have. Maybe she's still alive. She could be."

"Well, could be, but she would be pretty old, over eighty."

Clara pushed back her chair and started to her feet. "This is all getting to be more than I bargained for. It's as if...well, as if Chuck, we were strangers to each other. How can you be married for forty-four years and be strangers? Everyone said what an ideal couple we were." She picked up her handbag and turned away. "I think I'll go lie down now."

"Can I see you later?"

Clara looked at him for a moment and then slowly nodded her head.

She was awakened by the telephone. "Clara? It's past four. I just thought...." Sidney's voice betrayed his worry. What was he worried about? She wasn't going to commit suicide. Men!

"Yes. I'll be down in a few minutes." She replaced the telephone receiver and lay back on the pillow. She didn't want to get up, ever. She was tired. What did she really care about Thomas Pennan? Chuck shouldn't have just left her like that. He should be here now and sort this all out. Make love to her. They had still made love. Not often in the past few years, but nevertheless, they had made love. She had pretended last time that she was a geisha girl, all passive and so on. If that was the way geisha girls were. She didn't know, but what did it matter, it had pleased Chuck. He had often asked her just to lie still, perfectly still. It was hard sometimes, when she wanted to move so she could feel him in her. But she had accommodated him. She had always accommodated him and now here was all this. He hadn't ever accommodated her, not even with the truth. And then, he had just left as if she hadn't spent her whole goddamn life trying to make him happy. Clara found herself angry, her fists clenched.

She rolled over and thought about phoning Patricia's number again, and this time, leaving a message. Just to say she had been here and tried to get in touch. It had been good just to hear her voice on the answering machine. But actually, she had been relieved when Patricia hadn't answered. She had enough on her plate.

She reached for the telephone and rang Sidney's room instead. "Sidney, I'll order a bottle of bubbly. Why don't you come up here and we'll celebrate our small success." She leaned back and smiled slightly.

Later, much later, after a full room service meal and a bottle of wine, Sidney had wanted to stay, but Clara had managed to persuade him that what he really wanted was to sleep by himself in his own room. He looked very sorry for himself as he left. But they had had fun. It was a long time since Clara had felt like laughing and joking. The champagne, of course, helped. And they had gone over the day's events. A few minutes after Sidney left, Clara phoned him at his room again.

"I think I'm going to go to Regina."

"Regina?"

She could hear the TV in the background. "To see if I can find Peter Pennan's mother. Nell."

"I can't see the sense in that, Clara. Even if she didn't die when he was a baby, she must be dead by now."

"What makes you say that?"

"Well, Peter is sixty-four. That would make her probably eighty-four." The TV clicked off.

"Maybe she had him young. Sixteen or so."

"She'd still be eighty."

"Well, lots of people live beyond eighty."

"Don't you think you're being a little silly, Clara? What does it matter if she is alive or not? You've found out who Thomas Pennan is, or was."

"Is it that simple? Peter Pennan is Chuck's son, it seems. That probably means he has some claim on the estate, doesn't it? Maybe his mother does too."

"Really, Clara. Do you think it's wise of you to bring that all up? I mean, what they don't know, won't hurt them. They think he's dead."

"Besides, Peter's sort of my stepson. In a way." She looked down at her hands. "He doesn't resemble Chuck much. At that age, I mean. Odd as it may sound, I found myself hoping..."

Sidney was silent, although Clara caught the sound of a sigh. She steeled herself and picked up her handbag, almost protectively. "And there's something I want to show you. Something... Do you mind if I come down to your room? It's something that I haven't told you about."

There was silence at the other end of the line. Then, "Well, sure. I'm still dressed."

"Be there in a minute."

Sidney opened his door wide on her tap. Clara was hardly in the room when she blurted out, "Here, read this." She took the letter out of her bag and handed it to Sidney.

Sidney read the letter through twice, turned it over and looked at the other side, fingered the brittle edges. "This must be thirty, forty years old."

"I think probably more like sixty."

"I'm not a lawyer, but I guess it is sort of evidence. I mean, it is a confession. TV programs seem to emphasize the criminality of withholding evidence from the police. Have you shown this to anyone?"

"No."

"You're sure? Then, why not just destroy it? No one would know the difference."

"I thought of that. I guess I can't destroy the fact that I have read it. I've read it many times. It...Well, it's like a message to me from Chuck. He had hidden it, kept it in the inner pocket of his tuxedo. That's where I found it. If he's kept it all these years, it must be important, at least important to him. Maybe I was meant to find it. I don't know. I don't know what to do, Sidney, but I can't just let it all drop." She let her hands drop to her sides. "Besides, I want to know. I want to know what all this is about."

"You heard Peter. He thinks his father was killed in Spain. What is the sense of digging up all this old history?"

"It's not old history to me. He wasn't killed, was he? He came home, found work, met me, and married me. Are you telling me I lived with a dead man for forty-four years? But, perhaps I have been living with, with all this, this history, all these years. That I didn't know about. It's like, like...I don't know what it's like. I can't just let it drop."

"Well, Clara, I can't miss any more time at the office this week. If you are determined to go to Regina, how about I meet you there on the weekend? I can get a stopover on the flight back to Toronto." He reached out and held her hand. "Perhaps you could book the room. Ah, it's a bit difficult with the secretary. You know."

Clara didn't know, but found herself relieved to be going off on her own, and not entirely pleased with the prospect of Sidney joining her. But he did seem to care for her, and to be willing to look after her. It might be useful to have him in Regina. She refused to think about the complications of their both being in Toronto.

As the airplane descended, Clara looked out over the small prairie city, seemingly stranded in a landscape too big for it, a few office towers, a lake and a big football field, some suburbs, and then, just land, flat and reaching out in every direction like the surface of a giant balloon. All the years – decades – she had lived in Canada and she had never seen the prairies. Well, Saskatchewan wasn't exactly a holiday destination, although, much to her amusement, she had gotten a special tour price from the ticket agent, which included a four-day car rental. A nice man. Holiday destination or not, the sun was shining, the sky was an unbelievable blue, and the wheat fields, or whatever they were, gleamed pale yellow as far as she could see. Here was something that wasn't going to change too quickly, and she thought of their neighbours at the lake who had brought in a bulldozer and reshaped the shoreline in front of their cottage. No one was going to reshape this expanse of land.

As she waited for her luggage, a tall, erect Mountie came and stood by a pillar. Why he might be there was not clear, but he smiled at Clara and she smiled back. Then, as she reached for her bag, a red sleeve stretched out in front of her and took it from the carousel. "Why, thank you." "Think nothing of it, ma'am. Can I carry it out for you?"

"Surely, they don't have you working here as a porter." "No, ma'am. Regina is our training headquarters, so we are stationed here to meet the people who arrive. It's sort of a promotion for the force." "How nice – I mean, how nice for me. Well, I'm just going over there to pick up a car." Clara hadn't seen a Mountie in full dress since the last time she and Chuck had gone to the Royal Winter Fair. And this one, if she was not mistaken, was actually an Indian, or aboriginal, or whatever they called themselves now. He was very handsome. She thought briefly of Sidney.

Car keys in hand and suitcase rolling behind, Clara stepped out into the noon sun. A fresh wind was blowing and she automatically put her hand to her head, then stopped and let it blow through her hair. On a beautiful day Chuck would sometimes say, "Just like a Saskatchewan day." It always brought a laugh, but she could see there was some truth in it. She felt younger and more energetic. She was going to enjoy life and quit worrying. It would be fun to try to find Nell Pennan, and if she didn't, then she had had an adventure anyway. The story of the tall, handsome Mountie would make good retelling back in Toronto, back home. Home. She wondered if Chuck had thought of the prairies as home.

Much to her surprise, the hotel was large and elegant – dark blue walls, gold and white columns, chandeliers, dark wood. Somehow she had imagined that hotels here would probably be like motels along the highways in northern Ontario, with thin mahogany doors, frayed carpets, and the television set bolted to the table. Not that she knew much about motels. This was luxurious. Actually, nicer than the Royal York, as far as old railway hotels went. Certainly nicer than Vancouver's. She was becoming a connoisseur of Canadian railway hotels. Her room overlooked a small park, and once unpacked, she decided to go and explore it and the wide street running beside it.

The park was perhaps predictably named Victoria Park and it had the obligatory cenotaph in the middle. Someone in the Parks Department, though, had been particularly inventive and the flowerbeds seemed to be laid out in abstract designs. People were dressed casually and enjoying the warm autumn-afternoon sun. Across the street from the park Clara spied a cappuccino place; she bought a bowl of *caffe latte* and sat watching the people passing by on the street, Scarth Street. That was a little different. Albert, Cornwall, sometimes it seemed as if Canada was just one city with all the same street names. On the whole, the passersby looked like nice people. Business people, artists, farmers, a good mix. It was strange to think of Chuck having been here, having walked on these streets. Thinking of this as home. Probably with Nell. Clara in spite of herself felt a pang of jealousy. This Nell must have been his first love. Had he ever forgotten her? Had he ever thought of her when he made love to Clara? Silly to torture herself with such thoughts. She longed for him to be here with her now. In a way, he was here. But not really.

Tomorrow she would begin her search for Chuck's first "wife."

CHAPTER THIRTEEN

"She doesn't even bloody well know about Nell, does she? Does she? You're a bastard, Chuck. A bastard."
Thomas stood, fists clenched, face flushed, angrier than he had been in his entire life.

"Tommy..."

"Don't Tommy me. Are you going to tell her? If you don't, I will."

"Tommy..." Chuck reached out a hand to place it on Thomas's arm. Thomas jerked away and then swung at him. Chuck caught his arm and slowly bent it, until Thomas cried out in pain. Chuck forced him down onto his knees. "Now, Tommy, listen. Listen, I said. It's not up to me to tell Margaret. It is none of her business. I consider Margaret a comrade, nothing more. She understands that..."

"She doesn't understand that at all. She's obsessed with you and all your crack-brained ideas. She's obsessed – you've possessed her soul." His accusation sounded odd even to Thomas.

"Tommy, it's no use our fighting over this. You're just upset."

"You're damn right I'm upset. I could kill you." The words were said.

Chuck looked long and hard at Thomas and then let go of his arm. He turned and walked away, crossing the park in the direction of 12th Avenue. Thomas got to his knees, then ran and jumped on Chuck's back, grabbing him around the throat. Chuck staggered and fell to one knee, gasping as Thomas's arm tightened on his windpipe. Thomas tightened his hold and pulled back. In one movement, Chuck reached back, laid hold of Thomas's shirt and half-threw, half-pulled him over his head onto the walkway. Thomas landed with a thud and lay there stunned. Chuck caught his breath and stood up.

"Don't try that again, Tommy. Don't ever try that again." He stepped over Thomas and continued along the walk at exactly the same pace as before. A group of men had gathered at the corner of 12th Avenue and Scarth Street. As Chuck came up to them, they parted and then closed ranks behind him, glanced back at Tommy lying on the footpath, and followed Chuck across the intersection.

It was the July 1st long weekend, Dominion Day, 1935. The past two weeks had been a momentous time in Regina. On June 14 the Trekkers, two thousand young, unemployed men determined to take their complaints to Ottawa, had arrived on the boxcars – the "CPR Express." But now the Canadian Pacific Railway Company had issued a statement refusing to take the men any further. The company hadn't exactly agreed to carrying the young men in the first place, but perhaps it had seemed the better part of wisdom not to try to stop them. Two thousand young men were potentially dangerous. Not that there had been any trouble. The men were unbelievably disciplined. Everything was organized down to the last detail – a hierarchy of "captains" who kept order; food details; regular marching; lessons in politics and economics with, of course, a Communist interpretation; rigorous schedules and work details. All along the route through the Rockies, the police had kept watch, perhaps waiting for an opportunity to act. But as long as the CPR didn't complain and the townspeople welcomed the men, there was not much that could be done. It was clear, or at least it was believed by the men, that the decision on the part of the CPR to prevent them going any further by rail was a political decision made by the hated Bennett government in Ottawa. An attempt to leave Regina by truck had been stopped by the Mounties. Now, the men were growing restless, as were the city and provincial governments. And it was hot – sweltering summer heat and weeks of no rain. The rich had gone to Katepwa Lake to their cottages; the poor sought out the parks and the shade afforded by the trees around Wascana Lake in the middle of the city. By this time of year both had a green scum of algae along the edges.

Thomas got up and brushed himself off. He looked after the figures of the men, trudging east on 12th Avenue. They disappeared, headed for the Workers Unity League hall in all likelihood. He thought briefly of the office at the church where he had been working the past few months. He didn't go in very often anymore. The city was in an uproar over the treatment of the unemployed and crowds gathered every day to hear the latest news. What did Bennett say? What was the Premier going to do? What was going to happen? There were tag days in support of the "boys." Chuck was holed up with the leaders from the Coast. Margaret was God knows where. Nell was sulking. His parents weren't speaking. His ordered life seemed to be spinning out of control. In any case, Reverend Evans was busy pretty well full-time with the Ministerial Association. Thomas found himself weary of the constant hassles, the impractical plans. As if he could talk about impracticality, the Reverend had said when he complained. But the Association was helping to feed the Trekkers and Thomas had on occasion used one of the trucks to deliver food to them. Mr. Williams would not have approved. Mr. Williams deplored the presence of the trekkers in the city. And feared them. He had told the drivers to lock their doors. But it was mainly Margaret that was the problem. He found himself enmeshed in conflicting feelings. On the few occasions when he did see her, she was friendly, but she obviously thought of him as, well, as a boy who would have to grow up before she could take serious notice of him. She was the adult doing adult things. And, it was always Chuck this and Chuck that. Even the thought made him jealous – and angry. He had one evening told her he loved her. She had laughed, not maliciously, but, even worse, tolerantly, as if he was too young to know what he was saying. She seemed to blame him that Chuck no longer stayed at the Pennans'. He concluded from this that Chuck had not told her about Nell. Well, she would be able to see that soon for herself. Thomas pushed his fingers through his hair and took the other path through the park, in the direction of the cartage company. He was supposed to book on early today for another of Mr. Williams' secret jobs.

The sheds on South Railway Street where the trucks were kept seemed empty and cavernous on this holiday afternoon. Thomas checked himself in at the office and joined John and Eric and Mr. Williams. It was two minutes after four.

"Well, Mr. Pennan, good of you to get here finally. We thought maybe you were out strolling with that sister of yours." Mr. Williams beamed at his own witticism and John and Eric dutifully laughed. Obviously, John and Eric had told him about his sister showing up out at the Mountie barracks.

"Sorry. I got delayed coming down."

"Now listen carefully, all of you. First, what I want you to do this afternoon is to be kept absolutely, absolutely secret. Understand? Absolutely secret. Is that understood? Eric? John? Thomas?" Each of the drivers nodded his head solemnly. "Good then. You will see that the trucks have been outfitted with benches which fold up against the wall. That's for transporting some men. Mounties. You're going to go to the barracks, pick them up and bring them back downtown."

"Where to?" That was Eric, always the most inquisitive of the three. Why? was left in their thoughts, unsaid.

"You'll be told," said Mr. Williams mysteriously. "All in good time. You'll be told. Any questions? Well, good then. Let's get going." With an energy which belied his weight and pompousness, Mr. Williams swung out of the office and headed toward the trucks. The men followed him in single file like three baby ducks waddling after their mother. "I'll ride with you, Thomas." Mr. Williams motioned Thomas over to the first truck in the line.

The three trucks came out of the dark interior of the sheds and into the relentlessly hot sun, hot even as the after-noon began to edge toward evening. Thomas had the windows open and a hint of a breeze moved through the cab as the truck moved forward. The worn plush on the seats had its own sharp smell. Thomas turned out into the street, double clutched and clanked the truck into second gear. Mr. Williams winced and sighed.

"Now, Thomas, I've come with you for a reason. Eric and John will go straight to the barracks when they arrive, and pick up the men who will be waiting for them there. You and I have a special mission to carry out. I'll tell you where to go when we get there." Mr. Williams gave Thomas a conspirato-rial smile and patted him on the knee. "Drive on, son! Lock your door."

Chuck stood next to the makeshift stage at the side of Market Square and watched the people gathering. He was proud of the work he had done in Regina. Nowhere along the route had the Trekkers been better treated, housed, and supported. His flow of information had been essential in assisting the leaders in planning their negotiating tactics. And, gradually, he had been accepted as one of them, one of the leaders. He could see that they trusted him and, more importantly, the men trusted him. The meeting this evening was to explain to the people of the city what had happened in the discussion this afternoon between the Trek leaders and the Premier. The cutting off of all welfare and federal assistance had left the men dependent on the help of the city, and the citizens were now threatened with reprisals if they assisted the men.

But trouble was in the air; it had been brewing all week. First the statement that the trains would no longer carry the Trekkers; then, the use of Act 98 to prevent any citizen from helping the boys on pain of arrest. Now, the increased number of Mounties in the city; they had been coming in all week and had been transported secretly, they thought, to the barracks. Margaret had given him an endless stream of information about what was going on there, which she gleaned from the rather bewildered young men coming in from Eastern Canada. Chuck smiled. He probably knew more about these raw recruits than their own officers did.

Two of the Trek leaders from British Columbia came up to Chuck.

"Well, comrade, we hear there are vans moving in around the square full of Mounties. You know anything about that?"

"Vans? Nope. I'll have it checked out. They wouldn't be coming here in any case. This is a legal public meeting. There's no law against a public meeting."

"Them bastards don't need the law. They are the law."

"My information is it's pretty chaotic at the barracks. Lot of young guys, untrained, stumbling over each other. I don't think they're prepared to do anything. They've probably been sent down to sit and watch. If the reports are true.

Anyway, they're not going to do anything, not with this crowd here. Women, children, men in their Sunday best. It's not a crowd of trekkers. They wouldn't dare start anything." Chuck could see the skepticism on the leaders' faces and he wondered for a moment if their instincts were not right.

"Okay. Well, let's get going then. It's eight o'clock. Comrade Black's going to chair the meeting. Come on. Join us on the platform, Chuck, so we can say a few good words about your work."

Thomas sat behind the wheel of the truck, transfixed by the scene in front of him. Mounties were unloading machine guns at the back of the Grey Nuns Hospital. From his truck. He was sweating, desperately watching, unable to move. Mr. Williams sat back comfortably, smoking one of his hand-rolled cigarettes, smiling at the Mounties, lifting his cigarette every so often in a sort of high sign. The Mounties ignored them as they carried the guns to the back entrances of the hospital. The hospital would be the surveillance post, the watchtower, looking out over the stadium and the two thousand men housed there.

"Oh, God. God. What are they doing?"

"It's all right, son. Everything is under control. It's just a security move. Nothing to worry about."

Thomas stared. God, what was going on? He hadn't known. He hadn't known what they were picking up. How could he have known? Oh, God. He had just done what Mr Williams said. Stay in the truck. Just wait until they get everything loaded, he had said. Thomas clenched the steering wheel and felt his hands slip on the sweaty Bakelite. Bang, the back door of the truck slammed shut.

"Okay, son. Drive on. Tom? Drive on."

Thomas stepped on the clutch and pushed the floor stick into gear. The truck shuddered and jerked. The engine died.

"Now, son, you can do better than that. Come on."

Thomas pulled the stick out of gear again and pressed the starter with his foot. The starter whined and whined. Finally, the engine coughed, and in a rushing smell of gas, started. He put the truck into gear again and moved slowly and carefully forward, out onto Pasqua Street.

The meeting began orderly enough. J.M. Toothill, a member of the CCF spoke for about fifteen minutes. The crowd stirred restlessly. They had gathered to hear from the Trek leaders, and the introductory political speech seemed to be simply stealing time. There was, though, something of a festive mood in the air. Men and women were dressed in their Sunday best, perhaps not to celebrate the birth of the country, but more because it was a holiday and, even in these times of unemployment, a holiday still suggested a break from the ordinary workweek. Here and there, women fanned themselves with a newspaper or a book. The men were protective and hovering, strutting a bit in their role as attendees at a major political event. The square was bare, no trees or bushes; only the makeshift platform erected at the far side decorated the grounds. Here and there in the crowd, there were small groups of trekkers who had come downtown from the stadium where they were housed.

"What's going on, Mr. Williams? I can't..."
"Nothing. Nothing, my boy. Don't you worry now. It's just a security move."

"They're armed."

"Of course they are. Do you think they can maintain order unarmed? Just be sensible and wait here. I'm going to walk back to the office. You can bring the truck later. Okay? Tom? Okay?"

Mr. Williams climbed heavily down from the truck and crossed in front. He waved to Thomas and started up the alley to the street. Thomas watched him go and then turned to look at what was going on in Market Square. Someone was on the platform speaking. He could see Chuck sitting with three other men behind the speaker. The crowd of people had moved closer to the platform and the area around the trucks had almost emptied. He had to tell Chuck what was going on. What was going on? The Mounties in the back of the truck were quiet, no one spoke. It was strangely quiet everywhere in the Square, only the barely discernible voice of the speaker droned on. The Mounties opened the back door of the truck. Thomas pushed down on the door handle and his door swung open. Should he leave the truck? He stepped out onto the running board and looked over the cab at the backs of the crowd. Nothing seemed to be happening. The cab was too hot to place his hand on it. He jumped to the ground and went to the front of the truck.

Finally, Mr. Toothill sat down, to general handclapping, and the Trek leader in charge of finances got up on the platform to give his pitch for funds. Just as he began to speak, the strident, high-pitched sound of a police whistle pierced the air, and the doors of the fire hall and police station at the end of the square opened, disgorging rows of city police armed with truncheons. At the signal, Mounties clambered down from the trucks on either side of the square and started on the run for the crowd. They were similarly armed, with truncheons which looked as if they had been made from baseball bats. As the police surged into the crowd, swinging at anyone in their way, the Mounties headed straight for the platform. People screamed and tried to get out of the way. Here and there, a man or woman fell to the ground with a groan, holding their head or shoulder. The truncheons flashed and fell, flashed and fell. Paths opened up in front of the line of policemen. By the time the city police were halfway to the platform, plainclothes Mounties were already on the stage arresting the speakers and trying to drag them down to the ground. Suddenly, the crowd that had started to flee before the rain of police blows began to fight back, turning on the police as if someone had commanded them to stop and resist, picking up anything that might serve as a weapon. Shots rang out, people screamed, some fled, others fought. The wounded lay on the ground, battered by the fighting going on all around them. Men threw themselves in front of women, and women, frantic to get their children out of harm's way, fought their way through the melee. At first the police line faltered and fell back. The crowd cheered and surged forward and were then driven back again as the police regrouped. And again. On the far side of the square, near the end of the platform, a plainclothes policeman lay bleeding on the ground. A group of about ten men backed away from his body and ran. Tear-gas bombs were being lobbed into the milling groups of people. One went off next to the truck that the Mounties were loading the prisoners into. The occupants coughed and hung out the back as the truck jerked into motion, headed for the RCMP station jails.

Nell stood beside the fire hall wanting to see Peter but trying to stay out of sight. Suddenly, there was a piercing whistle blast and the entire scene in front of her burst into activity. Police swarmed over the crowd, swinging their truncheons. Dust, screaming people. She could see Peter and the men on the platform looking for a way to escape, but before they could get down, seven men had jumped onto the stage and surrounded them. She saw three of them grab Peter and pull him off the platform into the crowd. Just as they started to haul him away, Mounties from a nearby truck started to run toward her. She automatically held her stomach to protect the baby, and tried to crouch down out of sight beside the building. One of the Mounties swung and hit her across the head. She fell to the ground, her head bleeding from a long gash. The Mounties pounded past her into the square. Just as she was losing consciousness, she felt an arm around her shoulder.

"Nell, it's me, Jim. Can you stand? I'll get you into the hall here." The fireman stood beside her and yelled at the Mounties to leave them alone. "Can't you see I'm wearing a uniform?" He helped her up and half carried her into the fire hall.

"Peter." Nell tried to turn but the effort was too much and she slipped into unconsciousness.

Thomas gaped at what he saw happening. He couldn't believe his eyes. Police and Mounties were clubbing men and women indiscriminately. People were screaming, blood running down from head wounds; they were trying to flee, to escape the rain of blows, but every time they made a break for it a circle of police closed them off again. The Mounties from his truck were helping their fellow policemen who had seized the speakers on the platform and were dragging them towards the truck. It was his fault. He had dropped off armed Mounties and machine guns at the Exhibition Buildings. He had brought the Mounties to the square. He had...

One of the men being dragged across the square was Chuck, and at the sight of him, Thomas ran to the other side of the truck and started towards the three Mounties struggling to subdue him. Thomas ran around the edge of the melee and then waded into the middle, clawing people aside as he went. He pushed his way to where Chuck fought to get free. The Mounties had his one arm behind his back and were grabbing at his other arm. One had his truncheon raised, but seemed unable to decide where to strike without hitting his companions. Yelling at the top of his voice, Thomas came up behind the two struggling to hold Chuck's arms and grabbed their shoulders. As both of them turned to deal with Thomas, Chuck hit the third one. He staggered, clutching his stomach. Chuck turned and grabbed the two fighting with Thomas and smashed their heads together. They sighed and slumped to the ground. Thomas turned on the other Mountie, who, seeing it was now one against two, backed off and ran to get help. Chuck grabbed Thomas's arm and, pulling him along, ran for the alley between Apex Dye Works and the Auto Wrecking Company yards. It was a good move because the alley ran west, off from the police station, and most of the people were trying to run north and east. They started up the alleyway and were about two-thirds of the way along when a policeman appeared at the end, blocking their path.

"Don't stop, Tommy. We'll run him down."

But Thomas stopped and stared at the policeman. "Bob, what the hell are you doin' here?"

The policeman looked hard at them and then recognized Thomas. "Is that you, Tommy? Christ." He lowered his truncheon. Chuck and Thomas came up to him and he stepped aside. "Go on. Get goin' or I'll lose my job."

"Thanks, Bob. We'll remember this."

"Don't."

As they hurried down 12th Avenue, Thomas noticed that Chuck was limping and unable to keep up. "What's happened to you?"

"Bastard clubbed me across the knees."

Thomas put his arm around Chuck and half-carried him the remaining few yards to the back of the building where the Workers Unity League rented office space. As soon as they climbed the outside steps they could see that the door had been broken open and hung atilt on its hinges. They stopped inside the doorway and surveyed the chaos. Every desk drawer and filing cabinet had been opened, papers lay strewn around the room, typewriters had been thrown against the wall and lay smashed on the floor.

"Jesus, Tommy, they got here before us. They've got every name on the lists." Chuck bent down and picked up an old shell casing that had served as a paperweight and hefted it in his hand. "Who the hell organized this? I'm supposed to know what's going on. This is my fault, Tommy. Who did it?"

"How can it be your fault? They just chose today 'cause of the meeting. When I was dropping them off…"

"You were what?" Chuck swung around on Tommy. "What did you say?"

Tommy backed away a step. "I was driving one of those trucks."

"You were driving a truck, with Mounties in it? And you didn't tell me? You stupid bastard."

"I didn' know…I was mad when you…I…"

"Christ, Tommy. Don't you know nothin'?" Chuck started toward him, but stumbled and sat down heavily on the only upright chair in the room. He raised his head and looked out the front window. "Never trust a preacher boy." He swung around to Tommy again. "What'd you think it was, one of your acts of charity, a good deed to save their souls? How can you be so stupid?"

"I didn't know." Tommy stood like a repentant schoolboy in front of Chuck. "I wasn't thinkin'."

"You got that right. Shit." ·

"I'm sorry, Chuck. I'm really sorry."

Chuck sat silent for a moment and then looked up at Thomas. "Tommy, maybe now you can see what's what. This is the world you think you can patch up with faith, hope and charity."

CHAPTER FOURTEEN

Clara walked east on 12th Avenue. She couldn't remember when she had felt so full of life and energy. The morning was cold, crisp, and aflood with autumn sunlight. It had been a good decision to get out of Toronto, away from everyone feeling sorry for her, away from Mount Pleasant Cemetery. She had decided to leave the rental car in the lot behind the hotel and walk. It was good just to walk. Chuck must have walked down this street. Young, full of energy. She felt close to him this morning. Oh, if she had only known him then. She smiled at the thought of her being still a baby when he was here.

As she crossed Broad Street and started down 12th again, she could see the contrast of the houses and street from the more downtown section near the hotel. The houses here were dilapidated, and big, old cars were parked along the street. It was a bit threatening, and she began to regret not having driven. It was like San Francisco, where she and Chuck attended a conference once. There, two blocks off the main street with its upper-end boutiques and gourmet restaurants were tenements, x-rated video shops, and, let's face it, wall-to-wall blacks, as Chuck used to say. Only he didn't use the word "black." However, there seemed to be no one on this street. It was early, but all was strangely, almost eerily, quiet.

Clara's sense of foreboding increased; she felt she was walking into a sort of tunnel, cut off from the city she had felt so happy in just a few minutes before. At Osler Street she turned north. The so-called rest home was supposed to be somewhere in the next few blocks. As she approached the driveway of a small apartment building, she saw what looked like someone's legs sticking out from behind the garbage bins. She stopped, not sure what to do. When she turned to go back the way she had come, she saw the figures of three young men coming down the street toward her. Her heart began to pound. There was no one around except the three men and her, and, of course, the whatever behind the bins. Clara looked frantically at the windows of the houses across the street hoping to see someone looking out. Sidney had said on the phone to wait until he got there. Now she wished she had. The men were sloppily dressed and had long black hair. One wore the inevitable baseball cap on backwards. Their fancy sports shoes made no sound. Clara froze. There was nothing she could think of doing. The three men came up rapidly. They were bantering among themselves, but eyeing her up and down. The one on the outside clinked the coins in his baggy pants pocket. Clara could now see that they were Natives. She drew herself up and waited for the worst.

As they came up to her, the one on the inside, the youngest of the three, stepped back behind the other two, and the three of them passed by without a word. They walked a few steps further and turned into the driveway.

"Nick. Nick. Get up you lazy son of a bitch. Did your ol' lady toss you out again?" They kicked the prone figure behind the bins. "Did ya hear? Get up. Come on." The three bent down and after a struggle managed to get Nick onto his feet. They staggered a bit under his considerable weight, and then made for the front door of the building. Clara stood there watching and listening as her heart slowed down to its normal rate. She decided to walk back to the hotel and wait for Sidney, who had said he would be in on an early evening flight. They could look for Nell tomorrow.

The hotel had preserved the old marble sink and tub, and the black-and-white tile floor of the original hotel bathroom. They were comfortingly old and solid. Clara sat on the toilet seat and studied the floor pattern. It was three o'clock in the morning. She had been there for almost an hour, and felt the cold through the light silk dressing gown she had thrown over her shoulders.

Sidney snored in the other room, sprawled across the king-sized bed. He had arrived on time; they had met in the lobby; they had had dinner down the street at Danbury's, an old club which had been converted into a restaurant; they had come back, and, after a bottle of champagne, they...Clara stared down at her hands and the white band where her wedding ring had been. Why? She had felt sorry for him. No. She didn't know why. One thing had led to another. She sighed and the evening's events raced around in her mind.

When Sidney had undressed, she saw just how fat he was. His belly stuck out like a large melon and his genitals hid beneath, well, his erection was not exactly hiding. But he was a fatty, no doubt about that. Oh, well. Clara had leaned on the pillows, watching him struggle with his socks. He looked apologetic.

She had made a few somewhat negative comments about Chuck to Sidney over dinner, which she now regretted. *De mortuis nil nisi bonum.* The Latin phrase from Horace came back to her. Her grandfather had died when she was at university. Latin was one of her first-year courses, and the morning after his death, she had run across that line. "Say nothing but good of the dead." Not that what she had said wasn't true but she felt disloyal in any case. Silly. How can you be disloyal to the dead? Nothing was clearer about Chuck's dying than that, when he died, he was simply not there any longer. He was beyond being hurt by her words. He was dead; his body rotting in that shiny polished-mahogany box. Dead. But somehow she was still married to him. It was too soon after his death. Sidney had come along too soon. In spite of herself, she smiled at the thought. It was true he had come a bit too quickly last night for her liking. She looked at the white band of skin on her finger again and wished she had not removed her wedding ring. She had betrayed Chuck. Perhaps she was also betraying Sidney who was so, what? *enthusiastic* was perhaps the word, about her.

Well, *toujours gai, toujours gai,* there's a dance in the old dame yet. The Archie and Mehitabel line came back to her and she stood up and went over to the mirror to brush her hair. That was the trouble with hotel rooms, there was nowhere you could be by yourself except in the bathroom. She thought momentarily of getting dressed and going down to see if the bar might be still open, but sighing, she realized that she had to go back to bed. Which she did, as sneakily as possible, taking up hardly any room at all at the edge. Sidney groaned and threw his arm over her.

"Well, that was great, wasn't it?" Sidney bellowed. He seemed to be a lark, a morning person who gets up the minute he opens his eyes. She could hear him bustling about, getting showered and shaved. He didn't sing, but his words boomed out like an operatic aria. "You were great, my beautiful Clara. Just great." He came back into the bedroom. "Clara, means what, clear?"

"Bright and shiny, which I'm not." Clara rolled over and hid her head in the pillow.

"Bright and shiny, eh? You were certainly bright and shiny last night. Yessirree." Sidney chose a red tie and tied a double Windsor knot in it. "There. Are you coming?"

"Yes." Clara burrowed more deeply into the bedcovers.

"I'll be reading the paper in the lobby. Kiss?"

Clara pulled the pillow tightly around her head.

"Well, see you in a few minutes, dear."

"Oh, gawd, what am I doing?" Clara stared into the mirror, trying to find some answer to her question in the deepening wrinkles around her mouth and eyes. "How

did I get into this? What a fool I am." The litany of regrets
continued for awhile and then, "It is nice, though, to be held."

She deliberately turned her thoughts to Nell Pennan.
When she first arrived, she had phoned every care home in
Regina and just when she was ready to give up, one of them
over on Osler Street had said, Yes, they had a Nell Pennan
there. Yes, she could receive visitors. Yes, she was clear-
headed even though she was eighty. So, thought Clara, she
was right: Nell was still alive. She must have had Chuck's
baby, the words stuck in her mind, when she was very young.
She must have been only seventeen in 1935, but she had
never married. Well, Clara had been sexually active before
that age, but more careful than Nell, for no reason, as it
turned out. Different times. Chuck's baby. She didn't want to
imagine Chuck making love to another woman, not even that
long ago. He wasn't an angel, though. She remembered a
woman friend telling her that Chuck was having an affair.
She hadn't done anything about it. He travelled a lot, sometimes with women business colleagues. She had often
thought he was hiding things from her, but he always seemed
happy to come home to her. She never got up the courage to
confront him, not even when that woman phoned for him.
Why make herself and him unhappy? The fact, however, was
that they had never had children together, and he had had a
child with this Nell. He kept that secret all his life. Kept it
from her. There seemed to have been a lot about her husband
that she had not known. She had been, she guessed, a fool,
but that was all past now. All past. She carefully outlined her
lips with a lip pencil.

As she stepped out of the brass-doored elevator, Sidney jumped to his feet and came over to help her. Gawd, did he think she was incapable of walking across the lobby by herself? Attention is very nice, but enough is enough. Clara realized she was in a grumpy mood. Chuck had always ignored her moods. Sidney wasn't so clever at mollifying her.

"Something wrong?"

"No."

"I can see something's wrong. Come on, tell Sidney."

"No."

"My Clara..."

"I'm not yours."

Sidney looked at her warily and had enough sense to back off a bit. "Breakfast?"

"Yes."

They walked down the corridor to the large room where breakfast was being served. Businessmen sat here and there throughout the room, drinking coffee and reading the business news. A few of them looked up briefly to see who was coming in and to assess Clara. She passed muster and one man glanced up a number of times. Odd, she thought, how men think they are being so inconspicuous, when their interest and intent were so obvious. There was only one other woman in the room and she sat reading the same section of the newspaper as the men. She paid no attention to the new arrivals. How different it had been when she was that age, thought Clara.

"What will you have, dear?"

"Sidney, I am not your dear, either. I'll have two eggs, over easy, bacon, and a toasted bagel with coffee and juice."

"My, you do have an appetite this morning. Now, why would that be?"

"Let's get on with it. There is a Nell Pennan at a home on Osler Street. That's only few blocks away, but it seemed a pretty rough neighbourhood. I suggest we take the car."

"Okay." Sidney had finally seen the message written plainly for him to see, and he concentrated on the task at hand.

"I've been trying to figure out exactly what I want to know, what I want to ask her, I mean. If her brother is dead, as her son said he was, and now Chuck is dead – although Peter Pennan of course said he was killed about the same time, too – then really, I can give her more information than she can give me. Except she can tell me about Chuck when he was young. What he was like, what he did. Well, about her brother, too. And maybe she knows what this note Chuck had means."

"Are you going to show that note to her? I mean, she's eighty, and we don't know what the note really means."

"Why not? Maybe Thomas was the killing kind, a serial killer. After all, it must have been Chuck she loved, and she, I would guess, might understand why he would keep this letter from her brother, confessing to a killing. Maybe she knows who Margaret is, or was."

"And maybe it's a family secret that she doesn't want anyone to know about."

"Then we'll keep it a secret. As long as it isn't a case of murder or something."

Their breakfast plates arrived and they ate.

CHAPTER FIFTEEN

Clara stopped the car in front of a rundown building. The sign on the lawn announced in white letters on a fading green background that this was Grace Haven Retirement Home. Before they left the hotel, Clara had made Sidney go upstairs and change his tie. He now was wearing more casual clothes since the tie, it turned out, had been one of the two he had brought with him and the other had fallen victim to some spaghetti sauce in Vancouver. He was much less buoyant now, whether because of the loss of his tie or because of the rejection he had felt in Clara's cutting remarks at breakfast. He looked straight ahead, apparently waiting for her decision before doing anything.

"I'm sorry, Sidney. This means more to me than I thought and I can't think about anything else right now."

"I understand."

"No, you don't. But let's go." She undid her seat belt and opened the door. Sidney followed, scurried around the car to hold her door, thought better of it and stood rather awkwardly on the curb by the front wheel. Clara climbed out of the car and walked determinedly up the path to the door. A sign said Come In, with an exclamation mark after it for some reason. Inside, the place smelled not too awfully bad, a bit like a hospital and a certain stale smell, perhaps of old people, or just infrequent cleaning and scrubbing. A woman in a pink uniform with stringy blonde hair stood in the hall, watching them.

"Yep?" It was apparently a question.

"Er, do you have, or rather you have a Mrs. Nell Pennan here. We'd like to see her. I phoned. Yesterday, no, the day before yesterday."

"Miss Pennan. She doan like being called 'Mrs.' Took her two years to get that sorted out with the government. Old Age Pension and the like. I'll get her. Sit down in there." She motioned to the right with her hand and thudded down the hall and up the stairs, pulling herself along by means of the banister.

On the right-hand side of the hallway a double French door led into a sitting-dining room. About half a dozen residents sat in the room. A few looked up and then returned to their cross-word puzzles or magazines; some just stared in front of them; others seemed to be napping in their chairs. Clara and Sidney went over to a table beside the fireplace, that had four chairs around it. For bridge? Clara thought briefly of her bridge club and remembered that she had forgotten to phone Terri to say she wouldn't be able to come this week, well, last week. Sidney pulled out a chair for Clara to sit down and one of the old women on the other side of the room tittered.

"Sidney, just leave it, will you? I can sit down by myself." Clara almost hissed the words at him.

"All right. All right." Sidney held up both hands, palms out in a gesture of defeat and defensiveness.

The woman led into the room by the pink uniform was tall and erect with a stance that was both defiant and self-assured. Her hair was pulled back tightly from her face and, somewhat surprisingly secured at the back, like Clara's, with a decorative Spanish comb. She wore a grey dress, mid-calf, solid sensible shoes, dark stockings and a reboza, a Mexican shawl, over her shoulders. Sidney leapt to his feet at the sight of her.

"I'm Nell Pennan. You wanted to see me?" She held out her hand to Clara and then to Sidney.

"Thank you for giving us some of your time. I'm here on, well, on a sort of personal matter. I wonder if we could sit somewhere more, er, private?" Clara rose from her chair and the two women looked strikingly alike, almost like sisters, and in spite of the twenty years difference in age, they both had a certain agelessness about them.

"This way." Nell led them to the dinner table. "They won't be serving lunch for a couple of hours." They sat across from each other at the table and Sidney took the chair at the head of the table like a presiding judge. "Now, what is it you want?"

"My name is Clara Stemichuk." Clara paused and searched Nell's face for a reaction.

"I know. You left your name when you rang."

"This a friend of mine, Mr Penner, Sidney Penner."

"How do you do?" Nell reached out a hand and Sidney took it gently as if it were porcelain. Are fat men more gentle? Clara wondered.

116

Nell turned back to Clara. "Mrs. Stemichuk..."

"Please, *Clara*."

"Clara. As far as I know, the Peter Stemichuk I knew died over sixty years ago. I don't know what I can tell you. You must realize that I have put that behind me long ago."

"I know, but it is important that I hear about him from you. It seems he didn't die in Spain as you thought. I know how much of a shock that must be for you. But, for me, that he was even in Spain, that he had a, a child...It seems as if I never really knew the man I was married to for over forty years. I didn't know about you or, er, your son Peter. Not a word about that in forty-four years. It's as if he died as my husband, the man I thought I knew so well, and he has now suddenly been born again, a stranger."

"He was very good at becoming a stranger." Nell looked briefly down at her well-groomed fingernails. "Clara, even if what you say is true, I don't think you have any right to know that story."

"No right! He was my husband. We didn't have any children or family really, and now I suddenly find he had, had another life. I know it was earlier, but having children, a child, goes on and on. It doesn't end. I know your son has nothing to do with me but somehow I feel as if...It's hard to explain." Clara calmed. "I have a sister, but we're not close. Not even cards at Christmas. My parents died, well, they died for me a long time ago. Then they really died. I didn't even go to their funeral. They died in a car accident on the Squamish highway. Chuck didn't have any family either. At least, I didn't think he did. We only had each other. And when he died, I had no one. Don't you understand?" Clara's eyes filled with tears.

"I understand, but as far as I know, Peter died in Spain. My son never had a father."

"Oh, I'm sorry. I'm sorry. I forgot. I mean, of course you understand. Except you did have Peter, young Peter, I mean."

"Yes, I had Peter, young Peter. Clara, tell me exactly what you want to know."

"I don't really know what I want to know. Everything. Just tell me what happened. Did you love him?"

"Yes, I loved him."

"And he loved you?" Clara's tone was beseeching.

"I don't understand what you want. If you like, I'll tell you what happened."

"Please."

"Tommy brought Peter home one day and my parents offered him board and room while he was in Regina. He had my bedroom after I left to go teaching. I came home weekends. We fell in love. Or at least I thought we were in love. I was in love, hopelessly in love. I let him have his way with me. That sounds old-fashioned, doesn't it? At the time, it was not like that. One evening we could no longer stop. We made love out on the porch one warm, late winter evening. I can see in your face that that hurts you. I don't mean it to. It didn't last long. Our idyllic times. I became pregnant. He left."

"But why?"

"I don't know. We never talked about it. Maybe he didn't trust me. He said he left to serve the Revolution. That must sound silly to you, but back then it had some ring of truth. I think, though, that he was really in love with Margaret..."

"Margaret! Who is Margaret?"

"Was. She's dead too. Only I'm alive. And my son Peter." Some of her composure slipped and her hand went quickly to the lines on her cheeks.

"I'm sorry. Go on."

"There's not much else. Last time I saw him was across the street from here. The block in front of this building used to be called Market Square. The fire hall and police station are still there on 11th Avenue. Historic buildings they say."

"I saw them and wondered, well, just wondered. Did you meet then, here, one last time?"

"You've been reading too many romance novels." Clara blushed slightly. "No, he was arrested across the way there. Dragged off by some Mounties. That was the last I saw of him. They were hard times."

"Is that why you've chosen this retirement home? To be near, near your memories?"

"Yes."

Nell and Clara sat looking at and through each other. Sidney leaned back in his chair.

"We saw your son in Vancouver. That is how we got your name." Sidney said.

"My son? Where? Is he all right?" Nell was suddenly animated, girlish in her eagerness.

Sidney glanced quickly at Clara and continued, "He was, er, fine. We only talked with him for awhile, but he seemed fine."

Nell straightened herself and reassumed her more reserved manner. "I'm pleased to hear that. We don't see each other very often now, since he moved out to the Coast, and neither of us is much at writing."

"What happened then? After Peter was arrested?" The gentleness in Sidney's voice moved Clara and she looked at this man she hardly knew (but, she added to herself, knew in the biblical sense, which increasingly seemed like not knowing at all). Nell turned in her chair toward Sidney now.

"The men, the trekkers as they were called, were sent back to wherever they came from. Peter must have left with them. We, my brother and my parents, went up to Dewdney Avenue and watched them march off to the train station. But he wasn't with them. I remember one pretty girl put a pie plate on her head and marched along beside a very embarrassed young Mountie who kept trying to look dignified and keep his eyes trained in front of him. Some of the trekkers shouted, "That a girl Peggy." She was Peggy Ryan, Mrs. Ryan's daughter. People here were very supportive of the trekkers. There was a Reverend, Reverend Evans, who organized people to feed them and invite them over to their houses. Tommy worked for him for awhile." Nell's body began to relax as she slipped into her memories and Sidney and Clara sat quietly listening, for her story had, it seemed, become one that needed to be told.

"I guess Peter must have left too. He sent me a note through Tommy. I have it here. I brought it down for you to see. To prove..." Nell opened her handbag and brought out a small piece of lined paper. She handed it to Sidney and he opened it and showed it to Clara. It said simply, "I will love you always" and was signed *P.*

Clara went visibly rigid and pushed the note away. "It's not Chuck's handwriting," she said and glared at Nell.

"Oh yes it is. I know Peter's handwriting."

"So do I."

Sidney picked up the note and handed it back to Nell. "Perhaps handwriting changes over sixty years." The two women sat silently watching each other. Sidney leaned back again. "Then what happened, Miss Pennan?"

"Then? Nothing, I guess. Tommy got sick that winter, what they would probably call a nervous breakdown, now. I gave birth to my son. The next year Tommy left home. Later we found out he joined up as a volunteer for the war that was going on in Spain. Margaret left at the same time as the trekkers. I guess she went with Peter. I don't know."

"Can you tell us about Margaret?"

"It's hard for me to be very objective about her. She lived next door. Her father hanged himself, oh, sometime before all this happened, and she lived on in the house on her own. Her mother had left before. She was very beautiful. Poor Tommy fell madly in love with her but she didn't want him. She wanted Peter and I guess she got him. At first they just worked together. She would get the young Mounties talking by riding on the streetcar with them or meeting them down at the Trianon. That was the dance hall downtown. Men will tell women anything. Is that not right, Mr. Penner?"

"That's right, Miss Pennan." Sidney smiled hugely and turned to Clara for confirmation.

"Sometimes." Clara found herself uninterested in the conversation now. It obviously had nothing to do with her. Manners, however, prevailed. "I'm sorry, Nell. Yes, you're right."

"She would inform Peter of what she gathered from their conversations and, well, Peter worked for the Workers Unity League. You probably don't know what that was, but in the thirties it was a very powerful communist organization. Peter was very left-wing."

"Left-wing! Chuck? Chuck was a little right of Metternich." Clara exploded.

"Metternich?" Nell looked a little bewildered by the reference.

"He was a..."

"He was just someone who held right-wing opinions," Sidney interjected quickly and nudged Clara under the table.

"Well, Peter was a communist. Margaret gave him the information she gleaned from the Mounties and he passed it on to the leaders of the Trek. He became indispensable to them." Nell paused and looked down at her hands again. "She was his informant. Then, I guess, one thing led to another. They were together every day. Anyway, she left at the same time as he did. Her mother actually came back and mom and dad took her in and looked after her until she died. She never heard from Margaret. We never heard from Peter. It was as if they disappeared from the face of the earth. Then Tommy left. And he died. Eventually, mom and dad died, fairly close to each other, and then there was only me and little Peter left at home. I continued teaching and here I am." Nell stopped, looked at both of them a moment and then pushed back her chair.

"I know how hard this is for you..." Sidney began.

"Do you?"

Sidney suddenly reached out his hand and laid it on Nell's. She started to withdraw hers and then stopped. She bent her head and Sidney could see a long scar hidden in her carefully coiffed hair. He patted her hand.

"No, I don't know. But Clara here is suffering too, and you can help her, us, to deal with it."

"Yes."

Was it agreement or an invitation to continue? Sidney continued. "We need to know anything you heard or ran across that could shed any light on a matter which has come up in regard to the death of Chuck, or Clara's husband. Clara, why don't you show Miss Pennan the note you have."

Clara looked at Sidney thoughtfully. He had obviously changed his mind about showing the note. Clara then looked at Nell and decided to trust Sidney's instinct. She reached into her handbag, brought out the letter and said, "A note for a note."

Nell took it. She gasped, "Teruel!" Her hand shook slightly as she read it slowly several more times. Then, she shook her head. "No. Tommy would never have killed Margaret! Tommy wouldn't have killed anyone. He was so idealistic, head in the clouds all the time. Peter used to despair of him. He was so naive. He could get angry, but he would not have killed anyone. I can't even imagine him in the War." She handed the letter back to Clara dismissively. "You must have the wrong Thomas Pennan."

"I wish I could believe that. But I don't think so."

"That note could have been written by anyone. It wasn't written by Tommy."

After a few seconds of silence, Sidney moved a half-step toward Nell, "That's very true, Miss Pennan. It could have been written by anyone. We, Clara, just wanted to know if there was any chance it could be, well, have some significance for you. Miss Pennan?"

Nell looked up. She pulled her shoulders back in a way that suggested she had faced many things in her life with exactly the same gesture. She turned to Sidney and then back to Clara. "There were other times that I heard, not from, but about, Peter. I can tell you about that. No, first, let me go back a bit. All three of them, Margaret, Tommy, and Peter went to Spain. We didn't hear any news from them, but we were told they had all died in Spain. One of the trekkers came through Regina years later, after the War, and came to the house. He had been there once with Peter before the riot. He said he had served with them in Spain and that all three of them had been killed. Margaret at a place called Teruel, and Peter and Tommy during the Retreats, as he called it. He said they were fighting a rearguard action to let the boys get to the coast and onto ships and died in the trenches. But oddly enough, I later heard from a British war bride that she had met a Peter Stemichuk in a hospital on the Isle of Wight during the War. He had been hit by a mortar bomb in the landing on the beaches of Normandy, and was in hospital there for three years. I didn't give it any credence. For me, he was dead."

"My Chuck had been wounded. He had scars on his legs and chest from a mortar bomb. And thin slivers of shrapnel would come through his skin sometimes. All his life. It must be the same person. It must have been Chuck."

Sidney asked, "Do you remember her name, Nell? The war bride?"

"No, but I have it written down. I, well, I have kept a scrapbook, or at least I used to, when there were things happening I wanted to remember."

"Would you show it to us?"

Nell stood up. "I'll get it."

Clara and Sidney sat at the table looking at each other. "What do you make of her?" Sidney asked.

"I knew it. Chuck survived. Don't you see? He was wounded."

"If..."

"If, if, if. Oh, Sidney, I'm suddenly very tired. It all happened so long ago. What does it really matter? It's really none of my business, just as she said."

"She does look a lot like you."

"Like me? Don't be silly. She doesn't look anything like me. I need some fresh air. No, don't come with me. I can open the door myself." Clara stood up abruptly and caused a little flurry of reaction at the other end of the room.

"I'll stay here and wait," Sidney said to himself.

Nell returned to the room before Clara. She carried a large scrapbook which she set down in front of Sidney. She turned the pages to one with yellowing newspaper clippings.

"These are the clippings from the riot and some of the obituaries, my mom and dad, Mrs. Long, Margaret's mother, and here is the name of the war bride I mentioned. She was Betty Wigmore. That, of course, was not her maiden name. She married a handsome corporal during the war, and it never occurred to her to ask if he had any money. Or else, she did and he lied. In any case, they lived down the street from us in one of those tiny houses they built for veterans when they returned. I think she came from a fairly well-to-do family and was pretty shocked by what greeted her.

"And what is this written here?" Sidney pointed to a neatly written-out passage below her name.

"That's what she told me. Approximately. You may read it if you want."

Sidney read through it. "Did she say anything more about this Meg Stanhope, the nurse who actually looked after Chuck, er, Peter?"

"Not much. They worked on the same floor, where the critically wounded were treated. She and this Meg lost touch, with Betty coming to Canada, starting a family."

"Do you think we could talk with Betty?"

"No."

"Why?"

"She died, oh, fifteen years ago."

"So you never tried to contact Meg Stanhope yourself?"

"No. No reason to." Nell closed the scrapbook with a finality which signalled the interview was at an end. "I choose to believe Peter died in Spain."

Clara had returned and stood at the end of the table.

"Mrs., ah, Miss Pennan has found the name of the war bride and also the name of the nurse who cared for your husband, or this Peter Stemichuk, after he was wounded. Miss Pennan, one last question: You don't remember where either of these nurses came from, do you?"

"No. They were British. I think that's all I can help you with."

Clara came around the table. Nell stood up and shook hands with them. She picked up the scrapbook before Clara had a chance to look at it, and left the room.

"Well, she certainly didn't like me, did she?" Clara drove down Victoria Avenue toward the hotel.

"It was difficult for her to dredge up all those memories, I think."

"Still, we were in a sort of way married to the same man. You would have thought she might have had some sympathy for my situation."

"If it was the same man. There seems to be some evidence that her Peter died in Spain."

"Oh, nonsense. She just can't face the fact that he didn't want to come back to her. He obviously just dropped her. Anyway, she's a pretty unhelpful piece of goods, if you ask me."

"You weren't all that friendly and helpful yourself, Clara."

Clara accepted the criticism in silence, and then sighed. "I should never have started this. I wish I had burned that letter."

"It's too late now."

"I'd like to have my own room this evening, Sidney."

CHAPTER SIXTEEN

From the steps of the Workers Unity League building Thomas and Chuck could hear the roar coming from Market Square. Every so often shots rang out. It sounded like a full-scale war.

"We've got to get back to the stadium." Chuck said, starting down the steps.

"The stadium? Wait. Wait up." Thomas ran to catch up. "Why do you want to go there? The police are all over the place. With machine guns."

"Machine guns? What the hell...? How the hell do you know that?"

Thomas stood in front of Chuck and looked vacantly across the street.

"Tommy, what have you done?"

"Mr. Williams didn't tell us exactly what the trucks were going to be used for. He just...When they loaded the guns, it was too late to get in touch with you. Anyway, how was I supposed to know what they were for? They didn't tell me anything. No one tells me anything." Thomas looked almost pleadingly at Chuck.

"Machine guns are for killing people, Tommy. Didn't the Reverend Evans tell you that? Tommy, oh, Jesus Christ almighty, you have to be one of the stupidest men I have ever met." Chuck started up the street toward 11th Avenue.

"Wait. Wait, Chuck." Tommy hurried up behind him.

"No. I don't want to hear any more."

"Let me explain."

"There is no explanation, except that you are an idiot."

"That's not fair, Chuck."

"Fair?" Chuck stopped, exasperated, and then turned, favouring one leg as he hurried along. Tommy stopped, hesitated, then followed.

"Chuck. Chuck." Tommy felt tears starting up in his eyes. "Chuck."

As they turned the corner of 11th Avenue, they could see people running down the street in front of them. Smoke and dust rose in the air. Shots, screams. Then the crash of glass as store windows caved in. The shattered glass was picked up and used as clumsy weapons. Piles of bricks at the end of an alleyway just west of Broad Street quickly disappeared as men picked up as many as they could and ran for cover.

Chuck and Thomas slowed as they joined the crowd moving west on 11th Avenue. The police on horseback came up behind them, herding them down the street, clubbing the stragglers. At Scarth one of the Mounties was pulled from his horse and thrown to the ground. His horse ran riderless along the sidewalk. Men tried to grab its reins but it stamped and tossed its head high above the crowd, and people ran out of its way. Further along the street the crowd was turning cars over on their sides as makeshift barricades. From behind the still-spinning wheels, men, and women started throwing rocks, bricks, stones, anything they could lay their hands on at the police. Horses reared, some of them bleeding from the sharp bricks.

Chuck, with Tommy following, squeezed up along the storefronts. When he got to the corner, he surveyed the street and recognized a trekker, then another. He yelled at them to get together. He started grouping them, trying to get them in marching order, four by four. They gathered, fled in front of the horses, gathered again. "Line up. Line up." Chuck was screaming at them. "Back to the Stadium. Don't give them any reason to shoot." A phalanx of sixteen men got in line and started to march westward on the street, warding off the police as they went. "Let them through. They're going back to the Stadium." Chuck yelled at a mounted policeman. A policeman's horse reared and the rider clung to the saddle with one hand and swung his truncheon out at Chuck. The blow caught him on the shoulder and sent him staggering into Tommy's arms. Tommy placed himself between Chuck and the Mountie. The Mountie swung again and again. Tommy raised his arms and took the blows, until the Mountie pulled his horse around sharply and caught Thomas directly across the forehead with a back swing. Both Chuck and Thomas went down under the horse's hooves and the horse skittered over them. The crowd surged toward the policeman. He backed off his horse, swinging wildly now at the men grabbing for his reins. One caught hold of his foot and pulled him from the horse, shouting. They pummelled him, driving him back against one of the upturned cars. Two Mounties rode into the crowd and drove them off. The injured Mountie swung up onto one of the horses and drew his revolver. He's going to shoot. He's going to shoot. Men scattered and shots rang out.

"Tommy. Tommy. Are you all right?" Chuck shook Tommy and heard a groan. Tommy's head was bleeding; the cut was deep. He came to, groped desperately for Chuck's shoulder and then sank again into unconsciousness. Chuck heaved him to his feet and, staggering under his weight, pulled him around the corner where it was momentarily quieter. He looked down the street and saw Mrs. Ryan standing in the doorway of her café armed with a meat mallet. He half-dragged, half-carried Thomas toward her. "Get in here. Quick," she yelled. She stepped aside and looked menacingly up and down the street. Chuck heaved Tommy onto a booth table. He came to again, muttered, "I'm okay. I'm okay," and then passed out again. Other people hurt in the street fighting had found refuge there and sat or lay in the booths, holding their injuries close to them. Mrs. Ryan turned away from her vigil and saw that it was Tommy. "Oh, God, not Tommy."

"Some hot water and a bandage of some kind."

Mrs. Ryan ran behind the counter and grabbed a kettle from the grill and poured some water into a bowl. "Here. Let it cool just a little. I'll tear up this apron." Chuck examined the wound, wet the cloth, and began to clean out the wound. Tommy stirred and grimaced in pain. "Pour it on." Mrs. Ryan poured the hot water on the wound, and Tommy lost consciousness again. "Bind it up."

As they finished binding up Tommy's head, there was a crash at the door and one of the Mounties rode his horse right into the café, swinging at the men trying to put tables between themselves and the horse. The horse was panicked, rearing and crashing against the tables, its eyes rolling white. The Mountie almost lost his balance, apparently decided against going any further in, and began to back out. But by the time the horse was manoeuvred out, the café was a shambles, broken glass, sugar canisters emptied on the floor, chairs and tables smashed.

Mrs. Ryan ran to the door and threw one of the canisters at the horse and horseman. It missed, but the Mountie pulled the horse around and returned to the melee on 11th. Mrs. Ryan stood in the street and called out every obscenity after him she could think of. She returned to the café, shaking with anger. "Christly bulls. May they all burn in hell." She sat wearily down in one of the booths. "Look at this place." She was suddenly older looking.

"Don't you worry none, Mrs. Ryan. We'll clean it up. Won't we boys?" Chuck looked around the room at the men and they struggled to their feet and started putting the café in order again. "Come on. Tommy's all right for the moment." Chuck put his arm around her and led her to the back, got her a cup of coffee from the percolator which, remarkably, still bubbled on the grill and set it down in front of her with some milk and sugar. "There. We'll guard the door. Where's the phone? We got to get Tommy to the hospital."

"Over there, on the counter." Mrs. Ryan waved a hand toward the back of the café, and Chuck grabbed up the receiver as Tommy began to gain consciousness again. The bandage around his head was stained a deep red.

"Oh, Chuck, is he going to be all right? He's not going to...?" Mrs. Pennan stood in the middle of her kitchen, looking up at him. Chuck had headed out to Seventh Avenue as soon as he had Tommy looked after at the hospital. He had found only Tommy's mother at home. "I don't know where father's gone. Are you sure Tommy's all right?"

"Yes, Mrs Pennan. He'll be okay. He's lost a lot of blood, but the wound isn't too deep." He reached out and held her for a moment.

She pulled back, "And Nell? Where's Nell?"

"Nell? Isn't she here?" Chuck's face drained of its colour. "Where'd she go?"

"She went to that meeting. The one in Market Square."

"Oh, no." Chuck turned and started to run back across the prairie toward downtown. "If anything has happened to her...or the baby." He ran.

CHAPTER SEVENTEEN

Sunday morning dawned bright and sunny, and Clara wondered for a moment if people here didn't get tired of blue sky all the time. She felt like rain. She had always found the steady drumming of rain on the roof comforting. She wanted to be home. The session with Nell and the long walk along Wascana Creek with Sidney had exhausted her. Sidney had been kind and understanding. He was not a bad man. She just shouldn't have slept with him. Well, not so quickly. Sex was close to death. She had read that in a magazine once. Somewhere. It was still early, and Clara turned onto her left side and drifted back into a light sleep.

"Let's forget about all this – the Pennans and Chuck's earlier life. I'd like to just enjoy the day, go to the art gallery, perhaps look at the Legislative Buildings. Let's just have a little holiday today." Clara wiped her lips and set her empty coffee cup down.

"Good idea." Sidney always agreed, it seemed, but was he

really agreeing? Did she care? Sidney was now showing his enthusiasm again. "We could also go out to the Mountie museum."

Clara looked at him long and hard. He stopped, wondering what he had said wrong this time, then realized the implication of his suggestion. "Well, I guess it wouldn't be totally forgetting our search, would it?"

"No, not totally." Clara smiled. He was so boyish sometimes. She found herself liking that about him. But really a one-track mind. One-trick mind crossed her mind. However, she had to admit that the reason they were in Regina was to find out about Chuck. No, wait a minute, not about Chuck. They were here to find out about Thomas Pennan. It just always seemed to come back to Chuck. Anyway, the Mountie museum might be a good idea.

"The museums will be closed on Monday," Sidney added lamely.

"Okay. The Mountie museum too, but last of all and if we have time." She pushed her chair back and stood up. "Let's go, my cavalier." She laid her hand on his sleeve and he positively beamed his appreciation.

About 4:00 p.m. Sidney and Clara entered the Museum of the Royal Canadian Mounted Police. It was located at the RCMP training centre rather far out on Dewdney Avenue near Wascana Creek. They had almost walked that far the previous afternoon. Young men strode about among the red-brick buildings, and the entire setting was somehow more like a university campus than what Clara had imagined a police training centre would be. There was, however, a certain military air to the place, as in the curt, but politely correct answers the guard at the entrance to the grounds had given to their questions.

The artifacts in the museum were, on the whole, grisly or sad. A piece of the rope, actually three pieces of rope, with which, it was claimed, Louis Riel had been hanged; the handcuffs they had held him with; a carbine case of Chief Sitting Bull; various rifles, revolvers and other murder weapons. A stuffed horse. Even a Gatling gun. They learned that it was the first machine gun used by the Canadian military, and that this one had seen action in the Riel Rebellion at Batoche. When they came to the Regina Riot artifacts, they shuddered a bit at the brutal-looking truncheons which, the label stated, had been made by the trekkers to fight off the police, but the really interesting aspect of the exhibit was the enlarged photograph that formed the backdrop. It was grainy and very unclear, but you could see men running here and there in a large open space; others lying on the ground. A woman with a pram hurried across the square at the front. There were also broken store windows and the wreckage of cars in the street.

"It says that's Market Square. Things have sure changed since that picture was taken." Sidney leaned over and squinted intensely at the photograph. "Would you recognize Chuck?"

"Not in that photo, Sidney, but remember, I didn't meet him until he was fifteen years older than he was then." Clara paused and leaned closer as well. "I can't believe that Chuck could have been involved in that. It's just not possible. He was such a quiet man. He hated upset of any kind."

"Nell would have been standing almost where this picture was taken from. See the map? That building in the photograph must be the side of the fire hall. And the platform is over there. See?"

"I could see better if you took your finger away."

"Sorry."

Clara took his hand. "That's all right, Sidney. I just get grumpy when I think about it. I'm so confused about all this. I came to find out about a Thomas Pennan and instead I have found Chuck. A Chuck I didn't know, a Chuck that I can hardly believe is the same man I married."

"Nell didn't strike me as the type of person who would lie or even exaggerate very much, for that matter."

"No, you're right. One of those men in that photograph must be Chuck." Clara squinted at the dark shadowy figures caught in the past. She shook her head. "A communist involved in a riot, fighting the police. It is just too fantastic. There are two men there, running together. They could be Chuck and Thomas. We'll never know."

"Well, I suppose we don't even know for sure he was a communist."

"That's what Nell said."

"Yes, that's what Nell said." Sidney pulled Clara gently away from the exhibit and walked with her to the exit. "Let's go and look at the chapel. It's supposed to be the oldest remaining building in Regina."

Clara sat literally by herself in the large dining room of the hotel. Not only was Sidney not there, but no one else was in the room either. And it was fairly late. The hotel clock in her room had blinked out 8:00 p.m. before she had come down. Sidney had surprised Clara by announcing that he had put his bag in the trunk before they left the hotel and wanted to be dropped off at the airport to catch the 5:30 p.m. plane for Toronto. She had gone into the terminal with him and felt almost as if he was her husband flying off to a conference somewhere. Oddly, she had felt a loss at his going. Too many people going away. It seemed her Chuck was slowly becoming an indistinct memory. The more she found out about his earlier life, the more he became a stranger, sort of departing into a past she would never be able to share. And Sidney. As she sat waiting for her meal, she thought about Sidney. She did feel something for this man who had gone out of his way to help her and support her over the past, how long, only a week? He seemed to genuinely care for her. It was a good feeling.

But, she really wasn't ready for a new relationship. She had to be clear about that. It was too soon after Chuck's death. He was always on her mind, even if he was becoming less and less clear as she began to find out about his earlier life. It was somewhat odd, even understandable, that he had never mentioned the fact that he had been in the Riot or in Spain, but it was extraordinary he hadn't mentioned having a son. Yet he must have often thought about him, wanted to see him, know how he had grown up. His only child. At least as far as she knew. Clara got a little annoyed with herself for being so suspicious. She was not a very suspicious person usually. But a son he never even contacted, much less mentioned? That was a serious omission. More than that. It was simply irresponsible. He had left that woman to raise the child all by herself. Or had he? No. No, she was sure he had had no contact with her. That was, well, *inhuman* came to mind, but she pushed the word away. Still, what else might there have been that she didn't know about?

Then, Clara remembered that she had been surprised when they had gone to Mexico the first time and she discovered that he spoke passable Spanish. Learnt it in high school, he had said. It struck Clara now how unlikely it was that a high school in Saskatchewan would have taught Spanish in the 1930s. And he had never wanted to go to Spain. He had always said he preferred Greece or Italy. At the time, she had accepted these statements at face value, but now that she recalled them, they seemed to fit what she had learned from Nell. No wonder he spoke Spanish but didn't want to go to Spain!

Her dinner came and she began to eat slowly still immersed in thought. Pepper? Oh, yes. Sidney had suggested that she go over to the public library on the other side of the park and look up the newspapers from that time. She knew that she would do it, but she didn't feel like it. Her life seemed to have been discontinued in some sort of way. What had happened to the orderly existence she had had in Toronto – no obscure happenings, no unexpected revelations, no riots? It seemed gone. But, when she thought about it, her life in Toronto had had the same hidden surprises, only they had stayed hidden.

Damn Chuck! Clara clenched her teeth and let herself be annoyed, angry. What had he been playing at? How much else had he hidden from her? She had thought they shared everything. Well, maybe not his occasional peccadilloes, but their personal lives. If she had confronted him with her suspicions, she was sure he would have willingly owned up to them and asked her forgiveness. Or would he have? Anyway, she just hadn't wanted to know. Did she want to know now? She pulled herself together and resolved to be more businesslike. She'd focus on Thomas Pennan.

At ten o'clock the next morning, Clara walked up to the small, neat library. The sun shone into the glass foyer and had warmed the interior. She pushed open the door and stood for a moment just inside. Now, what would she find? Probably very little. It was just newspaper articles she wanted, and she expected they would not have much detail in them. She went upstairs, through the security door to the main floor, and walked toward the reference desk. To her right, she noticed an art gallery, or at least a large room that was labelled Dunlop Gallery. After a moment's hesitation, she turned and went in. It was an exhibition of cows. The sort of thing you might expect to find out here in Saskatchewan, she thought. Most extraordinary cows with wonderful names. On closer examination, she could see that these were also extraordinary sculptures, realistic and yet full of, what? independence and meaningfulness. Even humour. Clara smiled at their total involvement in their lives as cows and felt her heart lift. If you could take a cow and make it fit an art gallery, then she could take the mess of misinformation she was dealing with and make it into something, well, something that had meaning. A total non sequitur but it buoyed her up as she walked out of the gallery and headed for the reference desk.

Much to Clara's surprise, there was a lot of detail in the newspaper accounts of the riot and its aftermath.

Police Open Fire When 3,000 Jobless Wage Stubborn Fight: Detective Clubbed to Death.

REGINA, July 2- A policeman was killed, one man is dying and scores were injured here tonight when steel-helmeted Royal Canadian Mounted and city police charged a mob of 3,000 relief camp strikers and sympathizers in the Market Square behind the police station...

And then some lurid details:

Two strikers appeared in the lane opposite the Grand Theatre. They tossed rocks. Two Mounties rushed after them. The strikers took to their heels down the lane. Mounties yanked out revolvers and blazed into the darkness. They got their quarry, one striker being hit by bullets in both legs. He was taken into a restaurant at 1824 Cornwall Street. Two striker Red Cross men attended to him as he lay on the floor, blood welling in a dark pool...

This was serious stuff. Those two men could have been Chuck and Thomas. Although Clara was really not sure Thomas had been there. Nell had just mentioned Chuck. And 1824 Cornwall Street: the park was on the 1900 block, so the restaurant would have been just a block or so away.

Hard to imagine her Chuck running down these streets, fleeing the police. It was all here in amazing detail. As she turned the pages she came to a long list of the men arrested, carefully divided into those arrested by the Mounties and those arrested by the city police. And then she saw it, Peter Stemichuk, Ituna, Sask., and a little further on, Thomas Pennan, Regina, Sask. There it was in black and white. It was true. The article went on to state that Peter Stemichuk had been arrested "on warrant," and that Thomas Pennan had been arrested about 1:00 a.m. Tuesday morning in his home, 4529 7th Avenue. Clara ran her finger down the list of men charged and brought to court. Chuck's name was there but not Thomas's. Bail refused. But Chuck had been charged. By July 5, the newspaper was reporting the departure of the trekkers, mostly back to their homes or wherever they had come from, in "special colonist cars attached to regular trains." And that was all. The helpful librarian told Clara that she could read the minutes of the Royal Commission, that had been set up to review the evidence about the Riot, at the Archives, but Clara had had enough for now. Anyway, Nell's story was confirmed and expanded. She got up and walked back to the hotel, thinking, absurdly of course, she might still see some faint bloodstains on the streets. Too much imagination gets you into trouble, Chuck had always said.

And now she had the address where this Thomas Pennan had lived, where Chuck had met Nell. And next door would be the house where Margaret had lived. It was as if everything had suddenly become real. On the spur of the moment, Clara decided she would drive out and look at the house at 4529 7th Avenue where the Pennans had apparently lived all those sixty some years ago. Instead of going into the hotel, she walked around to the parking lot and picked up the rental car. It took a few minutes to find the simplified little map of Regina that the rental company had given her at the airport. Seventh Avenue. She found Dewdney Avenue easily and then Seventh. She and Sidney had actually driven within two blocks of it yesterday.

As she turned off Dewdney onto Connaught Street she past an odd mix of a few old houses mostly at the Dewdney end of the street, and then, clusters of bungalows from the sixties and seventies with their two-car garages and suburban lawns. Dewdney must have been Ninth Avenue once, or at least, it was two blocks to Seventh Avenue, and the one in between was Eighth. She turned right onto Seventh Avenue and stopped in front of the two houses on the corner. 4533 was still the corner house, although there was an empty lot on the actual corner. 4529 was a much smaller house, really just a shack, standing rather incongruously next to one of the suburban bungalows that lined the rest of the block. Clara parked the car in front of the shack and turned off the engine. The roof sagged a bit and the window and door frames hadn't seen a fresh coat of paint for a long time. How long? Clara got out of the car and stared at it, trying to see through the walls back into time. Then, she walked a ways back to the corner and stood in front of the larger house. A caragana hedge stretched across the front of the lot and was neatly trimmed. As she walked back to the car, a woman came out of the smaller house, pushing a toddler in a stroller. She looked suspiciously at Clara standing by the car, but Clara was engrossed in her thoughts about the Pennans, the riot, and her husband. Some of his life, an important part of his life, was played out here in this little house, in this neighbourhood. And he'd said barely a word to her about any of it. The little house still had a glassed-in front porch. Where Chuck and Nell had...He had kept all that from her. Why that bothered her so much, she didn't know. You think you know someone, all their habits, their stories, how their life has flowed along, and then you find that it was different, radically different from what you thought it was. She was beginning to doubt everything. In fact, their life together was taking on a certain air of unreality in the face of this overwhelming past.

She turned and got back into the car. Did it all change anything really, though? Their life together was just that. All those feelings and experiences were still there, were still hers. Chuck's absence was still there, both in fact and tugging her heart down like a weight. Tears came to her eyes and she openly wept, letting the rivulets course down her cheeks unobstructed. Her grieving had been like this, sudden, torrential tears without any warning. Her body shook, wracked with sobbing.

There was a tapping on the window next to her. She struggled to look up. The woman with the stroller was standing there. Clara rolled down the window.

"Is there anything wrong? Can I help you?" The woman's suspicion had given way to her natural empathy, it seemed.

"No. No. It's just, well, someone I knew once lived here, in that house. My husband actually."

"Oh. When would that have been?"

"A long time ago."

"We've lived there twelve years and it belonged to my parents before that. What was his name?"

"Stemichuk. Peter Stemichuk."

"No one by that name ever lived here. At least not since, oh, the thirties. My mom, she was an English war bride, and she came here, oh, well right after the war and my dad had lived down the street there on Connaught since he was a boy, like twenty years before that. More. He knew everyone round here, from the old days, I mean. He never mentioned a Stemichuk. And he would have, cause he didn't like them bohunks, as he called them. Oh, sorry. I forgot. I mean that's the way it was back then. Now, well, look at me, I married one." She smiled and tucked the blanket more tightly around her charge.

"What about Pennans?"

"Oh, sure. The Pennans lived there in the house we live in, until, well, they were there when my mom came. She and Dad lived in one of those little veterans' houses just right there on the other corner, over there." She pointed to the other side of Connaught Street. "We lived there where the stucco house is now. Mrs. Pennan, her mother, Nell's mother, was very kind to my mom when she came here. I mean, my mom was used to England and a big house and here she was in a little house out on the prairie. It was prairie round here then, edge of town, poor part of town, know what I mean?" Her run-on sentences were exhausting, but she looked proud of herself to be able to give all this information.

"You are sure they didn't live in that house, the first one there from the corner?"

"Think they did one time. Like later they lived in that one next to it. I don't know why they moved, like. But I seem to remember mom saying they did. Nell must've bought the little one we live in, 'cuz my dad bought it from Nell Pennan. She's dead now. My mom, I mean."

"Was there a Thomas Pennan?"

"The one that went off to war and didn't ever show up again? We heard plenty 'bout him. But not from Mrs. Pennan, that's old Mrs. Pennan. Like, I didn't know her personal like. She kept her lips zipped, she did. Least that's what my mom always said. No. It was like, gossip. You know people were pretty left-wing those days. Well, still are here in Saskatchewan, specially after the last government...Well, he, Thomas Pennan that is, well he, anyway this is what I heard, I don't know how much truth there is in it. But he was big for the church, this Thomas, like he studied to be a minister and stuff, but got thrown out or something and then he just went to the other extreme and became a communist. Like he, well you know, like he didn't believe in God no more and..."

"What happened to him?"

"I don't know really. Like he went off to war. Not the big war my dad fought in, but the one in Spain before that."

"Did your father, then, know Thomas?"

"Of course. Them days, everyone knew everyone."

"I mean, did he know him well?"

"Yeah. I think so. They were sort of pals, like all the kids would hang out together. Play kick-the-can on the road. But my dad was a lot younger, of course. Tommy, that's what my dad always called him, got hurt once in the riot. You heard 'bout the riot? Probably not. Well, there was this riot downtown..."

"I actually have heard about it."

"Oh? Oh, okay. Well, dad said Tommy got hurt in it. Hit over the head. He was never really right in the head after that and that's why he became a communist and went off to Spain and stuff. Got God knocked right outta him. Least, that's what my dad said."

"Well, you've been very helpful. Thank you." Clara put her hand on the ignition key.

"Glad to help. Sorry you're feeling sad, but my mom always used to say, It's all water under the bridge now." She waved a small wave and pushed her stroller over to the sidewalk, tipped it back so the front wheels were on the surface, and walked back to the little house. As she disappeared behind the hedge, she lifted her hand in another final, friendly wave.

Clara slowly rolled up the window, started the car and drove down the street. Nothing new in the information, but seeing the house and having talked to that woman made it all a bit more, what? perhaps satisfying. She had forgotten to ask about Margaret. Well, it was all water under the bridge.

CHAPTER EIGHTEEN

"If it hadn't been for Mr. Ader, I don't know what they might have done." Nell sat at the kitchen table while her mother bathed her head with a mixture of water and baking soda. Mr. Ader, his uniform creased and dirty, stood next to Nell's father by the kitchen door. "Shush now." Mrs. Pennan turned to Mr. Ader. "I want to thank you, Jim. For looking after my girl. These are troubled times."

"Oh, it's nothing. The least I could do." Mr. Ader shuffled his feet.

Nell's father looked out the small kitchen window, "Troubled times. Least you could do. I've done everything I can. I can't see what is going to happen now. It's just like that. It's all too much to comprehend. I'm lost somewhere now. There's no going back..." His voice petered out.

"That's all right, George. You just go into the other room and sit down." Mrs. Pennan handed the wet cloth to Nell and shepherded her husband into the sitting room.

"Is he all right?"

"Sometimes he's worse; sometimes he's better. What's a man to do when he can't get work to support his family?"

"Yes. I'm one of the lucky ones, I guess. Well, I best be getting along. The wife'll be worried." Mr. Ader put his hand on the doorknob and awkwardly put on his hat. "Maybe that cut needs some stitches."

"I don't know. But, thank you again, Jim."

"It's nothing. Think nothing of it. Hope she'll be okay." He left and skittered around the corner of the house, headed toward the street.

"Mother, it was awful. They beat up on everybody. Women, kids. It was awful. And they grabbed Peter right off the platform. They weren't doing anything illegal, Mom. They were just speaking to the crowd about the day. The police beat them. It was horrible."

"Did you see Thomas?"

"No. He wasn't there. Funny he wasn't. He's probably at work."

"I hope he's all right." Mrs. Pennan rubbed her hands on her apron and looked out the window.

"He'll be okay, Mom. The Lord's on his side."

"Now, don't make fun of him because he's religious. It wouldn't do you no harm to go to church, either."

"And have them all whispering? Look at that bad girl."

"Bad girls don't get pregnant."

"Tell them that."

Mrs. Pennan turned to her counter and began to roll out the scone dough.

Nell stood up, still holding the cloth to her head, "I think I'll lie down for awhile."

Thomas got home about 11:30 that night, his head bandaged, his clothes torn and dirty. He was utterly exhausted. Somehow Chuck had managed to get him into an ambulance and to the Grey Nuns' Hospital. There he had been put in a bed in the hallway and eventually seen to by a very efficient, no-nonsense nun. As soon as the wound was clean and bandaged, he was sent home and the next patient laid out on the bed. As he left, the sister smacked him lightly on the backside with a roll of paper and said, "See that you stay out of trouble."

His mother was waiting for him, sitting at the kitchen table, her hands folded in front of her. When he entered, she looked up at him. "You better get out of them clothes. I'll make some tea. Don't wake your sister."

He had hardly returned to the kitchen when Margaret burst in. "What's happened? Oh, Tommy. You're hurt." She reached out for him, stopped, looked around. "What about Peter? Where's Peter? Mrs. Pennan, have you seen him?"

Mrs. Pennan pointed to the kitchen table. "Sit down, Margaret. He got Tommy to the hospital and then he ran off to find Nell. I'm sure he's all right."

"Oh god, I hope so. Tommy, Tommy, you're hurt. What happened?"

"Nothing. We, Chuck and I, got into a bit of a scuffle, that's all."

"I've been asleep since supper. We were working so late last night, Peter and me. Is he all right, Tommy?'

Tommy sat down, took his cup and held it in his hands. "He's okay."

"Okay? What do you mean, Okay?" Margaret's voice rose.

"I mean he got battered about a bit but he's not seriously

hurt. He's...I don't know where he is now." Tommy set the cup down without drinking. "I was taken to the hospital. Last I saw him was downtown." He reached up and touched his bandage.

"Oh, Tommy. You're hurt." She placed her hand on his. He grasped it. She let him hold her for a moment then withdrew her hand and turned to Mrs. Pennan. "Can I do anything?"

"No, Margaret. I think we should all just go to bed and see what the morrow brings."

There was a banging at the door and Mrs. Ryan strode in. "The bastards, the cowardly bastards. Sorry, Mrs. Pennan, it's got to be said, it's got to be yelled out. They're shooting people downtown."

"Oh, no! Peter."

"Not Peter. He's been arrested."

"Arrested?"

"Dorothy, sit down and have some tea." Mrs. Pennan addressed Mrs. Ryan by her first name, even though Mrs. Ryan was always more formal with her.

"Tommy, you all right?" Mrs. Ryan sat down heavily on the wooden kitchen chair next to him. "My café. Ruined." She sank her face into her hands and let her body slump forward.

"You saw Peter, then?" Margaret moved almost involuntarily toward Mrs. Ryan as if to press from her an answer.

"Yes. He was in the café when...a Mountie rode his goddamn horse right into my café. Smashed tables, chairs. Stupid bull. I'm sorry but I'm not apologizing for the bad language. I threw every goddamn thing I could lay my hands on at him."

"And Peter?"

"He was there with me. He brought Tommy here in, half-dead. Laid him out on a table and then got the ambulance. I thought he was going to bleed to death. Tommy, I mean. How are you now?" She suddenly lifted her head as if she had just realized that she was talking about him in the third person as if he wasn't there.

Tommy nodded, "Okay."

"Peter came back after you left. Looking for Nell. But I heard he was arrested on 11th Avenue. They were trying to get the boys back to the stadium. Avoid violence. Bloody bulls wanted violence. Animals. They were thirsting for it, they were."

At around 1:00 a.m. the police arrived at the house and arrested Thomas Pennan on charges of public mischief and assaulting a police officer. Mr. and Mrs. Pennan stood and watched as Tommy was shoved roughly into the back of a van, parked in front of the house. The heat of the day still hung in the air and the sky was black and bright with stars.

CHAPTER NINETEEN

"They caught Chuck and threw him into jail. They got the Exhibition Buildings surrounded so the boys can't get out. The windows in R.H. Williams are smashed to pieces."

Thomas sat at the kitchen table, looking feverish and agitated, his head freshly bandaged with an old piece of sheeting that his mother had stored away to make underclothes. He didn't mention the machine guns mounted on the Grey Nun's Hospital roof and directed out over the buildings where the trekkers were. His mother was standing at the kitchen sink with her back to him.

"They got twenty guys in a cell at a time. Some of them bleeding, others can't stand up. One of them looked dead."

Margaret and Nell stood at opposite ends of the kitchen, Margaret at the back door and Nell in the doorway to the living room.

"You better lie down, Nell." Mrs. Pennan walked over to her and led her back into the room.

"Thomas, tell me how Chuck is. Is he all right? I mean, is he hurt or anything?" Margaret took a step toward him.

"Nah. He's okay. He's down there organizing the men to refuse to give their right names or where they come from. If they're forced to tell, he wants them to say they're from Ottawa or someplace in Ontario so they can regroup and confront Bennett."

"Just like him."

"Yeah." Thomas picked up his cup of tea and held it in his two hands. They shook a bit.

"You're shaking, Tommy."

"And the Rev is down there. At the station. He's insisting they arrest him too, because he says, he 'aided and abetted known revolutionaries.' They won't arrest him and they can't get rid of him. He's wearing his collar, so they don't know what to do with him."

Mrs. Pennan came back in, closing the door quietly behind her. She looked down at Thomas. "You should lie down too. It's been a long night."

Margaret turned to go, stopped. "Is there anything I can do, Mrs. Pennan?"

"No. Everything's all right now. I don't think there's much else we can do. Dad's lying down and once I get Thomas to bed, I think I'll try to have a bit of a nap myself."

Margaret rushed back in and put her arms around Mrs. Pennan. "Thank you. For everything. If you need anything, anything at all..." Mrs. Pennan let Margaret hug her and then she turned back to Thomas. He set down his cup and made to stand up, but his mother laid a hand on his shoulder, not exactly holding him down, but her pressure was sufficient to discourage him from getting up.

Margaret hurried to the door, turned, hesitated. "I'm going downtown. To see if...Maybe Chuck can be...I mean, he wasn't one of the trekkers." She started back at a quick-walk across the prairie toward downtown. Thomas watched her, half rising from his chair.

"Let her go, Thomas."

Thomas sank back down and looked up at his mother. "Mother, they beat us, like animals. And one of them..."

"Hush. It's over, for now. Just be glad you are safe."

"Oh, yeah. They let us, those of us that lived in the city, go."

"They don't want to get the people here angry. It doesn't matter about the trekkers. They come from somewhere else."

"What are they going to do with them? There are two thousand of them."

"Probably send them back to the camps or all off in different directions. Lot of people here won't be sad to see them go." She returned to the sink, taking Thomas's cup with her. She looked up and out of the window. "Did you see the Reverend Evans?"

"Well, no. Not exactly. I was talking to one of the men that was moved over from the Mountie's station to the city police station. He told me the Rev was trying to get himself arrested."

"That won't help the boys much."

"Oh, my head." Thomas held his head and started to shake it a bit from side to side.

"Don't do that. It may start to bleed again."

"I feel funny. As if everything...I've gotta go lie down." Thomas stood up, stumbled. His mother rushed over and caught him before he could fall.

"That's okay. Come on. You can lie down on the couch." She put an arm around him and guided him into the other room.

CHAPTER TWENTY

Slim, who had been one of the Trek leaders, Chuck, and Thomas stood on the railroad embankment just at the eastern edge of the Winnipeg railroad yards. They had walked out from the flophouse on north Main Street, where they had spent the night, and were headed east for Toronto.

Thomas had gone through a difficult time after the Riot with frequent dizzy spells and long periods confined to his bed. He was getting better though, and had recently begun looking for work again. Chuck, on his way East, had gone out to see Nell, but had been refused access to the house or his daughter by Mr. Pennan. When Chuck left the house, Thomas had run after him and begged him to take him East with him. Chuck reluctantly agreed and introduced him to an even more skeptical Slim. The three of them were an unlikely looking trio – Slim, tall, grey-haired and a bit stooped, a New Brunswicker with a gift of the gab; Chuck, shorter and stockier, serious, planning their next moves; and Thomas, putting on weight in spite of soup-kitchen meals, always a few steps behind the other two, seemingly sunk in his own thoughts. Thomas's clothes were a bit crumpled but still clean and pressed from his mother's insistence that he look "presentable." Chuck and Slim were grimier. They had gone from Regina to the Coast and back many times in the usual pattern of the unemployed, crisscrossing the country in what seemed a hopeless search for work. Except, they were going from town to town, from hobo camp to hobo camp, trying to rally support for the United Front, a newly formed organization that they hoped would act as an umbrella group for all the small unions across the country – another One Big Union – the idea would not die. Now, they were headed for Toronto to tackle the organization of all the disparate trade unions there that had so far resisted any attempt to unite them into a larger union. That was their stated plan, but there were also rumours of the civil war that had broken out in Spain. The call was out for men to volunteer. Both Slim and Chuck had spread the word up and down the railway lines that there would be recruiting offices in Toronto waiting for them.

"Knew a man once got his foot taken off in one of them couplings." Slim squatted down and looked under the box cars and up and down the tracks. "Thought he could cross over between the cars and the whole train shunted just as he stepped on the coupling. Swip. No foot." He pointed between the iron wheels of a boxcar closest to them. "Do you see any bulls? Bloody bulls. They're everywhere. Jumped into a boxcar out in Regina once and there was a goddamn bull nailed up on the inside wall. Crucified. And damned if I wasn't glad to see it." He peered under the cars again, then stood up and motioned Chuck and Tommy to cross over to the other side between the cars. "Quick."

All three of them scampered beneath the coupling and came up on the other side. The rusted wheels and the bright running edge where the rim of the wheel hit the track reminded Thomas for a moment of the pennies they had laid out on the track as kids. Flattened them. Saw some once at the Fair. Indians had punched a hole in them and hung them with beads on some leather string for a necklace. The doors of the boxcars on this side stood open. "Up and into it." Slim climbed with surprising agility up into the opening of the boxcar and turned and gave first Chuck, and then Thomas, a helping hand. "'Member when we used to ride on top? Through the mountains. Jesus, those tunnels were long." Slim rubbed his hands on his pants. "Whoa. The smell in here. Pigs."

"No, that's cows, Slim."

"Country boy, eh? Anyway, poor bastards whatever they were, off to slaughter. Just like us, eh?" Slim grinned. "Off to war. And let the crows eat us afterward; as if we give a damn. We'll smash those cocksucking fascists, eh, boys? You bet."

Chuck was collecting clean straw at one end of the boxcar and pushing cowshit down to the other end. "We'll sleep like kings tonight, Tommy. Nothing like straw. Lay your coat over it so it don't scratch and – bliss. No, don't close the door yet. We'll push all that shit out after we get going." Tommy felt his eyes water up from the dust and he wiped them furtively. Maybe he was crying too. He was already homesick.

Next morning, after a restless sleep, Tommy was up early and went and sat in the open doorway. The dilapidated, but neat houses of some towns along the track sped by. It was like a reverse movie. He had taken Margaret to her first movie just before the riot. It had been wonderful. No, it hadn't actually. She had hurried off afterward because she had an appointment with Chuck. Tommy looked back through the early morning gloom of the boxcar at Chuck and Slim still snoring in separate corners.

He turned again to the speeding landscape and tried to stop the houses by focusing on one far to the left and then watching it until it disappeared to the right. Once he saw a woman come out of a back door, tying her apron strings around her ample belly. It was early. Earlier still in Regina. Even his mother wouldn't be up yet. The rooms of the house would be dark and quiet, except for his father snoring in the back bedroom. Too early even for wind. Cool. What in hell was he doing riding in a boxcar somewhere in northern Ontario? He hugged himself against the early morning chill.

He would see Margaret in Toronto. Chuck had taken some of the money they collected on the tag days and paid for her ticket. She would get the paper work done for the boys. Tommy ached for her. Working with her occasionally in Regina after the riot had been marvellous. But whenever he had tried to touch her or ask her out, she had moved away or found an excuse not to go. "No, Tommy. I'm tired and there's still a lot to do. You run along." She talked to him sometimes as if he were a child. He had even dated a pretty Jewish woman who worked in the office, parading her out to the movies one evening. Later, Margaret had teased him about it. She hadn't seemed to mind at all. It made him so angry.

It was her sheer physical presence that overwhelmed him. He could see in his mind's eye the outline of her panties showing through her skirt as she leaned over the desk to reach for something. At the thought, even now, he felt a stirring. And then the memory of his housebreaking came back. Housebreaking – he had given it that name for some reason he did not entirely understand. Actually, he had gone over to her house one morning and knocked. The door had swung open and he had gone in and called out for her. Silence. Then, hesitantly, he had walked into the kitchen and through to the dining-living room. He had called out again, although by that time he knew he was alone in the house, in her house. There was a door off the room at the back. It was partially open and he could see the mirror of a dressing table reflecting the front window. He pushed open the door and stepped into what was obviously her bedroom. It was small and tidy, no frills, just a simple quilt on the single bed, a chair, small table, lamp, and the dressing table with a stool. Incongruously, there was a picture of a thatched cottage with a rose garden hanging on one wall. He had opened the drawers of the dressing table. The top one had mostly combs and brushes, but in the lower ones he found brassieres and panties, all neatly folded. He had touched the panties and...he was not ashamed of it. He had jacked off into one pair. He still had them stuffed down at the bottom of his sack. It was her fault. For what? For not taking him seriously? For not going out with him? Tommy heard someone stir in the boxcar behind him.

"Christ, Tommy, you're thinking so hard you woke me up." Chuck was sitting up, rubbing his head vigorously. "Wouldn't a cup of coffee taste good right now?"

"There's some milk left in the bottle, if it hasn't turned."

Chuck stood up, stretched and walked over to the opening. "Great morning, eh, Tommy? Great to be on the road, going somewhere. All the sitting around in meetings is a bit wearing, don't you think? Hey, Tommy, you there?" Tommy looked up and then got to his feet.

"Yep. I'm here, Chuck."

Chuck threw a playful punch at him, just grazing his shoulder. Tommy tensed and turned away.

From the back of the boxcar came a loud, long fart. "In the name of the Father, the Son and the Holy Ghost. Amen." Slim pushed back the dirty blanket covering him, stood up and stretched. He farted again, "And the Virgin Mary." Tommy blushed in spite of his effort not to react.

"I didn't know you were Catholic, Slim." Chuck threw the remark over his shoulder and, putting his arm around Tommy's shoulder, turned him to the open door again.

"Oh, Christ, yes. I was an altar boy. That's where I learnt 'bout communism and camaraderie. Jesus, those brothers were camradely." Slim joined them at the door. "Well, you two better step back because I am going to use the biggest urinal in the world." And he pissed out the door. "Hope to hell there's a bull somewhere back there just opening his mouth to yell at somebody." He buttoned up. "Now, by all the saints in Heaven, Holy Mary pray for us, let's hope this goddamn train stops soon so we can go and cadge a breakfast."

CHAPTER TWENTY-ONE

The Reverend Evans stood on a small platform at the front of the hall. About two hundred men and a few women sat in rows of chairs in front of him. A number of the leaders from the Trek, including Chuck and Slim, sat in a row behind him on the platform. Thomas stood at the back of the hall just behind Margaret. The Rev looked out at them, nodded his head as if to himself, grasped the edges of the lectern and began quietly to speak. The crowd hushed and then strained to hear.

"Brothers and Sisters, or should I say Comrades? (cheers from some in the front rows) we have witnessed in the last few weeks a great tragedy. There are so many tragedies these days, you are asking, which one? It is not the long lines of unemployed standing in front of the soup kitchens. It is not the poor making underwear out of sugar sacks. It is not children running barefoot in the streets, looking for scraps of food to take home to their brothers and sisters. It is not the tragedy of the young men beaten up and dispersed in Regina. No, I'm talking about a much bigger tragedy, much bigger, a tragedy that envelopes our entire country. Our country. We, or our parents or grandparents, came to this country to find a better life, to find the freedom that the old country could not give."

He stepped to the side of the lectern. His voice began to rise. The crowd sat back, tensely listening. "And for a time we thought we had found the Promised Land. It was that land of milk and honey, but a far better land than the one promised to Moses and the chosen people. True, it was a land we would have to tame, one we would have to earn through hard work and dedication, earn by the sweat of our brow, but we were willing to work, to work day and night, to do without, to sacrifice in order to build a society in which our children and grandchildren could be properly clothed and housed and fed and educated. Where they would be free. Well, that land is being taken away from us. That is the tragedy, that I speak of, the tragedy of our loss. We, the people of hope, once called the salt of the earth, have been deceived."

He began to pace back and forth, repeating "deceived." He returned to the lectern and raised his arms, stretching them out to the crowd. "For we thought we had created a new world. But, no, it is the old world, the old world of capitalist greed and state brutality, the old world of repression and censorship, the old world of dictators and moneymen. That is the tragedy we are facing. The minions of darkness have followed us here. They want this land that we have found and made into a land of hope and freedom."

"Yes. Yes. They want our country. You've seen them grow in strength. The enemy. And who is this enemy? After the Great War, men, and women, yes, women, who had given up their lives to fight in the battlefields of the old country, to fight for four long years against the forces of imperialism and oppression, came back home filled once more with joy and hope. And what happened? They were beaten and crushed in Winnipeg. And why? Because they came back to slave wages and slave working conditions and they had the temerity to complain, to protest, to say, we can do better than this, let us run the government for awhile and we'll show you justice, fair distribution of wealth and, most of all, freedom, what freedom is. We have fought and beaten the enemies of freedom and now we want to savour the fruits of our victories." Calls of "yes, yes," "right!" broke out. Fists were raised.

The Reverend waited until the crowd quieted and waited still longer, sweeping back and forth across the audience with his eyes. Then, he started to speak, articulating each word. "But the enemy was not on the battlefield. Oh, no. The enemy was waiting at home. The enemy was not dressed in grey battledress. Oh, no. The enemy was dressed in business suits. The enemy smiled and their weapons were the bankrolls they kept safely locked up in their huge mansions. The enemy smiled and made promises and came with hands extended, but behind them marched the armed lackeys of the state – the police, the soldiers who stayed in the army because they liked it, liked the violence and the killing. What did it matter if they marched in Ypres or Winnipeg? They were the puppet warriors of domestic imperialism."

The crowd hushed, strained to hear. "And then, there were the mining companies. Remember the mining companies? They said, Come on, bring your wives and children and we'll give you a house and provide a school for your children.

There's a store right there at the mine. It's steady work and you'll be looked after. Well, you know about the mining companies, don't you?" "Yeah's". "How many went out to Estevan?" Hands here and there in the hall went up. "See those hands, comrades, those men can tell you better than I can about our famous mining companies. They'll tell you, when you go down the mine, it's dark, and when you come out of the mine it's dark, and then, when you get your wages, you find you owe the company money for groceries and clothes for the children. That's when you begin to understand the mining companies. And, if you complain, threaten to strike, which is every worker's right, his only right –" "That's right, that's right." "Then you'll see the red coats of the police charging down on you. And are these police the upholders of law and order? No, no, we have found that these are another arm of oppression, another instrument of rampant capitalism in this fair country of ours."

"Then we come to the Trek. What a trek it turned out to be! Some of the men on this platform with me – Slim here, Red, Chuck – they have the scars to prove to you what a trek that was. We saw the face of the enemy and it was no surprise. We had seen that ugly face before. It was the face of oppression, the face of evil incarnate in our own land. It was the face of our Prime Minister, the Honourable R.B. Bennett," (boos, shouts) "Honourable! Lord preserve us from such honourable men. The capitalist papers have told you that the Trek was the beginning of a revolution, an attempt to overthrow the government. But was it? Oh, no. It was a cry for justice and it was a cry that will ring throughout this land forever, because it was a cry from the young men of this country, your brothers and sons, who were put into concentration camps for no other reason than that they couldn't find a job. Think about that. In South Africa, in Nazi Germany, they are put in concentration camps because they are the wrong race. That is evil enough. But to be put in a concentration camp because you cannot find a job. What does that tell you about our government? Is it any better than the Nazis?" "No, no!" "I am asked by the capitalist press if I believe in the Revolution and I tell them, the Revolution is not an event, it is a process, it is a goal toward which all Nature is striving."

Here and there men rose to their feet, delivered the communist salute and cheered the words of the Red Reverend. The Reverend motioned for them to quiet and sit down again. "In Regina we saw the beginning of that process. They shed the blood of the working class, and that is the beginning. And now, comrades, we must not despair. We must not give up. We must work for that Revolution which will create a society based on freedom and justice."

With this statement the crowd as a whole rose to its feet and cheered. The Reverend waited, his head bowed. When they were once more attentive, he walked to the front of the platform and half turned to the others sitting behind him. "I stand on this platform with the leaders of the United Front that will bring all of us, now separated into all sorts of small unions and societies, into one powerful union that can stand up for the little man, stand up and face these monstrous engines of injustice and intolerance. And, therefore, I say to you, my brethren, comrades, I say unto you, for God's sake keep a United Front." (Sporadic cheers) "No, no, even more.

Many of you here have found that injustice and intolerance reign in our churches as much as in the corridors of political power. And you have in despair turned from the oppression of the pulpit just as you have turned from the oppression of the sword. To you I say, If you cannot keep a United Front for God's sake, then keep it for Lenin's."

Amidst the final cheer, the Reverend turned and sat down next to the communist leaders on the platform. Few heard his "Thank you."

CHAPTER TWENTY-TWO

Clara stood in the hotel room again with the telephone in her hand. "Clara. Clara Stemichuk. That's right. I came to see you the day before yesterday? I wonder if I could ask you if you have any photographs of Thomas or Chuck. No. I know that Sidney saw them, but he has gone back to Toronto. No, I'm just...I'd just like to see a photo if I could. I don't know why. I guess it would just reassure me or something. Could I? Tomorrow morning, then, around ten. Thank you. Bye."

Clara replaced the receiver and looked down at her airplane ticket, lying on the hotel desk. She'd have to phone about the ticket and extend the car rental for a day or two. The world of Regina had somehow closed around her and she had trouble thinking about Toronto and what she had thought was her life. She should phone Sidney too. He knew when her flight was supposed to arrive and would probably be at the airport. That was a comforting thought.

And she had to find out more about Margaret. Could Thomas Pennan have actually killed her? What else could the note mean? Nell had seemed determined to reject even the possibility that her dear brother might kill, well, murder someone. But what did that mean? Could he have killed her here in Regina? She thought briefly about a missing person file or going to the police. No, he had said Teruel. Somewhere in Spain, Nell had said. The woman out on Seventh Avenue had said he got knocked on the head, not had a nervous breakdown, as Nell had indicated. Nell was probably just protecting her brother, her family. Fair enough. Anyway, Clara didn't particularly like her and her standoff ways. In fact she was beginning to dislike the whole Pennan clan. And Nell's ownership of Chuck. No business of hers, indeed. Clara picked up the phone and dialed Air Canada.

"I did bring all this material down last time, Mrs....Clara."

"I'm sorry. I was a bit distracted, what with what you told me about Chuck."

"I don't have many photos. We weren't that kind of family."

Clara, who had drawers of photos, all unorganized and unclassified, felt her incipient dislike increasing. "Could I see the ones you do have?"

"That's why I brought all this material down again." Nell turned over the pages of the scrapbook too quickly for Clara really to examine any of the clippings and other memorabilia, but she caught sight of a lot of programs for various school events, and, then, as Nell leafed back toward the earlier pages, more newspaper clippings – news stories, obituaries, and even a movie guide. "Here, here's a photo of the family. Tommy was gone by then, though."

Clara stared hard at the small black-and-white snapshot, with its jagged edges that were the style then. The four of them, mother, father, Nell and an infant, seemed to be out on the prairie. Well, in the distance there was a house. Nell, with the baby in her arms, stood behind her parents' chairs. The baby's face was hard to make out. "Is this just outside 4529 Seventh? I mean, looking, let's see, east?"

"How do you know our address?"

Clara stammered, "It was in a newspaper, at the library. I drove out there yesterday. Just to see where...Just to see the house."

Nell looked at her for a long time and then closed the scrapbook forcefully.

"No. No, don't. Please let me look a bit more carefully. I wasn't, I'm not trying to snoop into your family's business, but Chuck, it's all so, I...He was my husband." Clara stopped and looked pleadingly at Nell.

"I thought you were interested in Tommy, not Peter."

"Yes, but, well, I'm obviously interested in both of them. You must have a photo of the two of them."

Nell shook her head, not about to open the book again.

Clara hesitated, tried again. "I'm sorry. You and your brother must have been close?"

"Yes."

"And Thomas and Peter must have looked a bit alike?"

"No. Yes."

"Yes or no?"

"They resembled one another a bit. Same height. Peter was heavier. They looked quite a bit alike from a distance, I guess. Other than that, they were very different."

Clara, deciding she really had nothing to lose, took a deep breath and said, "The young woman that lives down the street from your old house said Tommy was hit on the head and was never the same afterwards. I just thought..."

"That's not true. He was struck down by a policeman in the riot, but he recovered from it. It was the stress of the times that got to him later."

"She said he had been quite religious and after he got hit, well, she said God got knocked out of him and he became a communist."

"Everyone was a communist or left-wing in those days. It wasn't unusual."

"So, you won't tell me any more then?"

"Look, I don't have to tell you anything. I don't see you have any claim or right to this information."

"Oh, for Christ's sake, Nell, he was my husband."

"Not Thomas. The one you're accusing. He wasn't your husband."

"No. Well, I guess I'm just trying to untangle the story, just to understand what, who Peter – Chuck – was."

Nell sat silently watching Clara, then she shrugged and began to push her chair back.

"No, wait. Margaret. Have you any pictures of her?"

Nell hesitated, then reopened the book and turned to a photo. It was a snap of a girl standing in a backyard near a garden of what looked like potatoes. She was dressed in a dark dress with a white collar. The dress was blowing out from her legs. She was strikingly beautiful with dark hair tied back and a petite figure. "That's Margaret."

"You didn't like her."

"No, I didn't like her."

"Because you thought, because she and Chuck, Peter..."

"Yes, because of her and Peter."

"But you really don't know that, do you?"

"No, I really don't know that."

Clara could see she was going to get no further with Nell on the subject of Margaret and Chuck. "Tell me about her and Thomas."

"He would never have hurt her. Never."

Nell looked up and out the window on to the back alley of the residence. For a moment Clara thought she was not going to say anything more, then she touched her cheek and said, "Tommy was very much in love with her, had been since he was small. He was younger than Margaret, two or three years. I don't think she ever took him seriously even when he was a grown man. She was friendly, but not in that way. He pined, that's the only word to describe it, he pined for her. He would sit at the kitchen table and watch her walk out the back way to catch the streetcar or go downtown. After he left, I found poems he had written to her. Never sent. They are the sort of poems seventeen-year-old boys write."

"Are? Do you still have them?"

"Yes. Well, I have my copies of them."

"May I see them?"

"Really, Clara..."

"Please."

Nell turned to the back of the scrapbook and brought out an envelope. "Here."

"Thank you." Clara felt a strange excitement in opening the envelope. The poems were written on lined paper obvi-

ously torn from a school exercise book. The handwriting
was very regular, schoolmarmish, Clara thought. The
poems were, as Nell had said, the romantic outpourings of
the boy, almost man. Clara read them through carefully,
however, and then again. "Do you think the dark threatening figure in the last two is someone, I mean, an actual
person?"

"Yes, I do."

"Peter?"

"Yes."

"Do you think Thomas knew there was something
between Margaret and Peter?"

"I don't know. Peter saved Tommy's life in the riot,
dragged him into a café, got an ambulance, saw he was cared
for at the hospital. Maybe that was why Tommy joined up
with him, in the communist party. Or he was just trailing
after Margaret again. That's all I know."

Clara could see she was in front of another wall. Nell,
though, seemed more relaxed now and more ready to talk.
Memories were obliterating the present. She sat down and
Clara sat beside her.

"Tell me about Reverend Evans."

"So you know about him too?" Nell stared out the window
for a minute. "He was our minister. A tall, handsome man,
always dressed in a sort of cutaway coat which made him
look like something out of a nineteenth-century novel. But
up close you could see the coat was very old. It had a sort of
green sheen to it, and the cuffs and lapels had been mended
many times. He was a wonderful man. He really cared for the
poor in the parish, no matter what church they went to. You

could call him anytime of the day. Funny, he too had been struck over the head in a riot, actually in the Winnipeg General Strike shortly after the Great – the First World War. He was the one who sent Tommy to the Bible college in Winnipeg."

"I didn't realize Thomas went to a Bible college. He wanted to be a minister, then?"

"Tommy was always wanting to be one thing or another. He didn't last long at the college. He lost his temper and they sent him home. He was erratic. Emotionally, I mean."

"A bit like Chuck." Clara stopped, "I'm sorry. I said I wouldn't..."

"It's all right. I've accepted the fact now that you are – must have been – his wife."

Maybe Nell wasn't so bad. Perhaps it was just her manner, a bit brusque, protecting herself from hurt. Clara could understand that. She steered the conversation back to the Reverend Evans. "Was he in the riot? The Reverend Evans I mean."

"Oh, yes. He was president of the Ministerial Association and, then, when the trekkers arrived, chair of the citizens' committee that arranged food and so on for the boys. And he gave a lot of speeches in their defence. Tommy was his assistant, his man Friday, as Peter used to say. Peter thought he was wasting his life. But he seemed dedicated to the work that the Reverend was doing. That's why we were all surprised when he went over to Peter's side. Not that he opposed Peter. Peter had got him his job with the cartage company and then, as I said, saved his life. And of course Peter boarded with mom and dad until..."

"And you think Thomas's going over to Peter's side was because of Margaret, not a knock on the head?"

"Yes."

"That certainly wouldn't explain the note I found."

"No."

Both women sat silent, each deep in her own thoughts and memories.

"I think mom was a bit in love with the Reverend Evans." Nell's voice sounded younger as she gave out this opinion. Clara said nothing.

CHAPTER TWENTY-THREE

Thomas and Margaret walked along a path in the Mount Pleasant Cemetery. There was still a chilly wind blowing from the north, but the day was fresh and sunny. Toronto was showing off its best side, hiding the last remains of winter and disguising its harsh face under the first days of Spring. The light streamed down through the leafless tree branches. It was hard to imagine that halfway around the world, in Spain, men were being armed to kill each other. Even harder to imagine that Chuck was there. Their talk circled and circled around Chuck.

"Where did you last see him?" They had stopped and stood looking out over the railings. Margaret had been staring at the crows squawking and coming in with a rush of wings for scraps of food people had abandoned. Perhaps she wasn't really seeing them. She turned to Thomas to ask the question.

Thomas felt, as always when he was with Margaret, the desire to touch her, hold her, but he feared, what? probably rejection. "We got off the train just outside of the city at one of the sidings. We'd come from Winnipeg." Thomas sounded, even to himself, curt and uninformative.

"Was he all right? I mean his leg and everything healed?"

"Yeah. He limped a bit still. Maybe there was something broken in the knee."

Margaret turned again to the crows and there was silence between them.

"He shouldn't have blamed himself for all that. It certainly wasn't his fault. We did all we could to make sure the boys knew what was going on." Margaret's tone was half assertive and half musing. "Slim said afterward that Chuck was a hero."

Thomas bristled and started to walk again. Margaret turned and followed, looking speculatively at Thomas's hunched back. Hunched with the chill or hunched to protect himself? "It was no one's fault." She said this extra loud and Thomas stopped and waited for her. "It was the government and this rotten society. Even the Mounties, they were most of them just young boys. Most of them were decent men. They just didn't know what was what."

"For not knowing what was what they sure beat the shit out of a lot of people." There was something like relief in Thomas's voice. And a belligerence. "My mother always said, Never trust the police if you know what's good for you."

Again, a silence.

"Oh, Tommy, I hope Chuck will be all right."

"He can look after himself."

"Yes." Margaret put her arm through Thomas's and walked along close to him. "He was lucky to have a friend in you. I'm glad you're with us now."

Thomas did not reply. They walked arm in arm. Like lovers, Thomas thought. He turned to Margaret, perhaps to hold her in his arms, but she was pensive, staring down at the path.

"Tommy, I want to go to Spain too."

"Don't be silly. It's not our problem."

"Chuck said it is a world problem and that we were all involved whether we liked it or not."

"I know. I know. That's what Chuck would say, isn't it? It's the proletariat's fight against the forces of fascism, and fascism is the outward face of capitalism. I've heard it all before."

"Yes. It's a world struggle against the forces of oppression."

Thomas stopped, "That's what we said in Regina too, Margaret. What good did it do? We lost and now they'll fight somewhere else and then somewhere else again. Perhaps the Reverend Evans is right, the revolution is a process, a very long process."

"The Reverend Evans is a good man but he doesn't see the bigger picture."

"Well, he sees heaven and hell and us in between, so that's a fairly big picture. I didn't leave the church because it wasn't a big picture."

"So, why did you leave then? You don't seem too interested in what we are trying to do."

"I left because...There were all sorts of reasons. I am interested."

"Committed?"

"I joined, didn't I? The card says I'm a bona fide member of the Communist Party of Canada."

"Oh, Tommy, you can be so, so difficult." She gave him a small squeeze and he turned to her expectantly. She stopped again and stared down a row of gravestones. "But, seriously, I want to go to Spain."

"You can't. They won't give you a passport for Spain."

"Oh, we know how to get them. Lots of men have got passports and tickets for Europe. They fix all that up at the Seamen's Union Hall, on Spadina near Queen Street. They go down to New York, get on a ship and when they get to Europe they just cross the border into the Republican sector of Spain."

"How do you get a ticket?"

"We set up a travel agency that does all that."

"We?"

"The Young Communist League."

Thomas scraped away some of the gravel with his toe and then looked up at Margaret, "Anyway, you're a woman."

"You've noticed." Margaret laughed her mocking laugh which always annoyed Thomas, because he could never tell if she was laughing at him, or just amused.

"I don't think you realize how serious this war in Spain is, Tommy. It's not like the riot in Regina. One killed, a few injured. This is a battle to the death."

"So what? It's in a foreign country. It's their problem. Anyway, they know the terrain, the language. You'd just be in the way."

"No, it's our problem too. It's everyone's problem." Margaret looked defiantly at Thomas. "You don't need to know the language to use a gun."

"You're just regurgitating the Party line."

"I want to go. It's my duty. You don't realize how serious this war is, do you? It's you who should be anxious to go. Why aren't you going? Tell me that. Hundreds of comrades are. Every day there's more signing up."

Thomas said nothing.

"Tommy, I think we have to go. It's our duty..."

"Duty?" Thomas exploded, "It's got nothing to do with duty. It's just plain stupidity. Why should Canadians go over to some parched, godforsaken country that can't even feed itself and get killed?"

"Because they're fighting for liberty and democracy and what's good. They're fighting fascism." Margaret glared at Thomas and held his eyes until he turned away. "Are you one of us or are you not?"

For a moment the parallel biblical phrase ran through his head. If you are not with me...Was he one of them? Did he even care? It was hard, though, to be neutral with Margaret. She demanded too much, too much loyalty, too much commitment, too much unreturned caring. He sighed, "I'm one of us."

"You sure sound excited about it."

"Getting killed doesn't excite me."

"What about innocent people, poor people, people fighting for a better life, to have a say in their lives?"

"What about them? They're no concern of mine. Anyway, if you want something to do, there's lots to do right here in Canada."

Margaret stepped back a little and walked over to the railing again. "That's true."

"Anyway, it's fine for you and Chuck. You don't have anything holding you here. No family, I mean."

"Okay, and you do."

"Yes, I do. You forget Nell has a baby now and she's the only money earner."

"I haven't forgotten."

"Well, your precious Chuck seems to have."

Margaret spun around and swung at Thomas. He caught her wrist and stopped the blow. They stood panting, fixed in position for the moment.

"I'm sorry. I shouldn't have said that." Thomas tried to pull her to him, perhaps trying to kiss her, but she jerked her head to the side and pushed him away. He let go of her wrist and she let her arm sink to her side. "It's just it's always 'Chuck this and Chuck that.'"

"Tommy, I love him."

Thomas stared angrily up through the bare branches at the clouds beginning to move in from the west. "Would Marx approve of that?"

"Oh, Tommy."

CHAPTER TWENTY-FOUR

"I wish I had let you answer that, Sidney. It was that bank manager I was telling you about. He needs a deterrent."

"Is that what you see me as? A deterrent?"

"Well, yes. But you're more than that, too."

"Well, that's something."

"A little more."

"Clara, you are a tease. I am very happy when I am with you." Sidney set down his whiskey and reached for her hand. He turned it over in his and lightly touched the place where her wedding ring had left a white mark around her finger.

"Here, let me see your palm." Clara turned over his hand and studied, or pretended to study his palm. "Ah, I see a certain confusion of lines in your palm. You are intellectual, but your heart line interferes with your thinking sometimes. I see you have a robust health line which does not break until you are, oh seventy-five or so, and doesn't end until you are well into your nineties. And then, it seems to end dramatically, perhaps a downhill-ski accident or a bungee-cord failure."

"Clara, you're making that up as you go along."

"Am I? Well, wait and see." She threw back her head and laughed.

"You are beautiful."

They sat across from each other in Clara's living room. The fire was going in the fireplace. The fireplace was sort of her first move in distancing herself from her memories of Chuck, or, maybe better, acting on what she wanted, rather than on what he wanted. He had insisted that they have a wood fireplace. It was somehow more pure. She had always wanted a gas fireplace, something she could turn on and have an immediate fire, and turn off when she was through with it. And no ashes. Now, the gas flames flared realistically behind the fake logs and she could simply turn them off when she left to go to the opera.

A month had past since their trip to Vancouver and Regina, and she and Sidney had been seeing each other regularly. Clara had resisted at first, but then had let herself fall into the pattern. Two of her friends had warned her that it was too soon, but she didn't feel like resisting the comfort of having companionship. Who could it possibly hurt? Except her, and she had to look after herself now. Anyway, Sidney was a kind and generous person. If he wasn't complaining, why should she? She was beginning to feel a bit tied down, though. Strange, after being married for more than half her life, to feel tied down, because she saw Sidney on a regular basis a couple of times a week. She wanted to be completely independent. She needed to be independent. Memory had taught her that. Too many memories, memories from when she had felt like an appendage, Chuck's wife. Not that Chuck had interfered with her freedom. He had been a wonderful husband in that way. No, she had just felt sometimes that she should be more independent. She had tried, had read Germaine Greer and the rest of them, and ended up doing no more than playing bridge every Thursday afternoon. Some freedom! Well, now she would be independent.

"Siddie, I'm thinking of going to England."

He hated that name and her using it always signalled something coming that he would not like. He had, however, learned not to react too strongly until he found out in which direction her thoughts were going. She wasn't an easy woman, that's for sure.

"Oh?"

"Is that all you can say? Oh?"

Yep, she was on her high horse again. Sidney raised his glass of whiskey and looked through it at the flames in the fireplace. "Strange you should say that. I was thinking of going over myself."

"Sidney, I want to go by myself." Clara was moving into fighting mode.

"So do I." Not true of course.

She looked intently at him and then realized he was having her on. She started to smile in spite of her determination.

"But first, hon, let's go to the opera. Okay?" Sidney vaguely motioned to the door and after some hesitation, Clara switched off the gas fireplace and went to get her cape. She let Sidney hold it, and she shrugged it on over her shoulders.

"I'm serious, Sidney. I want to go to England and see if I can find that nurse Nell mentioned. She could still be alive. I can't rest until I find out what's behind that note."

"You can't let it go, can you? A dog with a bone. Anyway, if I remember correctly, the nurse in England had looked after Chuck, not Tommy."

"Oh, Sidney, you're such a stickler for details. She still might know something."

"She might. Then again, she might be dead."

"That's what you said about Nell. Was she dead?"

"No." What he didn't say was, Sometimes, I wish she had been.

"Anyway, I want to go."

"Then, I am sure you will."

"Now, don't sulk, Siddie."

They were sitting on stools at the bar of the Park Plaza drinking Brandy Alexanders. An old-fashioned drink, but the waiter, who had been there as long as Sidney could remember, was obviously pleased to resurrect his old skills and shake up an Alexander. He set them down in front of Clara and Sidney with a flourish and a conspiratorial grin. "Best in Toronto. I guarantee it." Drinking them from a straw was a bit like being teenagers at a soda fountain. In fact, the Alexanders themselves were not unlike sodas, only with different effects.

Clara sat for a moment playing with the straw. "You know none of those stories may be true. I mean, what Nell and Peter said, even what that girl out on Seventh Avenue told me. It could all be a tissue of lies or, or poor memories or wishful thinking. Peter said his mother was dead, in fact, had died when he was a baby. She's still very much alive. Nell had reports that Chuck, Thomas and Margaret had all been killed in Spain and then heard that Chuck had been in hospital in England at the end of the War. And remember, I had a confirming story about Chuck's death from, what was his name?"

"Kroker, I think you said."

"Right. Bill Kroker. Who's to be believed? Anyway, it all happened so long ago, their stories have gotten mixed up, probably, with other things that have happened since."

"So, why do you want to speak with this nurse in England? It's just another story to add to the list."

Clara sat silent.

"Clara, you there?"

"Yes. I was just thinking, why do I want to talk to her? I think it's because there are so many stories. At first, I was just curious about that note I found. But now it's, it's, I don't know, interesting in itself I guess. I lived over forty years with a man and he had a whole life I knew nothing about. In fact, I lived with a man who has been reported dead to me by two people, and alive by another. And I buried him. And all that dying and living was done before I met him! Then there was all the living and dying he did with me. What really happened?"

"Probably, in the mix-up of the war or two wars, letters, records, reports were lost, and now memories are simply unreliable. It's unlikely we'll find out what happened. Just more stories."

"Oh, Sidney, you're such a downer."

"Well, down your drink and we'll order another."

"I really shouldn't."

There it was, lying on the foyer carpet under the mail slot. The letter she had hardly dared believe would come. Blue envelope with red and blue chevroned border, neat handwriting addressed to her, and a postal stamp, the address of which she could not make out. On the back, the sender was set down as Miss M. Stanhope, The Chapel, Fifehead Neville, UK.

Clara had taken Sidney's advice and asked the teenage boy next door if he knew how to find out on the Internet if there was a nursing association in Great Britain, and, if there was, did they have a list of past members. As he stood there, with the crotch of his blue jeans down around his knees, his T-shirt reading "They're all Scum," and his baseball hat on backwards, oh, and yes, his mouth hanging a little open from acned cheeks, Clara had had misgivings about the success of the venture. But he'd come back about an hour later with a printout of their web page, complete with address and a welcoming message. "Well, thank you. What do I owe you?"

"Owe me? Ah, nothing. It was dead simple." And he turned and left.

"Thank you," Clara called after him, and received a half shrug which she interpreted as "It's nothing."

She tore open the envelope and read the contents. It simply said that, yes, she was the Meg Stanhope who had tended the critically wounded in the hospital on the Isle of Wight between 1942 and 1947, after which time the remaining patients had been moved to other resident homes or hospitals. And, yes, she had indeed had a patient by the name of Peter Stemichuk, and, yes, she would be glad to meet with

Clara any time. It was a long time ago, but she remembered Peter as if it had been yesterday.

Clara felt a little guilty. She had, at Sidney's suggestion, told Miss Stanhope that she was Peter Stemichuk's sister. Sidney thought it would put Miss Stanhope more at her ease, rather than having to deal with a grieving widow. I'm not grieving. Yes, you are, and you should be. Oh, Sidney, I don't know. But, in the end, that was the alias she used. Well, it couldn't hurt. Clara read through the letter again.

They had fallen into a pattern of going out to dinner or the theatre. Sometimes Sidney stayed over, but more and more Clara wondered if that part of the relationship was worth the trouble. He was a very nice man, but...

This evening they lay in bed, Sidney still trying to convince her that it made sense for him to go with her to England.

"No. No, Sidney. I don't want you to come with me. I've got to get out and do things by myself."

"Well, I don't see why, but if you say you must, I guess you must. Still, if..."

"No, I said."

"Okay, okay. I hear you."

They were lying, naked, on the top of the bedclothes. Clara was amazed that she could be so casual about it all. Although a tummy tuck would have made her feel a little more comfortable under the constant surveying and, she had to admit, very appreciative eye of Sidney.

"Where did the scar on your thigh come from?"

"Sidney, I am not going to discuss all the blemishes on my body with you."

"Okay. I was just curious. You know I am interested in everything about you."

"Well, don't be." Clara rolled over on to her side and sat up.

"No, don't go yet. Massage?"

"No, I don't want a massage. I want to get up, shower and dress." Clara stood up and thudded away toward the bathroom.

Sidney swung his legs over the side of the bed. How can I be so lucky? he thought.

CHAPTER TWENTY-FIVE

You'll be issued another passport in Spain, for the International Brigade. And here are tickets for the train from Buffalo to New York. Josh and Peggy will get you to Buffalo. No, don't worry, there are ways to get across the border. Understood? When you get to New York, go immediately to the office at this address and they'll arrange passage on a ship to Le Havre. You will proceed from Le Havre to Paris by train. After that, the committee in Paris will arrange everything. Understood? And, oh yes, you will need to pick up some Spanish either here or there. Understood? Christ, of course he understood. He wasn't an idiot. But then again, maybe he was. The thought certainly came to him often enough. Thomas glanced at the pocket watch his father had given him when he had left home. Tick, tick, tick. Woolworth special. He jammed it into his pants pocket and put on his best smile for the woman handling the papers.

"Has Margaret left?"

"Margaret? Margaret who?"

"Margaret Long. From Regina."

"Oh, her. A few days ago."

"Oh."

Thomas sat in the aisle seat next to Peggy. The train swayed as it picked up speed along the flat river valley, heading east through New York State. In the end, crossing the border had been easy. They had simply waited for the right moment and walked across the train bridge. At night. Josh went halfway across with them and then returned to Toronto. Peggy and he were to travel on to New York City by themselves. Thomas looked at her and she turned and smiled at him.

"Well, honey, we made it."

"Yep."

"You don't talk much. Cat got your tongue?"

"No."

Peggy sighed and turned back to the window. She was dressed in a dark, mid-calf skirt, dark blouse and dark sweater. She had tucked her little sequined bag between her hip and the armrest, and she played with the handle whenever she wasn't talking. She crossed her legs and pulled up her skirt to examine her knee.

"Thought I scraped it when we jumped down from the bridge. Do you see anything?" She twisted around toward Thomas and pointed to her knee. He blushed, but looked.

"Oh, you are cute. I never." She pulled the skirt up a little higher. "Haven't you seen a girl's legs before?"

Thomas looked down the aisle. "Of course I have."

She pulled down her skirt and tittered. "Of course you have."

Thomas straightened up. "I'll be back in a minute."

Peggy smiled and gave him a little wave. Thomas went down the aisle toward the bathrooms, swaying back and forth with the train. The car was filled with a mixed bunch of men and women, a few businessmen, two or three couples, and some men he recognized from Toronto. They had not been told who was going when. Avoid suspicious clothing or groups. Just look like tourists. Stupid. Anyone could see that these men were not tourists. Some still wore pieces of the clothing that had been issued in the work camps.

He felt his erection subside. Actually, travelling with Peggy was a good disguise. She...She...Her bare legs flashed into his mind again. Thomas grabbed hold of the back of the last seats and waited until the toilet was free. He looked back and Peggy gave him another little wave. She was sort of pretty. When the washroom was free, he sat down on the toilet and felt the tension drain from his body. They had made it, at least this far.

It was Thomas's first time, but not Peggy's. She leaned against the pylon of the bridge and guided Thomas up into her. He came almost before she had him fully in. At which, she had sighed and then laughed out loud.

"Okay, let's go for a walk, honey, and try that all over again later."

Thomas was busy apologizing and doing up his buttons. Peggy waited and then took his arm in an almost motherly way. They scrambled up to the street. It was a poor end of the city, that's for sure. Tenements lined the streets, still hot from the day's sun. Vendors pushed their carts home or to another site; kids chased each other; groups of young men hung around at corners, chosen for some reason over others; storekeepers were taking in their fruit and vegetables. A newsboy shouted something or other above the noise. Peggy strode along; she seemed to be always in the best of spirits. She simply laughed, no matter what subject Thomas tried to broach.

"You take yourself far too serious, honey. No one gives a rat's ass what you think. Relax. Enjoy yourself."

"I don't understand you. Here you are going to Spain to fight for freedom and democracy and..."

"And nothing. If the Revolution's no fun, I'll do something else."

"You don't mean that."

"Honey, I don't mean anything. At the moment, I'd just like to be properly fucked."

Thomas had never heard a woman use that word before. He had never met a woman like Peggy. She didn't seem to have any...Well, she just...He couldn't get his thoughts straight. He trailed along at her side like a partially trained dog.

Eventually, she got properly fucked and then disappeared the morning the ship was due to leave.

"Oh, yeah, she was something else. A minx. Just run your hand up her leg and she'd come all over you. Shit, one time..." Thomas was in the midst of one of his stories. The men, his shipmates for the long, twelve-day journey, lounged around near him, half-listening, making comments, smoking and throwing the butts over the side, looking out over the expanse of water that had so far remained calm and endless. Gulls followed them, seemingly determined to exchange their American allegiance for European. They were eight men, housed in a freighter headed for France. Four to a cabin. Eggs and salt pork bacon every morning. Coffee. Throw everything over the side and watch it float away. "One time..."

"Why don't you shut the fuck up?" Cass, a large, bony miner of Polish descent stood belligerently in front of Thomas, his fists clenched at his sides.

"I was just telling the boys here..."

"I don't give a fuck what you was tellin' the boys. Just shut the fuck up."

"Okay. Okay. Don't get your dander up." His mother's phrase.

"I'll get up whatever the fuck I want to get up."

"Well, I sure got it..."

Cass grabbed him by the coat lapel and pushed him against the railing until Thomas's upper body was hanging over the water. Thomas flailed with his arms as if he would fly. The men laughed.

"I'll fuckin' drop you into the briny, if you say one more fuckin' word." He shook Thomas and pushed him further out.

"Okay. Okay. Don't."

"Let him swim for a bit."

"There's some nice shark down there just waiting for a tasty meal."

"You goin' to shut the fuck up?"

"Yes. Yes."

"I didn't fuckin' hear you. Say it again. Louder."

"Yes. I'll shut up. I won't say another word."

Cass seemed unsure what to do next, so he reluctantly pulled Thomas back onto the deck and dropped him. Thomas collapsed and lay looking up. He raised his hand in defence or perhaps to placate the figure towering over him. Cass reached down, grabbed his hand and pulled him to his feet.

"Now, you just shut the fuck up. You hear?" Cass turned and trudged down the stairs to the cabins.

Thomas was shaking. He laughed and gestured to the other men. A sort of shrug-it-was-nothing gesture. A let's-get-on-with-what-we-were-doing gesture. The other men walked off, leaving Thomas to deal with the events alone. He turned and took hold of the rail and held on. He didn't feel so well.

Thomas sat at the end of a single bed at the far end of a row of twenty beds. The hall, at a "certain address," had been turned into a barracks for the men being prepared for the last leg of the trip to Spain. It was cold in Paris. Paris. The hall was in the 19th arrondissement. You could hardly call it Paris. And it was cold and raining. Thomas sat alone in the huge room at the end of his bed, holding his head in his hands. He had got a cold or the flu or something on board ship and had spent the rest of the sea voyage and most of the past week feverish and running to the toilet every half hour.

The men he had come with were "shipping out" today. He was left behind. He still had to go through the course. Just as well. They were all a bunch of first-rate assholes anyway. He'd show them. Between running to the toilet and sitting there, he had been trying to memorize Spanish phrases from a small, soiled book he'd lifted from the office downstairs. One of his few attempts to go down to breakfast.

He'd just woke up from a mid-morning nap. He stood up. A little dizzy at first, then lightheaded but clear. For the first time in eleven days, he felt as if he didn't have to get to the toilet. He felt his forehead. Still dry, but not hot. He was hungry. He pulled on the heavy army sweater one of the men had given him and, staggering a bit, made his way to the door at the other end of the room. The building was quiet. The next bunch had not arrived yet and there were just a couple of Party members in the office. They nodded, and he went into the little room that served as a kitchen. The coffee was still warm and there was half a baguette lying on the counter. Thomas broke off a piece and poured a bit of coffee into a glass. He suddenly felt enormously good, perhaps even verging on happy.

If you collected scrap pieces of paper, folded them in half and carefully punched out the corner and folded it over, you got a pretty good writing book. Thomas sat every day at the back of the room, scribbling down notes from what the instructors said. He was determined to out-communist them all. And what they said made sense, in a way. He was working class, which had not sunk in before, and there certainly was exploitation. He thought of being forced by Mr. Williams to deliver guns and police to quell the riot in Regina. His father looking for work, day after day. Even the Reverend had pointed that out. And now, according to the men who stood at the front and lectured them, the world was moving toward revolution. Russia was the beginning. Then major strikes in England, France and Germany. Now Spain. An elected government attacked by its own army, by fascists. Fascists in Italy and Germany supporting them. These were the preliminaries, the fires flaring up, the build-up to the Revolution that would sweep all Europe and North America. Wipe out once and for all the capitalists and their lackeys in the Church and government. The final Revolution was inevitable. It was the goal toward which all nature was striving, just as the Reverend had so often said. Canada was not mentioned, but Thomas could see that it was all part of the pattern. What had seemed so exaggerated when Chuck had railed against the system in Canada, now seemed to have a ring of truth, perhaps was even rather tame compared to the bigger picture his instructors painted. Not Isaiah, but Marx. Scribble. Scribble. Every evening Thomas would review his notes and the next day ask questions, and scribble down the answers. In the afternoons, he studied Spanish with a little man who continually scratched his ear. Thomas felt an energy inside. He was part of a huge movement, seeking justice and goodness for the downtrodden. Only, he wasn't sure he wanted to go to Spain. He pondered the possibility of staying in Paris, as an instructor perhaps, or he could write brochures, or...But, then, there was Margaret. She was in Spain already. That much he knew. Thomas swung back and forth, but at the end of the week he was grouped with ten other men, who were all given their tickets to Perpignan, the last major stop before the train headed for the Spanish border.

The train was full. Men crowded in the corridors and stood in the compartments, holding onto the luggage racks. The air was thick with smoke from cigarettes and the locomotive's black billows swirling along the rattling cars. Thomas had found a corner at the end of the corridor where he stood, aloof from the men with whom he had boarded. At every stop more men boarded the train, most of them carrying their few belongings in sacks or cheap suitcases. They crowded into the corridors. Thomas put his knapsack behind him, waist-high, in the corner and leaned against it.

"*Vous, êtes-vous voluntaire?*"

"*Si*, I mean, *oui*. I don't speak French. *Je ne parle pas français.*"

"*C'est triste.*"

"I'm sorry. *Regret.*"

The man smiled, perhaps mischievously, "*Je suis désolé.*"

The man wore a heavy, dark green overcoat and carried a little suitcase that looked as if it might fall to pieces if he lifted it too suddenly. He gave off a musty smell mixed with a whiff of garlic. Thomas turned away and looked out the window. He hated crowds. The little man in the overcoat tried a couple of times to find some English words, but in the end gave up, either because of Thomas's curt replies or puzzled looks, or because it was too much work.

And still more men came. At every stop, they poured out of the station houses and onto the train, bringing bread and wine and sharing it out like it was Christmas. Thomas continued to look out the window and refused the wine and bread that was held out to him. Not a very serious bunch. The laughter turned into singing. First, the *"Marseillaise,"* and then the *"Internationale."* Thomas remained taciturn. The train rocked along, seemingly only mildly interested in getting to Perpignan.

It was late in the evening when the train finally pulled into Perpignan station. a crowd was on hand there too, this time not volunteers on their way to Spain, but well-wishers, mainly women, children and old men. Everyone seemed to have something they wanted to hand up to the arms stretching out the windows. Not just bread, sausages, olives and wine, but clothes, even guns. Everywhere, arms were raised in the fist salute. Police stood at the ends of the platform, their eyes averted. France may have declared itself non-interventionist, but the official position did not apply to what you did not see, and, apparently, the gendarmes did not see what was going on behind them. Some difference from the police in Regina. Even Thomas hung out the window, shook hands and ended up with a round of sausage and a bottle of wine. As the train shunted on its final run to the Spanish border, Thomas felt something like tears come to his eyes. When he looked down the corridor, he saw that many of the men who had been laughing and singing that afternoon, were now hastily wiping their eyes as they looked back at the disappearing crowd. A silence filled the carriage, until the city disappeared from sight.

passed

Little whistle stops past until they came to Cerbère, the last town before the Spanish border. A French customs officer pushed his way down the aisle, asking a few questions, looking at passports, and then slamming the door shut as he thudded off to the next carriage. Hundred pesetas for a hundred francs. Hundred pesetas for a hundred francs. Everywhere someone was always doing business. The train jerked forward, stopped, jerked forward again and came to a stop at Port-Bou on the Spanish side.

And there it was, hanging from the little, rundown station house: the huge black and red flag of the CNT-FAI, the anarcho-syndicalist organization they had been warned about in Paris. Confederación Nacional del Trabajo and Federación Anarquista Iberica, the crazies that had turned Barcelona and half of the east coast into a mishmash of collectivized trades and were now trying to collectivize the peasants. Thomas thought he could see something of the mishmash in what they wore as uniforms: a leather jacket and a leather cap, and any piece of clothing they happened to have. Many wore thick corduroy trousers. Some had on funny-looking rubber boots. Most wore pistols, but the butts said they were made by ten different factories in ten different countries. A scruffy-looking bunch. Thomas's heart sank, but many, if not most of his companions raised a sustained cheer at the sight of the flag and its guardians.

Most of the men were herded off the French train and over to the Spanish one, which to Thomas's amusement, ran on much narrower tracks, almost like a toy train. But it was getting dark now. Out of the station house, three men carrying Russian weapons hurried out to the train and assembled the men from Paris. They spoke to them in heavily accented English and then French.

"Over here. Over here, comrades. Identify yourselves." They had lists of names and as the men identified themselves, they were sent over to another very dimly lit platform. Their names were checked, one by one, off the list. Thomas hung back to see what they were going to do, but finally realized that these were Communist Party agents, the commissars, sent to separate the communist-trained men from Paris from the others. He went over to the efficient little men, had his name checked off and joined the others.

CHAPTER TWENTY-SIX

I t wasn't that she had not been in Heathrow airport before. It was just that she had never been there alone, standing in the middle of a throng of people, all of whom seemed to know where they were going and most of them coming straight for the spot where she was standing. Behind her and to the side, the heavily armed security for ELAL watched her, the dogs straining on their leashes. Chuck had always, well, she hadn't been there that often, but when they had come, Chuck had had a chauffeured car waiting at the terminal. It was always the same colour and always a Ford Taurus. She wasn't sure why. Perhaps the British banking company his bank was affiliated with only had one car. She held onto her handbag straps a little tighter, and followed the black-on-yellow signs to the luggage carousel with its disgorger already turned on.

She hated seeing her carefully packed, good-quality suitcase come careering out of the hole, jostle with all the other nondescript bags and finally head toward her at a precarious angle. What if someone else took it before it got to her? The

203

man next to her, immaculately decked out in a grey-checked, double-breasted suit and old school tie, seemed unconcerned, so Clara put a hand on her hip and tried to look like what she thought an experienced traveller would look like. At her movement, he turned and smiled at her. Before she thought about it, she smiled back. "Another nice man?" She could hear Chuck's slightly amused, slightly annoyed voice in her head. Her bag came and she began to struggle to break the hold the moving belt had on it.

"Here, let me help you." The man in the grey suit took hold of its handle and lifted it easily onto the floor in front of Clara.

"Thank you. Thank you, very much."

"You're welcome." He smiled again and turned back to the carousel.

Clara was, for a moment, a little disappointed. Then she pulled up the handle and started to roll the suitcase away from the throng of waiting people. She had, at Sidney's insistence, flown business class and had, also at Sidney's insistence, taken a Melatonin capsule, and had slept like a baby. She actually felt quite refreshed and a little excited at having got here by herself. Although, of course, once she was on the plane, there had not been many options. She felt ready for an adventure. In fact, she wondered if she really cared much anymore what the note and all the mystery was about. She'd just enjoy the search. Still, it was odd that in all those years, Chuck had never said anything, not one word to her, about it. Her emotional pendulum swung between anger and curiosity.

She queued up at the taxi stand and waited with anticipation to ride in one of London's black cabs that had been designed to carry a steamer trunk, and that made you feel you were sitting a luxurious distance away from the driver. How much do you tip taxi drivers in London? Chuck would have known. So would Sidney. She pushed them both from her mind.

In her hotel room, Clara, receiver to her ear, listened as the phone rang and rang. Obviously, Meg Stanhope was either out or dead. Since Chuck's death, Clara often found herself automatically thinking about death. Other people dying; herself dying. She now knew it was not an event that came from outside, some grim reaper of souls. We are all dying, even in the midst of life. It had not been something that had really occurred to her before. Or only very abstractly and at a great distance. If Meg Stanhope had died...She could have; she must be at least as old as Nell. The phone rang and rang. She tried to imagine the sound ringing out in the little village where Meg lived. It would be a sort of cottage like Jane Marple's, with a green-black door and brass knocker and a thatched roof. Clara finally replaced the receiver and stood biting her lower lip. Now what? She looked at her watch. It was mid-afternoon. Perhaps Meg was out at the shops, as they said here. She lay down on the bed, sighed, closed her eyes and fell asleep.

CHAPTER TWENTY-SEVEN

Thomas stood near the railway tracks, looking down into the valley, where the gleaming rails snaked along in the moonlight like some glistening slime trail. He was sick to the stomach. What the hell was he doing here? Everything in him told him this was the stupidest thing he had ever done. Could he turn around and go back? He looked at the men around him, dark figures sitting or squatting by the station building, a face here and there flaring into sight from a match or cigarette. They were all exhausted from the steep climb in the dark. They had been told not to smoke, but after that climb, the men had no patience with instructions like that. The mountain path, if you could call the rocky, treacherous trail they had stumbled along a path, would have been difficult to climb in daylight, much less in the middle of the night. The full moon had been both a blessing and a curse: on the one hand, it gave them some light by which to grope their way forward; on the other, it had distorted the shapes and distances and left them always fearful the border patrols would spot them.

"Want a snort?" One of the figures handed up a bottle to him.

"What? No. No, thank you." Thomas moved a bit away, stuck his hands in his pockets and turned his face into the cold gusts of wind coming down from the mountains. He listened to the murmur of voices in almost as many languages as men. He was supposed to feel comradeship, he guessed. What did he really have to do with any of these scruffy, hopeless-looking young men? Die with them. He was going to die with them, that's what he had to do with them. Unless he got out of here right now. Thomas looked back down the narrow path they had come up. There was a small roadside chapel or shrine about a hundred yards away. One of the men had stopped and pissed on it as they were walking by. Our Lady of Piss-all, another had whispered, and the wisecrack had been past down the line. Notre Dame de Pissat! Thomas thought of going back and pretending to take a piss there too, and then just disappearing. The thought of scrambling back down the mountainside by himself, however, was too daunting. He wasn't even sure he could find the way back to the town they had left just after dusk.

"Thinking about home?" The quiet voice was that of a slender youth who looked no more than sixteen. He hadn't heard him approach. When Thomas didn't say anything, the young man put his hand forward and said, "My name's Joey. I noticed back there that you're from Canada too." Thomas took his hand and shook it. "I come from Salmon Arm. You know that part of the country?"

"No, can't say I do."

"Everybody who's ridden the rails knows Salmon Arm. Where you from?"

"Regina. Saskatchewan."

"We all been there. I mean if we've ridden the rails." Thomas wondered if that was a put-down of some sort. He noticed that Joey was trying to keep his voice down an octave or so below its natural pitch. More manly? Older sounding? Less scared? Joey hunched up his shoulders and looked out over the brush and down into the valley. "Well, what d'you think so far?"

"It's bloody cold."

Joey laughed and scuffed his feet on the stony path where they were standing. He stood at Thomas's elbow, seemingly happy just to be near someone from home. "Got a cigarette?"

Thomas slapped his pockets in a mock attempt to see if he did and then said, "Nope, must be out."

"That's all right. I don't really smoke much anyway." He moved a bit away and also looked down the long gleaming tracks. "What'd we do without the trains, eh?"

"I hear they're not taking us any further by train. They're sending trucks up here to meet us." Thomas found a little importance in having this information. He expanded, "They're afraid the trains will attract too much attention, may even get bombed. Apparently," he added, regretting his talkativeness.

"Jesus, even up here? I thought this part of the country was still in loyalist hands."

Joey was right and Thomas felt defensive again. "That's just what I heard. It's better down the coast. Of the Mediterranean." Thomas added the last bit and found it no longer sounded so exotic as it had when they had been briefed in Paris. "Barcelona's the first stop, then down to some place called Albacete. That's headquarters."

"Shit, it's a long way from Salmon Arm. You carry a card?" Joey looked up at Thomas, perhaps willing him to say no.

"No. Yes. I am with them. I mean I support them. If it wasn't for the Party organizing all this, it wouldn't have happened. So, I took out a membership." Gawd, it sounded like the Boy Scouts.

"I don't. They was recruiting out in the camps. That's where I was. Not far from Salmon Arm where my folks live. I didn't want to join up 'til I knew a bit more about them. Well, my mother, she's always worrying about me. She doesn't know I'm here. She thinks I'm in Halifax looking for work." Joey giggled a bit, perhaps nervously.

"Lucky you got someone who cares. Me, I ain't got no family." The words didn't come easily to Thomas's lips. He was trying out Slim's way of talking. Sounded better. Anyway, as Chuck had said one time, Work on a need-to-know basis. No harm done in not telling everything. Even lying. Reverend Evans used to tell the story of the Doukhobors who got around lying to the Tsarist police by saying that it was not what came from a man's lips that counted, but what was in his heart.

"Geez, that's too bad. I mean, my family's all I got." Joey looked down at his shoes. "To tell the truth, I guess I'm a little homesick."

"You'll get over it, kid. We'll clean out these fascist bastards and be home in a few months." Thomas put his hand on Joey's shoulder and gave him a squeeze.

"You think so? Back there they said if we didn't get weapons and things through from France, Franco would overrun the country in weeks."

"They're just trying to scare you. There's plenty of weapons. Russia's sending them in by the boatload. Tanks, too." Thomas wondered if that was true. The commissars were convinced it was, and that there would be planes to deal with the screaming Stukas of the German Luftwaffe. Well, it made sense. Stalin wouldn't want to be beaten by the German corporal and his Italian stooge, would he? Or did he care? Did Thomas really care? He would soon, he thought, he would soon.

"Look. Here they come." In the darkness on the east side of the tracks, the momentary glare of headlights could be seen now and then, as the trucks manoeuvred along the mountain road. Every so often, probably on a straight stretch, the lights were doused and the only sign of the trucks would be the moonlight glancing off the wind- shields. The other men stood up, gathered around Thomas and Joey, and watched the slow progress of the vehicles. No one said anything. This was it. They were on the last stage of the trip. After this night, it was war. The strange silence of the night denied it; only the distant sound of the truck engines affirmed the ineluctable unrolling of events. Someone flicked a burning cigarette butt out into the night.

"Jesus living Christ, don't do that. The whole fucking mountain'll go up in smoke."

"Aaaw, your grandmother's got piles. There's nothing but rocks up here."

Slowly, the lights of the two trucks came closer. They could hear the clatter of the truck bodies as they bounced over the stony road and the fitful roar of the engines as the drivers geared down to get traction for the last climb. Then, silence, darkness. The lights had briefly swept over the group of men, pulling their faces out of the darkness like puppets dangling against the backdrop of the station building. They stood expectant, waiting.

"Albacete express. Leaving in fifteen minutes. All aboard." The voice was American, thick with southern vowels. The man suddenly appeared out of the night and sauntered languidly up to the men, who had now been lined up in a parody of military parade.

"Attention!" The commissar, who was in charge of the men, clicked his heels and saluted the man from the truck as he came to a halt in front of him. "All here and accounted for, sir."

"That's good, fellah." The man surveyed the men for a moment. "All right then, you guys, let's get movin'. Into the trucks."

The men scrambled down the path to the road below and started off, half jogging toward the trucks, some stumbling in the dark and cursing quietly under their breath. They clambered up into the back of the trucks and squatted down along the sides and front. The backs were open with railings along the sides. They looked like farm trucks but it seemed unlikely Spanish farmers had trucks. At least, all they had heard about were endless lines of burros, seconded from the farms and put to work hauling ammunition and firearms up to the front lines.

"Here, I saved a place for you." Joey pulled at Thomas's sleeve and Thomas squatted down next to him.

"This is going to be a cold trip." Thomas rubbed his hands together. He could feel the warmth of Joey's leg against his.

CHAPTER TWENTY-EIGHT

Albacete was a scruff of a town. It was now the autumn of 1937, and, with several thousand volunteers being moved through to training sites and shaped into soldiers, it was even scruffier than usual. Thomas looked around in despair. It did not look like what he had pictured it would. Certainly, no military bands and marching troops. The boys were there, everywhere, standing in groups, playing cards in front of cafés. The new arrivals were shown their quarters, which occupied the dining hall of a recently emptied convent. The men who had arrived earlier were housed in the former nationalist army barracks. They were on the second floor. No one wanted to sleep downstairs where some of the villagers, suspected of siding with the loyalists, had been shot. Joey told Thomas that he had heard that their blood was still spattered on the wall. In the big hall of the convent, a few men were lying on their bunks, writing letters or reading. But by this time of day, about 11:00 in the morning, most of them had been herded down to the bull-ring to be registered at the Estada Major, where the International Brigade had its headquarters, and given a taste of military training. That, or else they had been sent on to Tarazona de la Mancha or Madrigueras for further training and assignment . For it had been decided that democracy and freedom too had their limits, and that they had to become a disciplined army if they were going to fight the well-armed fascists equipped by Germans and Italians with the latest in warfare. There had to be officers, and commands had to be obeyed. No more militias taking a vote to decide if they were going to go to war or not. There were limits to the democracy preached by some of the groups. It was not all that different, Thomas thought, from the discipline of the trekkers in Canada, but Thomas had only watched the trekkers from the safety of his family, so to speak. At first, he had found himself annoyed by the peremptory commands of commissars and officers, dressed in outlandish parodies of military uniforms. It was bizarre to stand at attention in a bullring, or march in squadrons up and down in the dust and heat with mongrel dogs from the town yapping at their heels.

But by the end of the first week, Thomas was marching up and down with the rest of them. He found he was actually quite good at taking commands. He even liked it. It was Joey who complained. Thomas gruffly explained to him, man-to-man, why they had to be a disciplined army. Joey said he had thought everything here was going to be done in a democratic way and that the army was to be run by the men and not by officers and political bureaucrats. And Thomas said there couldn't be any divisions; there had to be individual freedom but they had to act as a group. At least, until the war was won. Etcetera. Thomas and Joey had become inseparable, Joey usually hurrying a couple of steps behind him, talking away at him. Joey was usually asking questions; Thomas usually grunting a reply. They were becoming a fixture among the International Brigaders, waiting for assignments or to return to the front. To one of the fronts, for the Loyalists were now fighting up and down Spain in an attempt to stop the relentless drive of Franco's forces northward to Madrid. At least they still held Madrid, Thomas told Joey, although Joey had heard the same talk around town. *Non pasaran.* They shall not pass. And the commissars told them endlessly that they were winning, – the breakthrough at Guadalajara, the victory at Brunete – even as the news of lost battles and lost territories mounted, the lists of dead lengthened, and the wounded and dying lay moaning among them. Thomas tended to believe the commissars, even though he called them Stalinist puppets; Joey tended to be more skeptical, even as he attended the endless education sessions given by the commissars. And so they strode through the town, arguing, or rather discussing the situation over and over. The boys had come to call them "Si and Pero," because they always agreed, except when, in the next breath, they disagreed.

The veteran brigaders told stories of the first months in Albacete when the shops were full of produce from the surrounding farms and the wine flowed freely, when victory seemed a matter of months away, when the mood was ebullient, backslapping and boastful. A year had brought drastic changes. Now, the shelves in the shops were half-empty, and the men scrounged to get cigarettes brought in. Behind even the most optimistic talk was the growing shadow of Franco's slow, methodical move toward Madrid, and the terrifying presence of German and Italian fighter planes and bombers in the air. Particularly terrifying were the Stukas, the "three Marias," diving with their three engines howling. The trucks and railway cars full of men returning from or to the front-lines had to pass long, trudging lines of refugees from embattled villages. The sun relentlessly scorched the fields and plazas, shrivelling the crops and exhausting the men before they even reached the battlefields. And then, the sudden rain storms, sweeping down the gullies, carrying everything before them.

"Tommy! Tommy! Over here." Chuck pushed his way through a bunch of men standing by the entrance to the bullring. "Here." He waved his hand above the loafing men.

Thomas heard his name and searched the crowds for the voice. Then, he saw Chuck. It would not be too much to say his heart surged, just as it had that day on the train when they met. His loneliness of the past weeks almost broke through his veneer of toughness. He placed a hand briefly on Joey's arm and began to run toward the advancing figure.

"Chuck." They literally fell into one another's arms before Chuck pulled back, perhaps remembering his position with the other men, perhaps just to look Thomas over. He held him at arm's length, examining him from head to foot.

"No fighting yet?"

"I just got here a week ago."

"Christ, Tommy, you've just about missed all the action. We've got the buggers on the run." The lie was perhaps for purposes of morale boosting. "I didn't think you'd make it."

"'Course I made it. I wouldn't miss this for the world."

"No?" Chuck's question momentarily dampened the excitement of the meeting. "I thought they were stopping all of you from leaving Canada to fight here." Chuck let go of Thomas's arms and looked at him appraisingly.

"They passed a law, but the boys are still being funnelled down to New York. We just walked over the railway bridge into New York and then took the train to New York City. I came with about a dozen of them. But there were hundreds more. No problem. We just acted like tourists, and no one bothered us. Of course, everyone knew where we were going." There was note of pride, even boastfulness in Thomas's voice. "How's Slim?"

"Slim?" Chuck looked down quickly. "Slim's dead. At Belchite. On a reconnaissance mission."

Silence. The autumn sun was hot and beat down. The awkwardness grew between them. Thomas shivered and, at Chuck's enquiring glance, said, "Someone must have walked on my mother's grave."

"Another of your mother's sayings? That brings back memories of better days. How is she? How's everyone out on Seventh Avenue?"

"Nell, you mean, don't you?" Thomas's anger flared. "What do you care?"

"Tommy, I care a lot. I care about her more than anyone else, but first there are things that have to be done."

"And there'll be something else after this, I suppose."

"Yes, and then probably something else. Europe is headed for disaster and it won't miss us. I'm needed here, but that doesn't mean I don't care." Chuck half-turned as if to leave.

"No, don't go yet. Nell is fine and the baby's growing and healthy. She named him Peter."

Chuck looked long at Thomas. "Did she? Peter," he said as if trying out the name. He was obviously deeply moved and tried hard to refocus on the present. A young man marched smartly up to him and saluted. "Sir, the men are assembled."

"In a moment." Chuck turned back to Thomas. "I have to go now. Later? At the taverna?" Thomas nodded and watched Chuck walk off, the man who had come to fetch him marching a half-step behind him. The other men, obviously on a break, looked in Thomas's direction with new interest after seeing the friendly meeting between their commissar and the new man. It would not be too much to say that Joey was awestruck.

"You know him? He's a hero. He's fought in every major battle, been wounded twice, saved I don't know how many wounded from being captured by the fascists. The men worship him." Joey was close to babbling.

"Yeah, I know him." Thomas tried to be nonchalant but he could feel his face redden a bit with what? pleasure? self-consciousness? pride? "Come on, let's get back to the parade grounds." Funny, that word came from his watching the Mounties on their parade grounds when he was a boy. That was before they had been identified as the enemy; before they had come to be called home-grown fascists.

"I wrote to her, a couple of times, but no answer. I can understand her anger." Chuck rested his arms on the table and leaned into the conversation with the same intensity Thomas remembered from the days in Regina. "I can't send her any money. She's just got to understand that, Tommy."

Thomas bit his lip and remained silent. He drank from his glass and held the red wine up to the light of the setting sun.

Chuck waited, maybe expecting some commiseration or, at least, recognition of his situation. Then, he grinned and said, "You like the wine, do you? Not a Saskatchewan habit." He raised his own glass, "To victory." Thomas raised his glass, "To victory. *Libertad.*"

Thomas raised his glass, "To victory. *Libertad.*" And both of them fell silent.

"Funny the Spanish word for blood, *sangre,* and for their red wine drink, *sangria,* sound almost alike. They're a brave people, blood and wine, good blood and good wine." Chuck smiled and laid his hand on Thomas's arm. "It's a bitch of a war, Tommy, but we're fighting for what's right. I feel if we win here, we'll win everywhere."

"Who's we? I hear the CNT are refusing to fight with us. And that the Marxists in Barcelona are trying to hijack the supplies coming in from Russia."

"You're a thorny person, Tommy. Yes, sure, there are disagreements. A lot of the groups that were powerful before have their nose a bit out of joint, now that Stalin has sent in so much support for us, for the Party. But there's only one cause. You know that."

"Do I?"

The silence came again. A slight breeze, cool even, had sprung up. Thomas stared at his glass and then drained it. "What about Margaret? Did she get here?"

Chuck grinned. "I wondered when you'd ask that. Yes, she did. She's in Barcelona, working, but itching to get into the thick of things."

"Fight, you mean?"

"Yes, fight. Women are as much a part of this war as men. They fight side by side, even if they do different jobs."

"Uh-huh." Thomas made circles with his glass in the bit of wine spilt on the tabletop. "How is she?"

"She's fine. Last time I saw her, which was about a month ago, she asked after you. Asked if I had seen you."

"Did she?" Thomas looked up.

"Still think you love her?"

"Yes."

"Well, I don't know how she feels, she's working day and night. She was working at headquarters, but...Now, she's working in a munitions factory, actually. One of the collectivized projects. Not much time for other things, not even for the Party. But she doesn't have another fellow, far as I could see." Chuck squeezed Thomas's arm and pushed back his chair. "Got to go. It's good to see you Tommy. Now we got our own battalion it'll be easier to keep track of each other. *Hasta luego.*"

Thomas raised a hand and said, "*Buen suerte.*"

"You're learning a bit of Spanish, eh? *Que bien. Que bien.*"

CHAPTER TWENTY-NINE

Oh, thank you, God, for the heavy traffic. Thank you, God, for the heavy traffic. Clara had invented this personal mantra especially for use in England. The palms of her hands sweated, greasing the nubbly plastic of the steering wheel, and every so often she reached with her right and then quickly with her left hand to make sure the gear stick was still there. The major blessing of North American civilization had to be the automatic transmission. Nevertheless she also gave thanks repeatedly that she didn't have to drive her Mercedes in this stream of little, dodging cars and huge, lumbering trucks, no, lorries. At least the traffic, on the whole, was moving slowly, and she could think her way through driving on the left-hand side of the road. The main problem was determining which lane was the fast one and which the slow. She positioned herself in the middle lane and tried to focus first on survival and then on any upcoming need to make a lane change. Damn Chuck for dying! Then she remembered how utterly hopeless he had been the one time they had driven in England, and she smiled. No wonder he liked chauffeured cars.

Once past Heathrow Airport the traffic thinned a bit, and Clara relaxed back in her seat. She realized that she had watched too many slow-paced, nineteenth-century, English dress dramas on public television, with their prancing horses and leisurely lives. This was busier than the QEW or 401 freeway at home. However, she managed to take her eyes off the other cars every so often to see the roadside vistas slowly change from industrial to rural. "A green and pleasant land." The phrase began to replace her desperate mantra and she picked up speed, heading determinedly westward.

Getting from the M3 to the A30 had been a challenge. Roundabouts made absolutely no sense to Clara, but everyone else seemed to know what they were doing, and after simply circling the little central knoll of grass and signs three times, she had made a break for the subsidiary highway and found the road reduced to two lanes of much less heavy traffic. There was no doubt that if she continued to be this successful, driving in England on her own could become confidence-building. She groped with her left hand for the knob to the radio. Music! Scarlatti. Life was not so bad.

The highway took her past Stonehenge. She thought of stopping to see it and Salisbury Cathedral, but a combination of seeing a gaggle of tourists wandering outside a wire fence strung around the famous rocks, and a certain trepidation about getting off the highway safely kept her on the road. The age of discovery was over and the age of tourism born.

Maybe witches and covens were genuinely something to fear in England. Or maybe people just kept writing their names on the stones. Anyway, she wanted to get close to her destination early, because she had a feeling from looking at the map of the area that Fifehead Neville was not going to be easy to find. Her map did not even actually show a road to the village, but there must be one. She'd stop at what looked like a fairly large town, Shrewsbury, to get directions.

Shrewsbury proved to be larger than she had anticipated, but she managed to park and stop a nice couple walking down the street. They directed her to Sturminster Newton and didn't ask her where she was from. She liked that. She had reserved a room in the Swan Inn in Sturminster Newton. It hadn't sounded as if there was a run on rooms at this time of year, and the man who answered had been almost obsequiously pleasant. Probably her North American accent boded well for tips. She shouldn't think that way. However, there would have been lots of North Americans in that part of the country, searching out Thomas Hardy sites. Now there was a really depressing writer. Of course, his was a pretty bleak time for a lot of people, especially women.

The car rental man had said it would take her about two and a half hours to get there, providing the traffic was not too heavy. "It doesn't take quite so long when you drive on the left-hand side of the road," he said with a perfectly straight face. She hadn't been sure whether to find it funny or be annoyed. She gave him her gold Visa card instead. "The insurance is covered." She had learnt that from Sidney.

She thought about Sidney. He had insisted on coming over when he could get away. He had said that it would not be later than the following week. She was glad. If Sidney had been here now, they probably would have stopped at Stonehenge.

A s she approached Sturminster Newton, the landscape slowly changed to rolling green hills uncluttered with factories or even many towns. White dots of sheep over the hillsides. Clara tried to remember if this was the part of England Constable painted, but while she could imagine him here, down in the valleys and glens seeking out the rural pathways and giant trees of Dorset, she could not remember where he had actually painted them. And Coleridge and Tennyson. Her knowledge was too vague, but bits and pieces of their work came to mind and seemed to be comfortable in the vistas of rolling land she saw on either side of her. She was now on an even smaller roadway; the smaller the road, the higher the number designating it. This one was the A3020 and, if she had read the map and the signs properly, should lead to Sturminster Newton. The English place names were a pleasure to say, even if the reality of the towns was often pretty shabby. It was nice to be irresponsibly romantic sometimes, though. Chuck would have been tight-lipped and noncommittal at her enthusiasm, perhaps afraid to let his feelings show. He had been a bit of a party-pooper at times, she had to admit. In fact, at times she had thought he was deliberately spoiling her fun, but then, marriage was not a smooth and easy run all the time. She could be difficult too, although nothing difficult about herself came immediately to mind. Sidney would have joined in and shared her pleasure, that much she could say for him. Still, we love who we love. Whom, Chuck would have said, whom.

The Swan Inn turned out to be everything she had envisaged an English country inn would be. Not large, on the narrow main street, a street so narrow that, as it came to a small bridge further down the street, the cars were allowed to cross only in one direction at a time. It was decorated in sort of early, unintentional Laura Ashley decor, and promised a full English breakfast. There were little shops across the road and a pub down the street. Across the bridge was a pub proudly called the Bull at the Bridge. There were even a good number of thatch-roofed cottages in the village and an abandoned mill on the stream, part of which was now a museum. Clara wondered if she could live in such a place, what it would be like. Well, it wasn't that simple. We don't just carry our lives around like change in our pocket. They were attached to some place, formed there, in some sense belonged there. Wet dripping trees of the west coast. Funny, one of the things that had always bothered her about Chuck was that he didn't seem to be attached to anything, or actually anybody, for that matter. He wasn't committed. Or he didn't share his commitment with her. Oh, he was always pleased to see her and so on, yet some part of him was elsewhere, or perhaps even most of him. But where? Regina? With Nell and little Peter? Since she had left Canada, he seemed to be constantly on her mind, even in her dreams. It was as if he was more present to her away from home, more present dead than alive.

Clara had enquired about the whereabouts of Fifehead Neville and found that it was quite close, about six miles or so away, but certainly not as the crow flies. She had written down the instructions and held a slip of paper with about twenty lines of complicated directions, such as: go to the corner just past the big house, that's the one back a bit from the road in some trees with the tall windows; then you just follow the road for about a mile until you get to The Willows, that's a cottage near the stream, the trees died out some time ago; and then at the next corner there will be some signs pointing to several villages; take the one marked Fifehead Neville; in about a quarter mile you'll come to a ford but don't worry that the water runs over the road at that point. The understructure is cement and you'll have no trouble, just drive right in and then, well, there's a vicarage, a large stone place to the right, and a little further on, the church, hidden behind the yews, but you'll see its towers and the graveyard; go left around the bend in the road, past the telephone box, and Miss Stanhope's place is on your left. But be careful, the road's pretty narrow in some places and some of the boys around here drive fast, far too fast, and, of course, there's often farm machinery on the road, so you have to be careful. You won't have any trouble, and you just return by following the directions backwards.

"How do I get out of town?" Clara's question brought a moment of puzzlement to the hotelier's face. "There's just the one road, ma'am, the one that runs past the hotel. Go left."

CHAPTER THIRTY

Margaret sat in the corner of the café, looking tired and dejected. She wore the bulky corduroy trousers and heavy sweater that were almost a uniform in the city. The only bright thing in the room was a red scarf she had tied around her neck. Her beret lay on the table in front of her. She was smoking, and a half glass of red wine sat next to the tin she was using as an ashtray. She seemed to have forgotten the cigarette hanging at the side of her mouth; smoke trailed up beside her face and mingled in her hair; the ash hung precariously from the end. Thomas stopped in the doorway and stood, watching her. He felt too, what? too frightened? too self-conscious? to walk over to her. He sighed and placed his hand on the casement of the door. The movement caught her attention. She squinted at him for what seemed a long time. Then...

"Tommy!" She jumped to her feet, upsetting the glass of wine and tin can. "Tommy. Tommy." She moved chairs out of the way and ran, falling into his arms. He wrapped his arms around her tightly and breathed in the smell of smoke from her hair. "Tommy. Tommy." He reached up and caressed her hair, pushing it aside.

They simply stood there, clutching each other. A couple of men in the café looked up and then went back to their conversations. Glasses clinked as the waiter wiped them and put them away. Finally, Margaret pushed Thomas back and looked up into his face.

"So, you came."

Thomas started to say something, but she reached up and put her fingers on his lips.

"No, don't say anything, yet. I just want to know you are really here. I just want to look at you and make sure. Come over and sit down. Come on." She took his hand and led him like a child to the back of the café where she had been sitting. She righted the glass and tin, and Thomas pulled out a chair. They sat across from each other.

"So, you're really here." Margaret took his hand and squeezed it. "How are you? Don't. Don't tell me. I just want to look at you."

Thomas felt his old impatience rise, but he kept his lips pressed shut. Chuck had not seemed to know exactly where she would be. He had finally located her by walking out to the shed they called a munitions factory and asking a Catalan-speaking woman there, in his very simple Spanish, if anyone knew her. *"Pero, desde luego. Margareeeta."* He had picked out of the following stream of words the name, the café and the street. Why she would know Margaret was in a certain café, had escaped him at the time, but he found out from Margaret herself that she lived in a room above it. But that was later. At the moment, he was thinking of nothing other than that he was actually with her. He reached out and took her hand. She let him. Tears came to her eyes and Thomas looked away.

"Oh, Tommy. It is good to see you. Okay, now tell me everything. Everything. No wait. You need a glass of wine." She half stood up from her chair and caught the waiter's eye. *"Uno mas, por favor."*

"I heard that there was no more of that in Barcelona. Everyone was equal. No more waiting on other people."

"Twaddle. They run the café now. The waiters and cooks. They're equals."

"Is this the famous collectivization, then?"

"Tommy. Don't be so thorny. You always did carry a chip around on your shoulder. Come on, tell me what you are doing, what's happened." The waiter set the glass down in front of Thomas and another in front of Margaret. *"Gracias."* Margaret raised her glass, *"Salud."*

"Salud."

Thomas related everything, or almost everything. He didn't talk about being sick in Paris, much less his ostracization by the men on board the ship. He told her about his training in Albacete, but only mentioned Chuck in passing. She asked about home and he told her about little Peter and described his sister's teaching position. Old news, because he had not received any letters since he left Paris. He said he wanted to get to the front lines as soon as he could. Which was true as he sat across from Margaret, even though at Albacete he was no more enthusiastic about the prospect than he had been in Toronto.

"And you?" Thomas looked at her and, for the first time, noticed the creases that had developed around her eyes.

She laughed. "I'm fine, Tommy. No reason to complain. This war...I'd like to get more involved, too." She looked past him for a moment, perhaps thinking about her desire to see action. "But, you, Tommy, how are you holding up in the army? Are they treating you all right?"

"You know, quick march, halt, quick march, kick the dogs out of the way."

Margaret smiled at Thomas's attempt to be humourous. "And Chuck? How is he really?'

"Really? He's the same as always. He said he had seen you."

"Did he say anything? About me?"

Thomas hesitated, turning his glass around and around on the marble top of the table. "He told me you were working in a munitions factory here."

"Nothing else?"

Anger flared for a moment. "No, nothing else."

Margaret looked down and then glared at Thomas. "I'm not surprised."

They sat silently for awhile, sipping every so often from their glasses. Margaret motioned to the waiter for another glass for each of them. Thomas slouched back on his chair and looked around the café.

"So, this is where you hang out."

"I live here. Not down here. Upstairs. I have a room."

"Oh."

The glasses arrived.

"Tommy, Tommy. It seems like an eternity since I saw you

last. I didn't think you were going to come. To Spain. What made you change your mind?"

"You."

"Me? I left."

"That's why. Margaret, I couldn't stay safe and sound in Canada with you over here risking your life. My feelings for you haven't changed, you know." He reached across the table and clutched her hand again. She let him. In fact, she turned her hand over and held his.

"Tommy. You are sweet."

"For god's sake, Margaret, I'm not sweet. I'm in love with you. Can't you understand that?"

"I can understand love. I care for you too."

"Care? Care?" Thomas gripped her hand, pulling her toward him.

"Tommy, that hurts. Now, stop it." She pulled her hand away. "It's getting late. I have to get up early tomorrow morning. Are you staying over?"

"Yes."

"Tommy, don't be that way. Where are you staying?"

"I don't know. Somewhere, I guess."

"It's not so easy to find a place. The city is full to bursting. How about staying with me? I have a couch you can use."

"No, I'll find someplace."

"Tommy, don't be like that. Come on, let's see if you'll fit." She laughed and stood up. Thomas stood up too, his hands dangling at his sides. "Oh, come on. You look like a bedraggled dog, that doesn't know whether to bark or run. Come on." She reached out and took his hand and led him to the door.

Thomas lay on his side, listening to the regular breathing of Margaret. It was dark in the room, but not so dark that he could not make out her shape on the single bed pushed up against the back wall. When they had first come in, she had turned on the light for a few minutes, but then turned it off because power was needed for other things. At least, that was what she said. They had talked in the dark, holding hands, sitting next to each other on the couch, like two teenagers on a first date. Then, she had yawned, stretched, and announced she was going to bed. She had simply turned her back to him, stripped to her underwear and climbed into bed. Her white flesh in the shadows of the room now hung in the air in front of him, more like a movie image than a memory. He turned over and closed his eyes.

He turned back over onto his other side and finally got up. Why did she never take him seriously? He walked over to the window and looked out onto the tiny street that led down to the dock area. No one was about. He pulled out his pocket watch and held it up to see the time. It was just about three o'clock. She still thought of him as the little boy next door. Shit, he was risking his life to fight in this stupid war. All because of her. He wouldn't be here if she hadn't...Thomas banged the window frame with his fist. He turned and stared in the darkness at the hump of her body under the blanket across the room from him. She had to know he was a man now. The floor was cold. He shivered a bit and clenched and opened his fists. This gesture had become a habit of late. As if he was grasping something and then letting it go.

If she only knew how he had longed for her, to see her, be

sure she was okay. All those months he had thought of nothing else. Now, she just undresses and goes to sleep. As if he wasn't even there. All she cares about is Chuck. Chuck. Chuck. Chuck. As if he, Thomas didn't exist.

Thomas walked stealthily across the room to her bed. Margaret slept motionlessly, almost soundlessly. Her dark hair had been cut short. One bare shoulder showed above the blanket. He looked down at her and then bent over the bed. Her smell came up to his nostrils. A sweaty, sweet smell. He thought of the smell of her underwear in the drawer of her bedroom that time. His whole body shuddered. Oh, god. He sank to his knees next to her bed and laid his forehead on the edge of the rough blanket. A moment passed, then he reached up and laid his hand on her hip. She stirred, squirrelled down under the blanket. He slowly ran his hand over her body. She tensed, turned.

"What the hell do you think you're doing? Get your goddamn hands off me." She spun around and, putting a hand on each of his shoulders, shoved him, hard. He literally flipped over and sprawled back on the floor. His head crashed against the couch arm. Margaret sat up and swung her legs over the side of the bed.

"What do you...Tommy. For christ's sake. What are you thinking? Idiot." She turned, lay down and pulled the blanket back up.

Thomas lay there for a minute and then got up and went back to the couch. Fucking women.

CHAPTER THIRTY-ONE

Meg Stanhope's cottage sat comfortably just off the main road. Its name was proudly displayed at the bottom of the steps leading up to the front door: The Chapel. The front windows and a round window high up under the eaves were still reminders of a time, now distant, when it served the people who preferred the stirring messages of travelling Methodist preachers to the ritualistic enactments of the Anglican church around the corner. But it had no graveyard attached, so in death parishioners must have opted to lie with their Anglican co-villagers, perhaps to ease the organizing of the eventual call to resurrection or, more likely, to assure they were not overlooked.

Clara pulled her car into the small parking place next to the steps. Wattle walls held back the encroaching greenery and wild and tame flowers poked out between the woven branches. Meg Stanhope was obviously a gardener, and her small front garden was full of neatly kept plants and flowers. Not a weed in sight. Clara felt an involuntary happiness as

234

she walked between the low, flowering shrubs and up to the dark green front door with its heavy bronze knocker.

Just as Clara reached for the knocker, the door swung open and a wizened little face stared into hers. "Hello." The voice coming from the woman could only be described, at least, that is how Clara described it later to Sidney, as chirpy. "Who might you be?" The woman rubbed her hand on her worn leather purse and straightened up as if making herself worthy of a serious answer.

"I'm Clara Stemichuk."

"Oh." The woman stepped half a step back and looked at Clara hard. "Oh. Yes." Still looking at Clara, she put her bag determinedly under her arm and stepped off the threshold of the door. "You should have phoned, dearie. I'm on my way to the shops." The fact that there were no shops in Fifehead Neville didn't occur to Clara immediately. "You'll have to stand aside so I can get past, you know." Clara obediently stood to one side and the little woman rushed past her, down the steps, and pulled her bicycle out from under some greenery overhanging the wall. "Make yourself at home, dearie." And she disappeared around the corner. Clara stood, arrested for the moment in time, and then turned to go into the cottage.

It was a fine cottage. Very simple, uncluttered, but comfortable. A small kitchen to the left; an eating area behind with French doors out to the garden; and, straight ahead, a sitting room, also with French doors leading out to the back garden, and furnished with comfortable sofas; a stone fireplace lined one wall and on the opposite wall, a writing desk and a few books. When Clara was well into the sitting room, she turned and saw that she had passed under a staircase which led upstairs, presumably to a bedroom at the front part of the house. The bathroom was located under that and there seemed to be a small guest bedroom off to the side. It was a thoroughly pleasant little house, and Clara was surprised to find herself feeling completely at home, even though nothing in the house or in the back view over farmers' fields could have been said to even remotely resemble her own Victorian, brick, three-storey house in Toronto.

She walked from window to window looking out at fields and, on one side, the barnyard of the farm right next door. She walked through the kitchen, opened a cupboard or two where everything was neatly located in its own place, turned a gas burner on and noted that it was a new stove, looked into the fridge, walked to the front door and checked up and down the road to see if Meg Stanhope was coming back yet, and finally returned to the sitting room and sat down on one of the comfortable sofas. It had been a tiring day, and she could feel jet lag asserting itself, her eyes falling shut on their own, her body getting heavy. She was looking forward to talking to the strange little elf who owned this house and who perhaps could tell her more about her late husband. She dreamt of wearing her wedding ring at a pool party, but it was loose on her finger and kept falling with a clatter onto the tiles around the pool.

"My, my, you did have a long sleep. You must be very tired, so I've made some tea and scones. Would you like some tea and scones? They're very good, if I do say so myself. They're my specialty. Do you like scones? Silly of me, you probably don't know about scones, coming from Canada as you do. Well..." Here Meg Stanhope screwed up her face and continued, "I think they're maybe Scottish. Don't say Scotch, that's what we were taught. And, now, they want to go it on their own. Silly really, but there you are. You can't understand what some people want. Where in Canada do you live? Oh, I remember: Toronto. Yes, yes, I remember now. Such nice letters. You express yourself very well, dearie. I didn't answer your second one, well, because I'm too old to be answering letters now. My garden keeps me busy and then I go over to the vicar's every day at 3:30 p.m. and make his tea. He likes it promptly at 4:00. Poor man. Not many go to church anymore. Not the Church of England. They go to those evangelical ones though. They don't require the same level of intelligence, of course. But I stay with the old church. Haven't always, but I do now. Even though I live in a low church chapel. The vicar says that's ironic. He's usually right, but I don't even think of it. Except of course when I have to explain it to someone such as yourself. Comfy?" The torrent of speech suddenly stopped and she leaned toward Clara and looked, questioningly, straight into her eyes.

Clara was startled out of her amused, lulling acceptance of Meg's talk, "What? Yes, yes, very."

"Good. Now eat up." Meg sat down across from her. Well didn't exactly sit, more perched on the edge of the sofa, wrapping her arms around her knees like a young girl. Clara wondered for a moment if she had ever had such an attentive audience. Chuck had always seemed a bit inside himself, a bit disapproving, not really interested in what she was saying.

Here was this little woman apparently avidly waiting for Clara to speak.

"I'm sorry. I must have dropped off."

"Aye. But don't be sorry. I decided, oh a long time ago, not to be sorry any more. Well, no one really believes you, do they? And it just takes time to say, so why say it? I think we should all just do whatever we are doing, and if it isn't exactly right according to someone or other, then that's too bad. That's what I think. Eat up." She pushed the plate of buttered scones closer to Clara. "And there's strawberry jam in the bowl there. I make it for the vicar. He does like his strawberry jam. We have a fete every year and it always sells out first. He says I make quite a contribution to the church funds every year that way. Well, I can't give much from my pension, can I? We all do what we can and if we can't, let someone else have a chance. That's what I say." Meg again lapsed into her very active silence.

"Miss Stanhope..."

"Oh, you call me Meg. That's what you Americans do, don't you? Go around calling people by their first names? I watch some of those shows on the telly in the evening and they are always calling each other by their first names. Sometimes I wonder if they have family names. They do all sound a bit alike, to us, I mean. But you just make yourself comfortable and call me Meg."

"And you call me Clara."

"Oh, I couldn't do that. Really. It's..." Meg threw up her hands.

"Fair is fair, Meg."

"You're absolutely right, Clara. Fair is fair. I think I'll have one of my scones myself. I don't usually, you know. Have to watch my figure." Meg giggled.

Clara patted her tummy. "I should too."

"Well, there's time for that. You're a young woman still."

"Young?"

"You couldn't be more than fifty-five, at the most."

"You are too kind. Would you believe sixty-five?"

"Yes. I believe whatever anyone tells me. I decided that years ago. Just believe them. It makes them feel good and it doesn't hurt me. Is that right, I say. Sometimes, if they're telling a real whopper, they back down and confess to a little exaggeration. But I always say to them, Stick with your story. As the Americans say on the telly, That's my story and if you don't believe it, ask my lawyer." Meg tried to put on an American accent but it didn't quite come off. Nevertheless she seemed delighted with herself for having attempted to accommodate what she felt sure were her visitor's cultural leanings. Meg liked to be accommodating.

"And how old are you?"

Meg looked a bit taken aback but squared her shoulders and stuck out her chin, "Eighty-five last birthday."

"You look remarkably well and young."

"For my age? Yes, dearie, I look after myself. For what or whom, God alone knows."

"How old were you when you knew Chuck?"

"Chuck?"

"Peter. Peter Stemichuk."

Clara felt as if she had raised a forbidden subject, more serious than weight or age. Meg drew back and then leaned into the cushions as if she would hide. She looked down at her hands.

"Yes. Peter. You see I used to feel awfully guilty about that." She stopped. "I was very young and so was he. And he was so badly wounded. It didn't hurt anybody. Really it didn't. But you know you can't dictate to the heart, now can you? No, it goes the way it wants no matter how hard you try to direct it. But, as I say, he was so awfully wounded and I didn't know if he would live or die. The doctors in those days never told you anything, not even the nurses. So, he could have been gone in a week, two weeks, a month. Or shipped out to another hospital or even back to Canada. He needed someone and I was there. I mean he was so wrapped up in himself. So I just let him think..."

"Let him think what?"

"I see you want the whole story, don't you dearie? Have some more tea. That's right. Tea is a comfort, I always say. I have to tell you, I was that surprised when I received your letter. Right out of the blue. He was a complicated man, I'll say that and, well, after, I mean after he was well enough to leave, I couldn't very well tell him, now could I?"

"Tell him?"

"Yes, tell him that it was perfectly natural for him to fall in love with his nurse. It happens all the time. You wouldn't believe how often, dearie. Married men, too. And old ones that can hardly shuffle their walkers along much less...well, you know, love does take a certain amount of doing, now doesn't it?"

"Fall in love?"

"Now, I don't know exactly what you want to know. I thought you wrote to me because, as his sister, you wanted to know about his time here. But families aren't close anymore, are they? And people are curious. You know, in those years, during the War, it was a tense time and life was lived at the edge. Later, I'd see him, you know, sometimes when he came to London on business.

"Meg..." Should she tell her? It had seemed a small fib when she had explained in her letter that she was Chuck's sister. It seemed, what? more appropriate somehow, than just saying she was his widow. She did tell Meg that he had died, but still there was a lot of difference between being his sister and being his widow. A sister might be expected not to know a lot of things that a wife would surely know. After all the stories she had heard about Chuck's life before he met her, she now decided that it had been the right thing to do. To tell a little fib.

"He wasn't my type. At least, that's what I told myself. And he wasn't very happy in his marriage, you know. Sometimes I'd just let him talk himself out. He needed to tell someone. It's really amazing how a woman can cause a man so much trouble. But as his sister, you probably knew that, or suspected as much. I told him, You made your bed, you have to lie in it." Meg looked at Clara enquiringly.

Clara sat quite still and tried to decide what to say.

Meg cocked her head and pursed her lips a bit. "You didn't look so well there for a moment. It's that flying. It's not healthy to be up there so high. You know the story about the poor young man that tried to fly and his wax wings melted. I think that was a warning to us all. You have a bit more tea and another scone and I'll take some lamb chops out of the freezer." Meg got to her feet.

"Oh, no, I couldn't possibly impose. I, I..."

"Nonsense. You want to hear my story and I want to tell it to you. You seem like a nice person to me. Nicer than that brother of yours, if you really want the truth. He didn't let anything stand in his way. No sir. He said he always got what he wanted. And he did. Even from me. Well, once or twice. But he sure didn't get what he wanted in his marriage." Meg chuckled, perhaps a bit lasciviously. "And, for all his declarations of love, I knew he got around a bit whenever he came to London. Two days business and three days fun. I wasn't the only one. Not by a long way. I'll be right back. You just sit there and relax."

Clara sat, absolutely stunned.

CHAPTER THIRTY-TWO

"I think they should sneak up behind them and just pick them off, one by one, blow up their supply stores, that sort of thing. They'd never know who was who, and I bet the people would be sympathetic, hide them." Joey gestured with his hands, emphasizing his points with quick flourishes. Thomas and Chuck sat back on their chairs and, perhaps good-naturedly amused, let Joey ramble on. It was late and they had all but finished the wine Thomas had picked up on the way back from Barcelona. Chuck had been moved to Tarazona de la Mancha and had brought Thomas and Joey with him. "And what about all those people Stalin is shooting in Russia. They're revolutionaries too, just like...Well, just like us. What about them? Is that what Communism is? I don't think so. It's fine for us to fight here against these fascists, but what about afterward? Are they going to start shooting people here because they were anarchists or what not?" Joey didn't hold his liquor very well and his speech started to slur after two glasses. Thomas looked over at Chuck. He felt slightly embarrassed at Joey's repeating some of the thoughts he himself had expressed to Joey. Chuck, leaning forward, his elbows on the table, listening closely to what Joey had to say, did not make Thomas feel any easier.

Chuck nodded his head. "There's a lot in what you say, Joey. But first we've got to win the war. Then we'll carry out the revolution. Isn't that true, Tommy?"

Thomas hesitated, not knowing whether he wanted to distance himself from Joey or from Chuck. "That's not the line in Barcelona."

"Tommy, Tommy, you don't understand. The CNT and POUM have put the cart before the horse. They're trying to have the Revolution before they fight the war." Chuck was moving into his argument with his usual passionate energy.

"Margaret says..."

"I know what Margaret says, and if she were here she'd realize that the discipline of the Party is going to win this war, not some vague ideals."

As usual, Thomas felt a surge of defensiveness. "She's still a Marxist. Even if she thinks the Party is wrong."

"Marx didn't have to fight any wars. We do. Marx was a prophet and prophets don't fight wars or carry out revolutions. You should know that, Tommy. No matter how right they might be."

"The CNT says..."

"The CNT has feet of gold and a head of clay."

Joey pulled out his notebook. "Oh, that's good." He wrote quickly in the book.

Chuck sat back, perhaps realizing it was useless to argue with Thomas. He gestured to Joey. "So what's that going to be, Joey? The definitive account of the war?"

"I just write down things. To look at when I get back home. Home." Joey's eyes watered ever so slightly.

Thomas was angry, angry at being dismissed, angry at being defensive, angry at Joey's adulation and sentimentality. He turned on Joey. "If you get back home."

Chuck threw up his hands. "Tommy, you are impossible. I got to go. You'll get your assignments soon." He stood up and gave Thomas and then Joey a hug. *"Buena suerte."*

"What do you think our assignments will be?"

"You mean, where are they going to send us to get shot at? Our death notices?"

Thomas was sitting looking out the dirty window, but aware of Joey, sitting beside him trying to clean his uniform, or rather the jacket of a French uniform that he had been issued when they had first arrived in Tarazona de la Mancha to train with the 2nd Battalion of the Brigade. They were billeted in a building attached to the church and their view from this window was of the square in front of the main doors. They had been in Tarazona barely three weeks.

"No, seriously, what do you think they are going to do with us?" Joey's voice showed some traces of the underlying anxiety he, and probably every man there, felt about being assigned to the front lines.

"Guess we'll find out tomorrow."

"Tomorrow?"

"They're going to give out assignments tomorrow."

"You never told me." Joey could not get used to Thomas's refusal, or, at least, failure to tell him things. He told Thomas almost everything, but Thomas seemed to like to hold on to information, even torment Joey with hints before telling him.

"Each of us will be assigned to a battalion and then trained for combat." Thomas tried to sound indifferent.

"Won't we be in the Mac-Paps?" The creation of the Mackenzie-Papineau Battalion had been a major event for the Canadian volunteers who previously had been assigned to various battalions, mainly the American Abraham Lincolns. Even then, the new Canadian battalion's military commander was American.

"Who knows? At the moment, they're even having one hell of a time distributing all those Christmas packages from Canada. Guys are all over Spain. The packages all have the same things in them, so it doesn't really matter who gets which one." Thomas lit a cigarette. "But they've got them all laid out over in stores and trying to get them to the names on the parcels. If they can't figure out how to do that, then I really can't say how they're going to sort out our assignments. But, that's the army for you." He blew out smoke over Joey.

"Well, they seem to be doing all right to me."

"No doubt."

Joey ducked out of the cloud of smoke and threw his jacket on the bed. He stood beside Thomas and looked out the window. "I hope we get assigned to the same battalion."

Thomas said nothing.

"Thomas Pennan – machine gun company."
"Joseph Flaherty – communications."

"Communications? What does that mean, Tom? Telegraph?"

"Nah. It means you're going to be a runner."

"Jeez, that's really dangerous, isn't it?"

"Nah. You just have to take messages from one place to another."

"But up in the front lines, all the time."

Thomas put an arm around Joey's shoulders. "You'll be okay. Just duck and run fast. Anyway you're too small a target to get hit." He gave Joey a squeeze. Joey turned and hugged Thomas. "Hey, you'll be all right." He pushed Joey away and gave him a mock punch to the shoulder. "I'll cover you. But why would they assign me to machine gunnery? I don't know the first thing about machine guns. I'm not even Finnish."

"Finnish?"

"Most of the guys in machine gunnery are Finns from Ontario."

"Maybe you could get me assigned there too. There's ten or twelve men with every gun."

"Do you think you could move an eighty-five pound gun carriage around all by yourself? That's why they assign big Finnish workhorses, to carry the machine guns."

"Then, I could be second gunner."

"Well, I'll see what I can do. But no promises." Through his connection with Chuck, Thomas had managed to get some privileges – better food, treats, passes. He was a bit leery of pushing too hard, however, because Chuck didn't know he was using his name. "I'll talk to Reg." He dropped the first name of their captain casually, knowing it would impress Joey. "But he probably gets his orders from higher up."

In fact, Thomas was panicky about being assigned to the machine-gun battery. They were the first and slowest to move in and the last to leave. They dug in and stayed; they covered the attacks and the retreats, if there were any.

What followed was a month and a half of disassembling, assembling, cleaning, oiling and loading an old Maxim WWI machine gun, interspersed with long "educational" sessions on what they were fighting for and the relationship between capitalism and fascism. Discipline, Hierarchy and Organization. *Libertad y Tierra,* was the regular Spanish army cry. Theirs was, Liberty or Death! And very little actual firing of the guns, because ammunition was in short supply.

On December 15, 1937, word came to the Brigade that an offensive had been opened in the Aragon mountains, at Teruel, where the Spanish Popular Front army was moving rapidly to take the Nationalists on their weak, eastern side, thereby drawing them away from Madrid. "A hundred thousand men," Thomas told Joey. The nationalists held the city. A major assault and no volunteers this time. Nevertheless, on December 17, 1937, Thomas, Joey, and the unit were ordered to pack up the Maxim and load it and the remaining ammunition onto a truck. The battalions of the International Brigade were being moved into position, just in case. They celebrated Christmas in the little village of Mas de la Matas. The parcels from home were opened, wine and brandy flowed, warm socks were put on, beards were shaven off, the men danced and sang. Thomas stood in the square every evening, watching the merriment. Even communists apparently celebrate Christ's birth, was his comment to Chuck, who had been appointed as their political commissar. For a few days, the war was a long ways away. Then, on December 31, the call came to pack and move up into the mountain ranges where the battle for Teruel raged. Bitterly cold weather and heavy snow awaited them. Take lots of brandy, they were told. The water to cool the machine guns freezes up, so you've got to use brandy. That was the story that went around.

CHAPTER THIRTY-THREE

"Now, where were we, dearie?" Meg settled back into the sofa across from Clara and folded her hands in her lap. "No, no, I remember. I forget a lot of things now but not everything. The vicar says I'm a marvel. Well, that's his job, isn't it? I mean, making people feel good. Not like in the old days when they preached all about hell and brimstone and the poor suffering souls in eternal fires. Nowadays, they like to make it a bit more attractive. Flattery, not fear is how I see it. But that's nicer, don't you think? Who wants to be told they're going to go to hell? I ask you. I like a little flattery sometimes, don't you?" Meg stopped and waited.

"Yes, yes I suppose I do. If..."

"I know. There's got to be some truth in it, or it doesn't turn your crank." The phrase was bizarre coming from the lips of the proper little English woman across from her, and Clara smiled, almost in spite of herself. "Something I said, dearie? Or did you have a thought I shouldn't know about?"

"No. I mean, yes, it was what you said." Clara felt a determination to hear this story through. "But about Chuck...Peter."

"Ah, Peter. I'm just going to get us a little something and then I'll tell you all about Mister Peter." Meg scurried over to the desk and brought out a nearly full bottle of Scotch whiskey and two glasses. She set the glasses down on the coffee table between the sofas and poured a generous helping into each glass. "There. I know you Americans, Canadians, too, I should think, like ice in their whiskey, but it isn't right, you know. Better to drink it neat, I always say. Maybe a little water, but just a smidgeon. Would you like a little water?"

"No, let's drink it neat. But, first, I did tell you that Peter died, didn't I? Last year."

Meg's face fell for a moment, then she nodded her head. "Yes." She pulled herself together, very much like Margaret Rutherford playing Miss Marples. "It comes to us all. Never mind, my dear. Let's drink to all those that have passed on before us." She raised her glass and saluted Clara, who did the same. "Well, welcome to merry old England. Not that we're so merry anymore, not after that terrible woman from the flat over the grocery store. I'm no snob, Mrs...Clara, but she just ruined this country, and I think it was all because she didn't know anything about government. Grocery stores are one thing; countries are another. You've got to be born to it." She took a drink and cocked her head a little to the side. "But that doesn't interest you, does it?" She sat down. "You want to hear about Peter."

Clara took a drink of her scotch and nodded.

"Peter was brought to the hospital where I worked...that was on the Isle of Wight. It was just days after the landing on the beaches of Normandy. A lot of boys came in after that; even more, you know, didn't come back at all. Peter was one of the lucky ones, if you call not getting killed lucky. They were terrible times. I wouldn't want to see them again." Meg's face fell and she looked as if she was on the verge of tears. "I'm sorry. Just a personal sorrow. You see, I lost...But, you don't want to hear about my troubles. Anyway, those ones are all far behind me now. I went out and found some new ones to take their place." She smiled and then grew serious again. "Peter was badly wounded, shrapnel from a mortar bomb, other wounds, slipping in and out of consciousness. Let me tell you the odd thing about his arrival. I was standing by his bed after they brought him in, making sure he was as comfortable as I could. I had a lot of boys to look after, but I tried to give them each a little special attention. After what they'd been through, and they were all Canadians on my ward, come all that way to fight for us, as if they owed us something. Well, my family was never very keen about the Empire, as we used to call it, but we appreciated the help. Anyway, as I stood there fussing a bit with his pillow, he turned his head and said, quite distinctly, 'Margaret.' Now, that's my name. They call me Meg, but my name's really Margaret. Well, I was that surprised. Only my mother had ever called me Margaret. Here was this soldier I had never seen before, and he turns to me and says my name. Yes, I said. But he was gone again. That's how it all began. The special relationship between Peter and me, I mean.

"Now, let me just think a bit." She sipped from her glass, passed the bottom of it over her hand and carefully set it down on the table again. Clara started to nurse hers, then changed her mind and took another good drink. "Don't warm up that whiskey too much. That's fine for brandy, but whiskey likes the temperature of the room. Least, that's what someone I knew once told me." Clara took another drink and set her glass down on the table. "And don't take too much at a time. That's strong drink, you know."

Clara smiled. She liked to be looked after. She could feel the warmth of the whiskey. "You're right. Sidney tells me the same thing. It's just a nervous habit."

"Sidney? Your husband?"

"It's just someone I met. Just a friend. It doesn't matter. Go on."

"From that day on, I was Margaret for him, never Meg. Oh, after, well, it must have been three or four months, he didn't confuse me with…Let me go back. When he was delirious and drifting in and out of consciousness, he thought I was Margaret, not me, of course, someone named Margaret, someone he said he loved very much. His voice would take on a soft, almost pleading tone when he said her name. He thought I was she. He'd talk to me about things we used to do, people we worked with and knew. Sometimes, he'd take hold of my hand and thank me for coming back and other times he'd ask forgiveness. I never found out where I was supposed to have come back from or what he needed forgiveness for, and I didn't ask him then because he was so ill and later, well, it didn't matter. Anyway, I don't know anything about this Margaret, except I gather they fought together in Spain before the War and they knew each other in Canada. I couldn't make out from the bits and pieces of his conversation what they had done together, but they'd fought together, that I know, because he'd talk about carrying ammunition and men being killed and the gun overheating and her being there. I don't think they were lovers. Maybe Peter loved her and she didn't know it, or maybe she loved him and he didn't know it. He thought he loved her. Anyway, they were comrades-in-arms, that I know, because he sometimes relived in his mind some battle and she would be there. I mean, he'd think I was in the battle with him and he'd say all sorts of things, like, Why did you come, It's too dangerous here, Please, please, I can't, and other things I didn't understand. Sometimes he'd refer to himself in the third person. As if he were standing outside himself and addressing himself."

"Yes. Yes, dear Chuck. He'd dissociated himself. Somehow. Just for a moment."

"Dissociate. That's the right word. That's what he would do. Then, he'd say something. Then, he'd contradict it. But I'd agree with him or say, I'm fine, don't worry about me, and, you know, things that would calm him down. And then he'd fall back into an almost comatose state. I don't know. He was badly wounded, but he was also deeply disturbed, in his mind, I mean. It took a long time before he could distinguish between me and this Margaret. And when he did, he decided he loved me and not her. Some sort of substitution, I guess. I never encouraged him. I was just kind to him."

"But you said he saw you. Later." Clara was moved by the picture of the sufferings her Chuck had gone through and which he had always refused to talk about. But why had he come to see this Meg when...after they had met...after they had married?

"Yes, he could be a passionate man, and then just forget all about you. He said he loved me, but I knew that it was just fanciful thinking. You know, he'd married badly, probably just jumped at the first thing that came along, and then thought he would create this mythical romance." Meg smiled slightly. "He was like that, believed that whatever he dreamed of could become true, rather than face reality, like the rest of us. Maybe he was just escaping from that wife of his." She glanced at Clara. "But you probably know more about that than I do."

Clara felt her cheeks reddening, both with embarrass-ment and anger. "I..." Clara stopped; Meg bowed her head and seemed to be immersed in her memories and unaware for the moment of her listener.

"Anyone who didn't live through those times can't under-stand how it was. Everything was either immediate, right now, or else a dream of some far-off future. It was as if we had only two buttons and when you turned on one, it was all pain and vomit, and if you turned the other one on, it was all moonlight and champagne. We just let ourselves go. I mean, we didn't act as we would in normal times. So, it didn't seem strange for Peter to love me. And I, well, I let him, and, to be honest, joined in the game. It wasn't as if – well, he was all bandaged up and pretty well unable to move. We thought he was going to die. So, I made him feel good. Caressed him; that sort of thing." Meg picked up her glass and fiddled with it for a moment, before setting it down again.

Clara took a drink and let the liquor assault her throat. She momentarily closed Meg's rambling tale out and let her thoughts dwell on Chuck, how he'd looked those days before he died, the flesh losing its muscle, subsiding around the skeleton.

How much she had loved him. Her heart ached. The whiskey was also making itself known. That and jet lag. She drifted. She didn't care about Meg's story anymore. What did it matter? Through half-closed eyes, she seemed to see the elfish face of Meg change into something more impish. It was getting late. Meg's voice rambled on. Perhaps it wasn't even true. The fantasies of an old spinster. Clara took another drink and set the glass down with a clatter.

"...it was..." Meg looked up, startled by the sound. "Are you all right, dearie? Not used to strong drink, I see. Shall I get you a drink of water?"

"No. Go on." Clara was abrupt, almost rude now. Meg squinted at her and took another sip from her glass.

"Well, there's not a lot more I can tell you. He was, in fact, moved out, to another hospital, before he was sent back to Canada. I didn't see him until some time later, after the War, after he'd married, when he came back here on a business trip. Maybe he did really love me. Maybe it wasn't just a wartime fancy."

Clara reached for the bottle and poured herself another drink.

"Perhaps I had better put on something for us to eat." Meg started to rise.

"No." It was almost a command. "Go on. Please."

"As I say, there's not much more. I guess I can tell you, we made love once or twice, on the first trip back. But, after that, well, he was married and I...To tell the truth, I did care for him ... I cared for him more than I let him know, but I could see he wasn't the faithful type. Lived too much in his head, if you know what I mean. Lot of fantasies. But that was all years ago now. Water under the bridge. I'm sorry to say these things, you being his sister and all, but well, you've come a long way to hear them, so I better tell you everything. Anyway, you can read his story about all that. Not about us, but about going to Spain and then the War."

"His story? You mean he wrote down the story of...all that?"

"Oh, yes. Well, he didn't actually write it down. He couldn't sit up, you know, so I wrote it down while he talked, at night, when I was on duty. He slept in little catnaps and, of course, I was on duty, as I said."

"And this story? I didn't find it amongst his things."

"Oh, no, you wouldn't have. I have it here. He asked me to keep it for him. He swore me to secrecy and told me that I must only send it when he died. When, not if... And afterwards, well, afterwards I just kept it. It was a memory, I guess. I had nowhere to send it, anyway. And he never asked me about it, or I, of course, would have given it to him. Perhaps he forgot, or..."

"You have it? Here? May I see it?"

"Yes, of course. He did write it for you, you know." She glanced up, a small smile on her lips. "To tell you the truth, I didn't quite know what to do after I received your letter. I thought of sending it to you, but then when you said you wanted to come visit, well, I thought, it can wait another few weeks, since it's waited this long. Everything's too much of a rush nowadays, don't you think?" Meg folded her hands in a self-satisfactory way and waited.

Clara, now attentive, tried to figure out what exactly Meg was talking about. "It's a letter? For..."

"Oh, yes. Anyway, there's nothing in it that would, uh, compromise his memory. And I changed some of it, when it got too raw, I mean. He was sort of delirious some of the time, and he imagined all sorts of things that I am sure never happened, so I just recorded, you know, the main story, as it were. And, later, when he came back, he changed some things, and then I got it all typed up, nice and neat. But I don't think it was so important to him later, as it seemed to be when he wanted it all written down. Anyway, it isn't very long."

"I would like very much to see it, if I could." Clara gulped down the rest of the whiskey and then felt it rise again to her throat. She coughed, choked, and then swallowed the now bitter liquid.

"Yes, I better get us something to eat." Meg got to her feet and scurried out to the kitchen, leaving her drink almost untouched. Clara filled her own glass again.

CHAPTER THIRTY-FOUR

The mood at the beginning of the march was ebullient. The men marched in straggly lines, singing at the top of their voices, raising their right arms and clenched fists as they past the cheering villagers. *Salud! A la frente!* Perhaps the veterans of the earlier battles were a little less exuberant than the new volunteers. But battle stirred the hearts of everyone. Crush the fascist bastards! *Tierra y Liberdad!* And, liberty or death!

Fear was forgotten.

La Pasionaria had said, "It is better to die on your feet, than to live on your knees."

Remember that.

That morning Chuck had gathered the men of the XVth under his command and instructed them in detail about the battle, the taking of the city of Teruel from the fascists, the capture of d'Harcourt and all his officers and the bishop, and the liberation of the townspeople. He pounded home the message, We're on the move, This is the beginning of a sweep of the North, Victory will be ours. Chuck had developed, Thomas noted, into a moving orator. His words poured out and swept any doubt before them. The men looked at him, transfixed. Or so it seemed to Thomas.

"He would have made a good preacher," Thomas whispered to Joey.

"Tommy, your unit moves out first." It was apparently a special honour.

T he mountain roads were treacherous. Narrow trails clinging to the hillsides. The snow and rain had washed out sections, other sections were like grease underfoot. The men plodded, slipped, fell. Burros loaded down with supplies stumbled and were tipped over the edge by their heavy loads. The trucks ground forward in low gear. A bitterly cold wind swept down from the highlands. Reports said the heavy snowfalls of the previous two weeks had abated, but in their wake the temperature had plummeted to -20°. Men were already wrapping their sleeping blankets around themselves to keep warm. The sky was a brilliant blue.

Thomas's unit of twelve men in some ways had the best of it. They were the first after the scouting parties to use the trails and roads and, if the tracks were full of unexpected danger, they were also not yet torn apart by the movement of equipment and men. Still, the clumsy Maxim machine gun had to be carried up the mountains. Even broken down into three parts, it was a constant fight to keep moving forward under its weight. The shield, although the lightest of the three sections, caught in the wind and threw the man carrying it back onto his compañeros. The cans of ammunition hung heavy on the backs of every man.

Long before they moved into the highlands just east of the city, they could hear the regular booming of artillery guns and the snap of rifles. Then, silence. Then another barrage. No sound of the dreaded German planes that had terrorized everyone on the roads as they came in low to strafe soldier and civilian alike. The winter weather had one thing in its favour; the planes were still grounded. With the pounding sounds ever closer, Thomas could feel his heart pound as well and the sweat of fear beading on his forehead. What a stupid place to be, he thought. The habitual thought came to his lips. Then: but exciting too. He could almost feel the pulsing hearts of the men slogging and slipping along the track behind him. After five hours or so, they stopped to rest in a small mountain meadow; no, meadow is too grand a name, a rocky piece of ground at the end of a ravine. Long drifts of snow streamed out from every rise. The temperature had dipped and the men huddled around their loads. A bottle of brandy passed from hand to hand.

Chuck came down the lines, talking to the men, slapping some lightly on the shoulder, cracking jokes about the coffee, encouraging them with talk of victory. "Won't be long, Tommy. I'm glad you're here with us. Looks like you're keeping that gun good and clean, Joey." Thomas felt a surge of pride in spite of himself. He patted Joey on the shoulder, but before he could turn back from seeing how his men were responding to the praise, Chuck was down the road, dispensing his seemingly unending supply of energy freely on all sides.

"He's turned into a goddamn grandstander," Thomas muttered and his spirits sank at Chuck's departure as rapidly as they had risen a moment before. His thoughts kept circling like scavenger birds: we're being led up here to die. For what? He stood apart from the men and looked up at the hills towering over them. Look at this godforsaken country. Thomas turned from the vista of rough, bare mountains to the faces of his unit. The men lay on groundsheets or hunkered down, perched on stones, smoking, talking animatedly, laughing at some joke, wanting to get into action. Wanting to die, Thomas thought. Christ, this was a mistake. A huge mistake. Thomas walked off a ways by himself and lit a cigarette. His hand trembled.

From far off they could hear cheering, rising in volume as it was picked up by closer units. Then, the sound of gears grinding down as the vehicle ploughed its way up the mountain road. Thomas and his men stood up and gathered at the side of the road to see what was coming. In a few moments, the front of the vehicle came around the last curve, spraying out the muck from the slick surface of the road. They jumped back to let the truck go by, and joined in the cheer when they saw it was an ambulance. Not any ambulance, but one of the ambulances sent over by the Communist Party from Canada. It was the pride of the battalion and manned by Canadians. The clenched fist salutes went up all along the road. The doctors and nurses waved as the ambulance passed, mud spraying out from the spinning tires.

"Let's move out! Up and at 'em!" The unit commanders lined up their men and the trek began again. Thomas turned to his men and pointed to Cass, who had ended up in his unit, "You. You take over moving the gun carriage up the rest of the hill." Cass smiled a big smile back at him and put his shoulder to the carriage. "Bastard."

CHAPTER THIRTY-FIVE

Teruel was the first city Thomas had seen torn to pieces by war; the little city in the bleak winter mountains had been shattered by weeks of heavy artillery shelling and then systematically ransacked, street by street, as the city was wrenched from the hands of the defending fascists. The extraordinary buildings of the city lay in ruins, with their unlikely patterned brick and ceramic towers still jutting into the sky. Ancient walls were filigreed by the pounding of shells and sniping bullets. Craters, rubble, dead horses not yet pulled out of the streets and squares, stinking even in the below-zero weather, doors hanging from hinges, windows smashed, and in the ruins, the people, still looking dazed as they tried to clean up the debris, setting up places to live in the skeletons of houses, scrounging enough to eat and, before all else, trying to feed the children, who ran about in the cold in bits of ill-matched clothing. And everywhere the smell of cordite and despair. Many of Thomas's men had been at Belchite and had seen worse. They knew even victory was a hollow thing for the civilian victims.

They listened to the constant sound of gunfire in the background as the fascist forces threw their weight against the republican units holding La Muela, a high ground just west of the city. Tonight under cover of darkness the Mac-Paps would move down into the valley and set up a defence to hold the valley at the base of El Muleton to the north. The German and Italian planes were now coming in waves from first morning light until the sun dropped behind the Aragonese mountains. The heavy artillery of the British battalion, dug in on the Santa Barbara cemetery hill, over-looking the battlefields in the valleys below, pounded out its answer to the not-so-distant fascist guns.

Thomas stood with Joey in what had been the Plaza del Torico; as Thomas leaned against one of the huge, pock-marked pillars along the east side of the square, a rather stupid memory came back to him of the Reverend Evans saying in his Christmas sermon, "Even a stable is not such a bad place to have to spend the night." What did the Reverend know of real poverty, of devastated lives, of war? But he must have served in the Great War. He probably had some cushy padre's job. Thomas wouldn't be here in this hellhole if the Reverend hadn't abandoned him for politics. He would have stayed and worked for the church if he had just said he wanted him to stay. But the Reverend had no time for him. Oh, no. He had to hurry off to one meeting after another, grunting goodbye or God bless as he went out the door. Thomas wasn't his wife; he didn't have to put up with that. Then Chuck had got him a job...Here, Thomas abruptly quit remembering and turned to Joey. "Let's get in the grub line."

"These poor people," said Joey.

The thirteen of them ran, scuttled would be a better word, bent over, crouching, hurrying, stumbling in the dark. There were three fixed-rifle points below the *escalinata* (a series of staircases cascading down from the city into to the valley), across to the railway tracks and then along the ditch to the building where the communications were housed. The fascists had set up permanent, mounted rifles aimed at these gaps in otherwise concealed track along which the men had to move; at each gap any movement would bring a burst of rifle fire. They manned them twenty-four hours a day, but especially at night, when the scurrying men would be less wary and often lit up suddenly and unexpectedly by a burst of artillery shelling. The rifles were firing from a distance so their accuracy was not great, but gradually they had found the range and running through these gaps was always extremely dangerous. Dragging the heavy Maxim machine guns past those points was the most nervewracking of all. Thomas went ahead, leaving Joey to run up and down the line and give the men the signal when to move forward. In spite of the intense cold, the men were sweating heavily by the time they got the gun sections and ammunition to the communications post.

Thomas bent over the map spread out on a table and lit by a coal oil lamp. Chuck stood across from him, while Reg, the military commander, pointed repeatedly to places on the map. He indicated first the key concentrations of the fascist units and then the line of defence the units of the republican regulars and the brigaders were expected to hold and advance. "Here are the Thaelmann, on El Muleton; here the British, who'll be firing over your head at the fascist positions here and here; our 2nd and 3rd companies are along here." He pointed along a westerly line, "You're here." He pointed to the mouth of a valley to the west of El Muleton. "There are three small hills there. Get behind them. You've got to have the guns set up and ready before daybreak. Your job is to stop any movement down the valley. There'll be three machine-gun posts. They will be set up here and here and here. Understood?" Thomas nodded. Shit, they were being sent right out into the open valley. He peered out the doorway into the dark.

Chuck came up beside him. "Tommy, before you go out, there's someone here you might like to see." He motioned Thomas to a back room. Thomas handed his papers over to Joey and followed. The second room was smaller and obviously served as a combination kitchen, hospital, and bedroom. At one end of the room a figure was hunched over a low cabinet, perhaps washing. "Here's Tommy, Margaret." And he left them.

"Margaret."

She stood erect and turned to him.

"Surprised?" He ran to her and took her in his arms. She struggled free of his hold and stood apart. "Whoa! Give a girl a chance." They laughed. "And Barcelona? – how long – what have you been doing – how did you get here – supplying parts – Christ, what a surprise – yeah, machine gunnery – nothing – luck." Chuck called from the doorway, "Got to move out," and Thomas moved away reluctantly, walking backward. "Right." He turned, left the room and walked over to where Joey was standing. Margaret followed him to the door and watched him turn to Chuck for instructions.

Chuck watched out the window for a few minutes, then, "Okay, let's move out." Thomas passed the command on to Joey, and Joey ducked out of the building to tell the men outside. Chuck came around the table and put his arm around Thomas's shoulders.

"Tommy, it's up to you now. Good luck." He hugged him. Jesus Christ, easy for him to say, safe in this building. With Margaret. Thomas gave him a clumsy hug back and stepped out into the night.

CHAPTER THIRTY-SIX

The hillocks were what on the prairies would have been called hills. North and east of them the Aragonese mountains towered, rising up in slow undulating levels. El Muleton towered alone and white between valleys of the dry bed of the Jiloca River and the small, winding Alfambra River. The snow in the lower reaches and in the valley was patchier than higher up. In the darkly illuminated night, it seemed to have its own light, and the men ran from shadow to shadow, from bare patch to bare patch to stay out of its luminosity. Behind the hillocks the Spanish regulars or perhaps the brigaders who arrived earlier had already dug trenches, which ran to the eastern side of El Muleton and then on to the Alfambra River, which was the only source of water for both men and machine guns. If the guns freeze up, use brandy, not water, the regulars had told them. Under Joey's direction and with the skill of northern Ontario loggers, Thomas's unit built a log buttress on either side of the machine gun, so that only the barrel stuck out, but the gun could still be manoeuvred to sweep over a wide arc of the valley in front of the hillock. The gun had to be cleaned and oiled; the ammunition set out for immediate use. The men had worked together before and knew what had to be done, but Thomas ran back and forth checking, fretting, and cursing. Jesus, we would have to pull a greenhorn – look at him – like to give him a clenched fist right up the arse – Okay? Okay, all in place – stand to – Christ's wounds, it's cold – freeze the balls off a brass monkey. Shh! You, shh! Up fuckin' yours too, whoreson (too low to be heard).

Slowly, the day began to lighten. The hour or so before dawn was the most dangerous. That was the time of attack. Into position in the dark; attack from the high ground at first light. And the heavy rumble of artillery guns pounding, pounding the hillsides, softening up the defences, literally blowing off the tops of hills; like sheet lightning, the sound of its thunder rolled down the valleys. And then nothing. Then, rifle fire, machine guns rattling somewhere behind them. The heavy British artillery now answering, firing over their heads. Christ! But nothing, nothing moved in the valley. It was if the gods were fighting it out above them and they were waiting there huddled in their trench for the divine fury to exhaust itself. Only it never did. The pounding and counter-pounding went on and on. And then the lines of planes appeared in the western sky, flying into the sun, low; first, small, fast strafing planes and then the bombers dropping their steel parcels onto roads, railway tracks, buildings, screaming in frustration when they missed, screaming in triumph when they hit, and rising straight up to expose their underside for a few minutes, long enough for a hundred guns to open up on them. A hit! Cheers rolling down from El Muleton. Then, quiet, a column of black smoke rising up from the somewhere in the valley, gently drifting off in front of the light morning breeze. The heavy guns began again.

All day long.

Thomas sat shaking with cold and fear. Joey took his turn at the gunsights. The men stamped their feet and pulled their blankets more tightly around them. Christ's wounds, it's cold. Three times during the day, Chuck arrived with coffee, food, news and his usual joking and encouraging. The Party line is that it's ambrosia; the reality is it's horse piss! But it's hot. The men held their tin cups and let the steam flow up over their stubbly faces. Come on, Tommy, we got some new reports from the front line. Thomas ducked down and, crouching, ran after Chuck back to the communications post.

"Here. Here. Here. That's where we've got to hold. Don't spare ammunition. If anything moves, blast at it. They have to be forced out into the open over here where the regulars can deal with them. The main fight is here on La Muela, but if they get a foothold in the valley, they'll pincer us. Bloody planes!" He looked up involuntarily.

Thomas looked intensely at the map. "They're gaining ground."

"Nonsense. The line's impermanent. Moves back and forth. That's why we have to hold here, so we can throw in all we've got over there." Chuck ran his fingers over the map almost caressingly, then stabbed at the key points with his index finger. "Here's where we can crush them."

"They've got thousands more where these came from."

"Tommy, listen, just this once, listen. We are going to win. Got that? We are going to win."

Thomas stood silent, staring down at the map. "Can I see Margaret again?"

"She's busy right now with the wounded from No. 3 Company."

"She's not a nurse."

"No, she's not, but she's getting men ready for the train out of here tonight."

"Where are you taking them?"

"First, Benicasim. Then, Denia. Valencia if necessary."

"Do you run them out every night?"

"Yes, long as there's no moon. Now, back to your post. I'll be by at about fifteen hours."

Fifteen hours! Instant soldier. You'd think he knew what he was talking about. He should try being in the front lines with only a few logs between him and the enemy. Thomas turned, ducked out the door and ran back to his unit.

In the late afternoon, the shadows in the valley lengthened until the sun went down over the range of mountains. The long drifts of snow held the light, but gradually the valley darkened, canopied by the blue-black of the sky. The stars seemed almost peaceful. There was a lull in the artillery fire. A rifle cracked somewhere. Few sounds. In every trench the men were on the alert to any movement in the valley. It was a good time to attack, when the night promised some respite from vigilance. The night settled in and nothing moved.

"All right, we're going for water. Both Joey and I'll go. You and you come with us. You, you, and you, stay with the gun. You, get back to the communications post and say all's well. Come on, Joey, let's go."

Bloody hell, he doesn't even know our names. Couple of poufs.

Joey hesitated. "Don't you think I better stay? So one of us is here, I mean."

"Do as I say. Bring the canteens." Thomas crouched down in the trench and started to move toward the river. It was a good ways away and the trench along its length had a number of fixed-rifle places. At each gap, they stopped and then scooted across one at a time. Each time, rifle reports and the pecking of bullets on the other side of the trench.

At the river they broke the ice and dipped in the canteens and containers. The water was black in the jagged frame of ice. Thomas thought of his father scooping water up from under the snow in the ditch at the front of the house in the springtime. His mother washing her hair at the kitchen sink in the soft water.

"That's enough. Let's get back. Move it."

They crouched down and ran to the trench, this time running more awkwardly under the load of vessels filled with water. They cleared the first gap and stopped to get their breath. At least, running warms you up. They set out again, curving around westward. Then, the next gap. First, Thomas, then the men, then Joey. A grunt. Thomas stopped with the men. "What's the trouble? What's going on back there?"

"It's Joey." Thomas pushed back along the trench to the gap. Joey lay at the bottom of the trench, tucked up in a fetal position. "Get him out of there. Pull him here." The man closest crawled back and took hold of Joey's arms. As he began to pull, he raised himself. Crack. The bullet caught him in the back and he sank to his knees. "Bloody idiot. You, pull them in here and for Christ's sake keep down." The second man grabbed the feet of the first rescuer and pulled him to safety, then caught Joey under the armpits and pulled him out. Bullets spit around the gap. Thomas stared down at the big burly man lying at his feet. He was dead. Thomas's first dead. Christ. He felt sick. It was the guy's own fault. Christ, why didn't he keep down? He moved over to Joey. Joey lay on his back, gasping for air. "Joey, where...what?"

Joey reached up and, with enormous strength, pulled Thomas down onto himself. "What the fuck..."

"Don't let me die, Tommy. My mother...Don't let me die."

"For Christ's sake, Joey, let go. Let go. Okay. You're not going to die."

"Yes, I am. Tommy, come closer. I want, I want to say something." Thomas leaned over and put his ear close to Joey's mouth. "Tommy, I want you to kiss me."

"Bloody hell."

"Please." Thomas drew back, but Joey pulled him down and kissed him full on the mouth.

"Tommy, two men lost. How in Christ's name did that happen? And one of them your second gunner. One of you was supposed to be with the gun. At all times. How often have I told you that?" Chuck was pacing up and down, his voice menacingly quiet.

Thomas stood in front of Chuck in the communications room. He stared defiantly at Chuck, then dropped his eyes.

"Christ, Tommy. You are one fuck-up, you are."

"It wasn't my fault."

"You're responsible. Two good men gone, wasted by your incompetence. Who are we going to put in as second gunner?"

"I know how to handle the gun." A woman's voice. Margaret stood at the end of the table. "I was in supply in Barcelona for awhile. We had to know how to take them apart, put them together. Had to check for parts missing. I know that gun like the back of my hand."

"No, I can't let you go out there."

"Why? Because I'm a woman?"

Chuck looked at her. Thomas continued to stare at the floor. "Okay. You're first gunner. Tommy, you're second now. Get back out there."

CHAPTER THIRTY-SEVEN

Meg carefully unlocked the drawer of the small desk under the window and drew out a small sheath of papers. She brought them over to where they were sitting and began to read.

This is my last will and testimony and a history of my life over the past ten years. It is being written primarily for you, whom I have not written to in all that time and who deserved better. I want you to know that there has not been a day in all those years that you have not been in my thoughts. There is no excuse for my having not contacted you and I want you to know how sorry I am. That cannot be corrected now, but I want you to know how those ten years were spent.

"You can see, he was very caring. He thought he was going to die and he wanted to make amends. He wanted you to know, dearie, that he cared."

"But, Meg..."

"Here, I'll let you read it." She stretched over the table and handed the papers to Clara. "Now, you just read and I'll try not to bother you. Well, unless there's something you don't understand. I'll come over there and just sit and read with you, if that's all right. It's a long time since I've read it, but I used to read it every so often."

"Meg..."

"I know you've had a little too much to drink, but it's good for you. That's what the doctors are saying now." She patted Clara's arm. "Now, I'll be quiet."

It's hard to know where to begin.

"I just added that bit because...Well, it does make it flow a little better, don't you think?"

It's hard to know where to begin. So much has happened to me. So much loss and pain. So much sorrow. It is difficult to focus my mind. It is as if just thinking about things is like a spoon stirring up thousands of memories that all seem important in some way. All swirling around. All demanding attention. What isn't important?

"Chuck was a little bit poetic, a little fanciful, wasn't he?"

We sailed for Le Havre on the 7th of July, 1937 from New York and went by train straight to Paris.

"He talked a lot about things in Canada. Things that happened before that. Freight trains and communists, a reverend somebody or other, people, walking by the lake, crocuses, oh, all sorts of things. But I couldn't put them in any order, so I just started with the trip over and let him talk until he got to interesting bits. Do you think I did the right thing?"

"Yes, my Meg, you did the right thing, the absolutely right thing. Now, I wonder if you could go and get me some Kleenex, what do you call them, tissues?"

"Of course, dearie."

After several weeks in Paris, gai Paree was not so gai. We had endless educational sessions and lessons on Spanish history and capitalism in Europe. The World Fair was on and we went out there to see it one afternoon. I keep using the term "we" but there was no one in my group whom I had known before. We weren't close yet, not as we were later as comrades-in-arms in Spain. It was early August before we set out for Spain. We were sent south in small groups and had contacts in various places en route. Secret agents were to meet us! Some secret. The villagers all knew who we were and where we were going and came out to cheer us on. They'd cluster around our contact person when we arrived, inviting us to dinner or a visit, and then raise a clenched fist to send us on our way. We Canadians were heroes to those people. It was all a bit humbling and yet we were proud to be going to fight against fascism.

My nurse is writing this down for me so I can't go on too much. I do want you to know, however, what happened. In case you hear stories. There are always many different versions of anything that happens. It's important that you hear this all from me. And believe it.

We arrived in Spain on foot. We had to cross the mountains in the dark to avoid border patrols. The Spanish government then sent us for training and we were eventually assigned to a special unit and a company. I was assigned to the machine gunnery and made head of my unit. That's like a captain in the regular army. By that time, I had got to know most of the new men and some of the veterans and we were like a family. When I left with my unit, they gave us a great send-off party. That was in December of 1937, just after Christmas, and we were sent to fight in the mountains southwest of Barcelona, to a small city named Teruel. These names will not mean much to you, I know, but you can trace them on a map when you have time.

Clara stopped, fingered the page, and looked across the room at the darkened windows. Teruel. Teruel.

"Are you all right? There, there. I know how hard it must be, dearie. Now, where are you? Oh, yes. You know sometimes he would speak with such eloquence and other times, well, it was as if he were a different person, hardly able to speak at all. He'd get all guttural, hard to understand. When that happened, I'd just write it myself, the way he would have said it if he weren't talking that way, if you see what I mean."

"Yes, Meg. I wonder if maybe I could read this on my own."

"Oh, dear, I've been talking too much, haven't I? That's what we old spinsters are like though, dearie. We don't talk to anybody for days, then we just babble."

"I'm...I didn't mean...It's just...Well, maybe another small drink and then we can read on."

"Do you really think you should? I'm just asking because, well, I am old enough to be your mother, and it seems to me you've had enough."

"No. Please. I would like another. Okay?" Clara turned the page.

"Oh, I see. Yes, I understand. You need something. I shouldn't be such an old fuddy-duddy. You just keep reading and I'll pour you another." Meg got up and reached for Clara's glass.

I had twelve men under me and we were a smooth-working machine by the time we were assigned to the front. My job was to stop any offensive by the fascists that threatened the city from the north. I should say the city had been held by the fascists, but we had retaken it, over Christmas. A cold Christmas even for us from the prairies. And snow, which I guess you wouldn't usually associate with Spain. Many of us got frostbite; some died of the cold. I don't know, counting the civilians, perhaps as many died from cold as from bullets. Be glad you are safe on the prairies, far from the horrors of war, safe from this war too.

Well, my dear sister, this is not the place to boast,

but you should know that the family's honour was upheld in the terrible battle for Teruel. My unit was on the front line and we held against incredible odds. They threw everything they had against us. We fought to the last man. I only escaped because I was wounded and had to be evacuated just before the city fell to the fascists. We lost the battle but we fought like demons. My heart aches to say it, but every man in my unit was killed. I was later given what the Spaniards call "prueba de corage," that is, a proof of courage, and I had the names of all those men inscribed on the back of it. It was one of my most treasured possessions until I lost it in the flight to France the next year.

"Oh, Chuck." Clara started to weep and then sob uncontrollably.

"There, there. You poor dear. How you must be suffering. But he was a brave man in war, no matter what he was like otherwise, don't you agree?"

"Yes, very brave. I didn't know any of this. He never..." She blew her nose and tried to stop the flow of tears. "He never told me." Meg handed her the glass filled with a good shot of whiskey. "Thank you, Meg."

"Of course, dearie." She talked over her shoulder as she poured a whiskey for herself. "Well, these things are not things they like to talk about. Terrible memories, comrades wounded and killed. The savagery of men. Maybe he would never have said these things if he hadn't thought he was going to die. Well, I didn't really think he would live and so I wrote down what he told me, in good order of course. Well, not everything. He told me some pretty tart things. Anyway, he made me swear to send this off to you when he died. Though how he thought I could…But, then, he didn't die after all, so no matter. They were hard times and he was so alone. This Margaret. She must have been someone very special. He would mumble her name in his sleep and, sometimes, he would weep. He trusted me, and, well, I was a nurse, and perhaps he thought I would understand. But I just left some things out. Here's your drink."

"Oh, Meg." Clara turned and hugged Meg. "Meg, I've been misleading you. You'll have to know this sooner or later. I'm – I was – his wife."

Meg stopped patting Clara's back and just sat there for a few moments. Then, she said very quietly, "There, there. You're tired. Perhaps that's enough for tonight. I've made up a bed for you."

"Oh, I can't. I mean, I have a room at the hotel in, in whatever that town is, with the bridge."

"Yes. Yes, I'll phone them. Now, you just come with me." Meg helped Clara up and led her to the little guest bedroom. "There's everything you'll need there and you know where the bathroom and toilet are." Clara sat down heavily on the edge of the bed. Meg turned back at the door. "We old fools rattle on without thinking. Don't pay any attention to me. He was a brave man and…well, those were hard times."

"Oh, Meg, you are so good to me, aren't you?" Clara tried to stand up again, but fell back onto the bed. Meg covered her with a blanket.

CHAPTER THIRTY-EIGHT

A t the doorway, Meg turned and looked at her somnolent guest. Clara had fallen asleep immediately. The little sitting room was darkening into evening. Meg picked up the pages she had kept so carefully in the desk drawer and put on the light over the sofa. She sat and read the familiar words.

They evacuated us to Valencia where there was a good hospital and a villa outside the city where we could recuperate. I remember the gardens and the roses blooming. My wound was serious and by the time I was well enough to go back to the front, word was out that we, those of us in the International Brigade, were to be sent home. The fascists had broken through at Teruel and then Ebro and the Spanish Government arranged with the CPR to transport us out of the country and back home. None of us wanted to leave before the fighting was finished. But that is war. You never know what will be expected of you. All of us felt a tremendous sense of past and, in an odd way, future loss.

We left by boat to Barcelona, stayed there until the early part of 1939 and then walked back to France. There we were put on a train which was sealed so we could not leave it and were sent straight through to Paris. We were all mixed up together. I found I was travelling with British brigaders, so I didn't know anyone on the train. But, even as I contemplated the loss of so many friends and fellow brigaders, the thought of going home and seeing you all again was uppermost on my mind. The trip seemed endless. And then they sent us on to England. That was February, 1939.

Why did I not come home? A question I have asked myself again and again. The ship was waiting; I had a ticket in my pocket. Certainly, my heart was pulling me away from Europe and to home. But a voice in my head kept saying to me, You've come to Europe to fight the fascists and the fascists are stronger than ever. I waited and watched. My wound needed time to heal. In Germany, the Nazis were growing bolder by the day. The people of Britain knew that appeasement was not working. I couldn't leave the job half-done. I had to stay and see it through. Can you understand that? Sometimes, there are things more important than family, friends, love, even country.

In effect, I delayed returning day by day, week by week, month by month, until war on Germany was finally declared. I was a prime candidate for recruitment. I was a veteran, trained for war, young, idealistic.

I knew the enemy, had fought against them, hated them. I joined the British commandoes and then transferred to the Royal Winnipeg Rifles. I wanted to be in the thick of the fighting. I was prepared to die if that was what was needed to stop the Germans.

I was with the Rifles when the regiment landed on the beaches of Normandy. Not many of us survived that assault. Those of us not killed were wounded. And although I survived and was brought back to England, I am not long for this world, as the Reverend would have said. But I want you to know that we died fighting for what we believed in, against an enemy that can only be described as evil incarnate. You may hear all sorts of stories, but please accept this account by a dying man as an attempt to tell you what has happened.

So, my dear sister, that is my story. I have asked the nurse to send this to you when I die, which will not be long, I think. She has looked after me as no one else could have. With such love. Her name is Margaret Stanhope and I have grown to love her in return. My regret is that it is too late. I would have liked to have brought her home to meet you. It will be hard for the people of these islands after this conflict is finally resolved. If she ever is in need for anything, I hope you will come to her assistance.

Remember me to little Peter. Tell him that his uncle thought of him fondly.

God bless.

He hadn't wanted to give his sister's name and address, though. Kept saying he would tell her "when the time came." Well, it never came. So here she was, and none the wiser about where to send this. She might have guessed that Clara was no sister, coming all this way to ask after him. Just the little sparrow of a wife he complained about. Likely his real sister was long dead.

Meg read to the end the pages she had so often read. She sat quietly on the sofa, finishing Clara's drink and, then, with a sigh, she gathered up the pages. She held them carefully, smoothing out the creases, which by now had cut and erased parts of words. She had loved him, from the beginning. Had she really thought his mistaking her for the other Margaret would someday be a transference of love as well? No, he seemed to have been incapable of loving anyone deeply. That was clear. She walked over to the desk, picked up a box of matches and went to the fireplace. Stooping down, she laid the top papers on the grate and lit fire to them, one by one. Just a dream. She took the last page, folded it, and pushed it down into the pocket of her apron.

"The past is always, in part, a lie," she whispered to the flames.

CHAPTER THIRTY-NINE

Chuck sat back on his haunches in the trench and peered out between the logs. "It's too quiet. Something's brewing out there." It was early morning, but light. The men of Thomas's, now Margaret's unit, waited. Chuck turned to them and Margaret, perhaps deliberately excluding Thomas, perhaps just focused on the job that had to be done. "You've seen this all before. How do they set up their offensives?"

"Diversionary. They set up an attack in one place and then pour everything they've got into another. Bastards!"

"Do you think they'll come in from this side?"

"Why would they do that?" Thomas asserted his presence.

Margaret turned to him. "Because the railway line is directly behind us. Because the communications centre is here. Because this would distract our forces from La Muela. Because this is the quickest way into the city." Chuck nodded his head as she spoke.

"Okay, you're the key post. You have to hold. Your flanks can look after any side action and set up some crossfire. But it's up to you. Right! *Buen suerte.*" Chuck slipped over the edge of the trench and ran back to the communications building.

"We haven't seen hide nor hair of them so far. Why would they suddenly decide to attack here?" Thomas fiddled with his belt and holstered revolver.

"Tiny, Kalle, Nik. You stay on that side, so you can feed the gun directly. Karlo, Niilo, Cass. You get on the other side. I want you to cover those ammunition tins in case we get a direct hit. Red and Eli. You stay with me. Is the gun cleaned and oiled? You're also responsible for cleaning and oiling the gun. Every day. You hear? Tommy, you get over there and be ready to spell me off. Boys, I've got a gut feeling he's going to give us some action today." Odd how they referred to the Nationalists as "he." As if it were just one man.

The men moved quickly into place and, stamping to keep warm, took turns watching the valley. Mother of God, it's a beautiful day.

The attack was more sudden and more bizarre than anyone could have imagined. It came mid-morning, just after the coffee had been delivered. Cups were dropped, men scrambled back to their positions. The hot spilt liquid steamed up from the frozen ground of the trench.

Christ! They're on horseback.

Down the valley, far in the distance, and then rapidly moving in a long line up the dried riverbed, spreading out as they approached, Moorish horsemen charged toward the machine guns nestled in their parapets. Their shouting and rifle fire echoed and re-echoed down the valley. "Don't fire! Wait! Wait, until they're closer. Wait until they're almost on top of us." Margaret set Thomas behind the gun and hurried along the trench, checking, patting the men on the backs. "Jesus, they're sitting ducks." Bububububu. "Tommy, I told you to wait." Bubububbu. Thomas had pulled the trigger in his nervousness and let off a round by accident. Margaret ran to the gun, pushed Tommy aside and swung the gun onto the advancing horses.

Line after line of horsemen charged and were cut down by the streams of bullets from the three machine guns. Horses reared and fell; men screamed. Then another line, trampling on the one before it. "More water! Keep this goddamn gun cool." Nik turned toward her, a surprised look on his face, and fell face down into the trench, blood seeping out and steaming on the ground. "Behind that horse." Margaret raked the ground and the dead horse. A man behind the horse rose up as if to speak and then fell back. "Got him. See to Nik. See to Nik."

There was no let-up. Horsemen who tried to turn back were shot at from behind. The machine gun in No. 1 placement overheated and seized up. "Kalle, get down there and see if you can get that gun going again." A grenade arced slowly through the air toward them. "Get down." It landed harmlessly in front of the trench, spraying dirt and snow into the air. Margaret shook her head and swung the gun onto the place where the grenade had come from. Another from the other side. This time, a direct hit. The hurriedly constructed parapet around the gun collapsed and fell back into the trench. Their right side was exposed; now they had to almost lie down to keep out of the line of fire. No. 3 placement, though, kept up such a steady fire that the horsemen, scrambling to get under cover, couldn't take advantage of it. Not yet. But Margaret knew they were easy targets now. Every time they raised up, rifles cracked and bullets picked at the dirt around the trench. Cass, Eli, Niilo fell. Margaret was protected by the Maxim's shield and she kept the gun swinging back and forth over the battlefield. "Thomas, for Chrissake, the ammunition! Get over there!" Thomas crawled over near where the men lay and started to feed the belts into the gun. "Not that way. Lift them up. Straight in. That's it. Tiny, can you give him a hand? Red, you take the gun for awhile." Margaret turned back from the gun nursing one hand. It was burnt and already red. She poured some water over it and tied the scarf from her neck around it. As she went to pull over another ammunition case, she twisted in pain. The bullet caught her in the shoulder and spun her around and against the wall of the trench. "Margaret. Margaret, are you hurt?" Thomas clambered along the trench to her. "Get back. Get back. Get back to the gun, you stupid bastard." Thomas stopped and looked at her, started back. The gun fell silent. Only No. 3 placement kept up its steady din. Margaret stood up and stumbled back to the gun. Another bullet grazed across her neck and she cried out, but stayed on her feet. "Get out of the way!" She placed her boot on Thomas's chest and shoved him backwards. "Red, feed it. Feed it." She took the gun again and raked down a half-dozen men who thought the gun was knocked out and were running toward the trench. Blood coursed down her coat. "Margaret." Thomas was weeping and trying to hold her. She shook him off. "Get off, you fucking coward."

What had seemed minutes had taken hours and the darkness was already settling. The horsemen who were still alive, if there were any, stayed hidden and the two machine guns still operable, quieted. Margaret slumped over the gun. Tiny had been hit by the shrapnel from a grenade and most of one side of his face and head had been torn off. Red lay moaning beside Margaret. Thomas crouched behind, holding himself and shaking. Night fell, and with it came the steady noise in the valley of reinforcements being moved up. "Go down to No. 3 and see what's happened there." Margaret's voice was barely above a whisper. "Go!" Thomas scrabbled down the trench, trying to avoid stepping on the bodies of the men who had fallen. He returned in a few minutes. "Dead. They're all dead." "Did you bring back some ammunition?" "No." "Christ. Oh, God. Chuck, where are you?" Thomas's hand shook as he tried to help Margaret back from the gun. "Chuck," she whispered and lost consciousness.

CHAPTER FORTY

Clara had awoken the next morning with a splitting headache. The first thing she'd heard was the clatter of pans and dishes from the kitchen and a small, high voice singing "Greensleeves". She had looked around for her clothes and found them all neatly folded on a chair at the end of the bed with a bathrobe draped over the back. There was a towel, facecloth, soap, and even some body lotion on the small table under the window. And an aspirin. It was not until she had finished washing and dressing that she had gone out to the sitting room and, almost as if guided, walked over to the fireplace and found the remains of the charred pages. She felt angry, betrayed. What right...?

"Crazy old bat!" Clara was driving on the M1, fast, headed back to London. Stupid woman! Jealous. She's jealous that someone else would weep for her lost love. She was jealous that I had been his wife and not her. I shouldn't have told her I was his wife. That's what upset the apple cart.

Clara swerved around a truck in the middle lane, gunned the car into the fast lane and back into the middle lane.

Dried-up old spinster, living out her fantasies with my husband. Chuck, Chuck, what in hell were you thinking of, talking to that, that woman? She just kept that story for her own selfish reasons. What'd she care, all snug in her goddamn little cottage, making the bloody vicar tea every afternoon. Clara drummed on the steering wheel and pressed the accelerator. She was travelling too fast. She knew it. And now, his sister would die and never...Clara grabbed the steering wheel. My dear sister...? Clara swerved to miss a car. Horns blared all around her. She forgot she was driving on the left side of the road and, braking a bit, yanked the car over into the right lane, thinking to get into the slower traffic. She had to think. A black car, coming fast, loomed into her rear-view mirror, and she tried to spin the car over into the middle lane again. A huge lorry, brakes squealing, caught the front of her car and lifted it into the air and over onto its roof in the fast lane. Her car flipped over again and leapt the guardrail, coming to rest on the thin strip of lawn separating the east-west traffic.

When she opened her eyes, she saw three Sidneys looking down at her from what seemed like a great height. "Oh, Sidney..."

"Don't try to talk." He held her hand and gently caressed it. "You're going to be all right. You were a very lucky girl." Tears came to his eyes. "I'm very lucky. I don't know what I would have done if you...Anyway, you are going to be fine."

"Wha..."

"Your car flipped over and you were caught upside down behind the wheel. Fortunately, an ambulance was going by on the other side and picked you up right away."

"What..."

"You have a broken jaw, two broken ribs and a broken leg. But the good news is, you have no internal injuries. We'll get you back to Canada, as soon as they let you go."

"Oh..." She fell back asleep.

"No, Sidney. Let me do it myself."

"All right. You must be feeling better. You're your old cantankerous self."

"I'm not cantankerous. I just want to do this myself."

"I was not finished. Your old cantankerous self, that I love more than God's own sandals."

"Sidney, that's blasphemous."

"Well, what do you think he wears?"

Silence.

"Are you thinking about that?"

"No, I'm trying to make this fucking walker go."

"Clara. I've never heard you say such words before."

"Well, you're going to hear more of it. I'm sick and tired of being the dupe. From now on I'm running my own show."

Silence.

"Are you thinking about that?"

"Clara, I was thinking two things. First, that I love you, and second, that as long as I've known you, you have been running your own show. And mine too, for that matter."

"Have I?" Clara looked genuinely surprised. "Have I?"

CHAPTER FORTY-ONE

Thomas lifted himself carefully up to see over the remains of the parapet; nothing in the valley moved that he could see. In the blackness, he groped his way back to where Margaret lay. She had slipped further down into the trench behind the gun. Thomas raised himself carefully again and looked out past the shield. He swung the gun, sweeping the valley width. Nothing. It was dark except for the occasional patch of snow that had not been torn up in the battle. No movement; sounds far off. The silence now seemed as unnatural and threatening as the tumult of the past hours had before. He turned away and bent down to Margaret.

Her breathing was heavy and laboured. He felt for the pulse at her neck and felt only the thick blood already coagulating. "Margaret." She stirred and by passing his hand over her face, he could tell that she had opened her eyes. "Don't die, Margaret. Please, don't die." He struggled with her body, lifted her and held her in his arms. He tried to cover her with a blanket tangled up at her feet. "Please, don't die."

"Tommy," Her voice was barely audible. "Go to Chuck. Tell him. Tell him..."

"For Chrissake, Margaret, I can't."

"Tell him, I love, love him."

"You love me. You love me."

"No."

"Yes, you love me."

"Never forget."

"Forget. I'll never forget. You know I'll never forget. Please, don't die."

"Forget what you did."

"What did I do?"

"Betrayed."

"I never betrayed you. I never. Am I not still here at your side? It was you betrayed me."

"Kill me."

"What? What? I can't...No, no.

"That's an order. I want to die. Oh, Chuck, is that you?"

"It's me. Tommy. Chuck's dead."

"No."

"Margaret, Margaret. He doesn't love you. I love you."

"I hope..."

"I'm here. I am. I'll never leave you."

"I hope you burn in hell."

Thomas let her fall back. He stared at her dark form in disbelief, looked up at the sky, down the black slit of the trench. He was all alone.

"Margaret, don't leave me." He touched her cheek and felt the weight of her head fall on his outstretched hand. He put his hand under her head and held her like a wounded doll.

"I can't."

She lay quite still, her breathing very slow now, a sort of hissing of air and then gasps. She reached out and grabbed hold of Thomas's coat. "Order you."

He drew his revolver and reached around her head until he felt the slight depression at the back of her skull. He placed the barrel against her wound, hesitated, closed his eyes and fired. Her hand gripped and then let go of his coat.

Along the road running parallel to the river, the men had dug out caves where they could take turns sleeping between watches. *Cuevas.* They were dug out of the soft, red stone and soil, some of them quite elaborate with stairs going down into a room. Others were just holes dug far enough into the mountainside to hold a man and his equipment. They called them home. Their dark spaces were empty now. Thomas had half carried, half dragged Margaret's body along the trench, ignoring the fixed-rifle gaps, which, in any case, elicited no rifle fire now. Once on the protected side of the mountain, he lifted her body up onto the edge of the trench and then clambered out into the still night. He bent down and picked her up and carried her in his arms to the *cueva* closest to the road. He laid her inside, folding her arms over her chest and straightening out her legs. He knelt beside her trying to make out her face in the dark. He lit a match. The orange glare bounced off the walls of the cave. She looked as if she was sleeping peacefully. He reached and pushed up her jaw to close her mouth. He tied it closed with his handkerchief. Then, he lay down beside her, close, body to body, and closed his eyes.

How long? When he arose from her side, the night was silent. No gunfire, no shouts. He reached out to touch Margaret, but she didn't respond. He shook her shoulder. He knew she loved him. She did. It was just the war. He bowed his head and thought about praying. But, there was no god. He was sure of that.

Thomas backed out of the cave. He stumbled back, tearing at his hair and twisting this way and that. He sank down to the ground and curled up at the side of the road. He was a dog at his mistress's feet. His thoughts just stopped and then...Bitch. That's what she was. I...She...Gradually, the cold penetrated his awareness and he got awkwardly to his feet. It was still dark, but now there were sounds in the valley, coming closer. Engines. Tanks. Overhead the batteries of artillery from both sides started up again. Thomas stood, undecided what to do. He had dropped his revolver in the trench somewhere, and now his hand unwillingly fingered the empty holster. Served her right. He began to walk toward the city. Flames outlined the remains of its buildings against the eastern sky. Then he remembered the ambulance train.

CHAPTER FORTY-TWO

When Thomas reached the railway tracks, he was thrown into a melee of men trying to get the wounded onto stretchers and the stretchers into the train cars. The large white circles with red crosses on the railway carriages stood out in the low light. Figures came out of and went into the darkness. But it was all carried out in a strange, whispered quiet. For all the confusion no one seemed to bump into anyone else, everyone seemed to know where they were going and what they were supposed to be doing. From where he stood, he could see something of how the movement of the wounded was being organized. The critical cases first, then down the line to those who could still partly look after themselves. He stepped back into the shadows to be less conspicuously idle. He realized that he had to get onto the train. It was the only way out. The body would be found. It was murder, not war. He had killed her. She asked him to. Who would believe that? He was numb with some deep, internal hurt.

Across from him and near the end of the carriages, new arrivals were being laid out for the doctors to examine. Thomas watched as the doctors ran from this task to the job of bandaging and sedating, and then back to deal with the next batch of wounded. Some of the men laid out had been crudely bandaged at the front. Others bled quietly or held scraps of cloth torn from some part of their clothing over wounds. Some lay still.

Thomas crossed over to the carriages to a place near the wounded men who, he thought, had not been examined yet, and realized that the ones by the end of the train, who lay so still, were in fact those who had been pronounced dead already. *Los fiambres.* The cold cuts. He waited for an opportunity and then bent over one of the dead and carefully removed a blood-soaked bandage from the man's head. The blood was cold now and the bandage stiff with sweat. Crouching down, he carefully wrapped the bandage around his own head. He pulled one side down partially over his left eye and felt to make sure the rest of the bandage was snug around his head.

He then went through the man's pockets and found some cheese and bread wrapped in a cloth. He stuffed the package into his pocket. Then, inside the man's jacket pocket, Thomas felt his passport. He took it out and laid it carefully on top of the body. He looked quickly up and down the train, took the passport out of his own pocket and slipped it into the jacket of the dead man. Thomas picked up the pilfered passport and flipped through it. A piece of paper fell out. It was too dark to make out what it was, so he shoved it with the passport into his own pocket. Thomas Pennan was dead. He patted the pocket and stepped back into the shadow. Dead. He was someone else. He didn't know who.

He slipped under a coupling between the carriages to the other side of the train. Here no one was in sight and he walked up to the side of one of the carriages near the engine. The doors were propped open. He climbed up the stairs and went through the right-hand door into the front carriage. It was full of men, some laid out on stretchers piled above one another, some sitting on benches, some even smoking. No one seemed to pay any attention to Thomas as he sat down on the floor. Then, "Here. There's room here. Shove over you guys." American voice. Thomas slowly raised himself from the floor and took a place on the bench and leaned his head back, pretending to be in such pain that he should be left alone. No one really wanted to talk anyway.

Later, much later, the train shunted back and forth and then hissed its way out of the chaos and into the night. The unfamiliar rocking of the train drew moans and gasps of pain as the men's bodies were jerked and shifted from positions in which they had been rigidly holding themselves.

It was a night of starts, stops, long waits in the pitch-black. No lights allowed. Blankets over the windows. The wooden slats of the bench cut into Thomas's thighs but he did not dare move. The man next to him had fallen asleep and his head rested on Thomas's upper arm. Thomas looked down at him, at his drooping face, two-week stubble, his big hands hanging uselessly between his legs. Thomas stared at him closely. There was no doubt. He resembled Margaret. He could have been her brother. Her father. Thomas wanted to touch his face, to wake him. No, he mustn't think about it.

Suddenly, the train gained speed. The wheels clattered over the unmaintained tracks; the carriages rocked and banged; loose pieces of equipment, odds and ends of hospital paraphernalia slid back and forth along the runnelled floorboards. Thomas gripped the edge of the bench to steady himself so the sleeping man would not feel the jarring so much. And then, just as suddenly, hissing steam, the train came to a stop. Silence. Shouts. Men running alongside the train. Carriage doors opened and slammed shut again. Thomas listened to the fragments of Spanish. *Prisa!* The track was out and had to be repaired. *Prisa!* The men in the carriage started to stir. Some stood up and cautiously stretched. One man in the corner moaned. A couple of men in the stretchers lay suspiciously still. Thomas felt panic rise in him. He had to get out of there. Away. He had to get home. He carefully pushed the man next to him upright. The man lurched the other way and then forward, face down, onto the carriage floor. The back of his jacket was black and wet with blood.

As several men tried clumsily to turn the man over, Thomas stood up and edged toward the carriage door. He pushed back the door and felt the cold night air rush in. A couple of men looked up but bent back to their tasks or their sufferings. Thomas stepped out and quietly closed the door behind him. He leaned out, looked up and down the track and then jumped clear of the train. He rolled and stumbled down the embankment and came to rest against a low stone wall. Above him the long, dark shape of the train stretched out against the night sky, the white circles on the carriages gleaming faintly in the small reflections and glimmerings of light.

CHAPTER FORTY-THREE

Chuck desperately ran back and forth along the lines of No. 2 Company, relaying the tactical instructions and organizing parties to bring in the wounded. Now, at a momentary break in the shelling, he peered out of the besieged communications building. There was no way to get out to the machine-gun nests. They were stranded in the midst of a raging battle. But they were holding. The rattling of the guns was constant, then one failed. The other two kept up the fire, stopped, started up again. Then only one. Then, silence. Above, the heavy artillery hammered away. A brigader ran in from the back door.

"They're knocked out. They're knocked out."

Chuck grabbed him by his jacket and yelled in his face. "Who? Where?"

"They've knocked out the machine-gun posts."

"Follow me." Chuck ducked and ran out toward the hillocks where the machine guns were now silent. He drew his pistol and crouched behind a low wall, what was left of a low wall. A shadow moved. He took aim and followed it as it made its way down past the first machine-gun post. It stooped and held up something that gleamed in the starlight for a moment. The bastard was going through the pockets of the dead. Chuck fired. The figure pirouetted on the edge of the hillock and fell. Silence. "Come on. We're going down there."

Chuck and the brigader scuttled down the slope, keeping in the shadows, avoiding being silhouetted against the snow. But no one else moved. The scene of the ferocious battle was quiet, almost peaceful. In the distance, the dark shapes of the horses and men that had tried to swarm the machine-gun posts looked like rocks and debris. As if they had rolled down from the mountain.

In the trench and shattered wooden nests the brigaders had built, the bodies lay, seemingly thrown this way and that. Thrown away. One still had his finger on the trigger of the machine gun. It now pointed at the stars. Another had fallen over a case of ammunition he had been carrying. Red, Kalle, Niilo, Cass. Where were Margaret and Thomas? Chuck held up his hand to stop his companion from coming any closer and then looked up and down the trench. He scrabbled down the trench a ways. No one. No one alive.

"Okay, let's get outta here." Chuck turned and practically pulled the other man up the slope and back to the communications building. He stopped by the table and scooped up the maps and ran for the back door. The hospital train was a distance away, but there seemed, strangely enough, to be no gunfire. The dead and wounded were being carried to the train from every side. Chuck ran up to a man with a Red Cross band on his arm, who seemed to be in charge, and pointed back to the valley. "There's some dead back there."

"We're trying to look after the wounded. The dead will have..."

"Get them. I said, get them. We're not leaving them here."

"Yes, sir."

La Muela had fallen. Had it? No. Yes. The Nationalist army was on the move. He'd be there before dawn. The artillery had started up again. There was no holding out. Retreat. The word was out everywhere. Retreat. Chuck searched and found as many of the men from his unit as he could and started collecting food and ammunition. Fourteen men. Chuck led them around the city and out onto the road they had come by such a short time before. The fascists were now close, keeping up a constant barrage, rumbling their tanks into position, strafing the hillsides.

Before the march to Teruel, one of the reconnaissance groups Chuck had sent out had spotted an old medieval fort on a hill overlooking the valley. It had been abandoned perhaps hundreds of years ago, but its walls were still standing and so were the stone tunnels leading up through the hill and underground to what had been a courtyard. It commanded a view of the entire plain to the west. At the time, he had marked its location on the creased map he always carried in the inside pocket of his leather jacket. Just in case. Now, he counted on its thick walls to assure that at least no rifle fire could penetrate. They'd be safe for a couple of days. When the fighter bombers found out where they were, it would not take long to drive them out, but if they could slow "him" up, give the boys a chance to get back. If...

They set up camp in the ruins of the building and began a twenty-four-hour watch from the walls. Already the next day, Chuck could see with his binoculars the distant movement of the nationalist troops. It was an orderly, relentless movement across the plain, an army now sure of victory, carefully sweeping everything before them. No hurry. Behind, in the interminable hills and valleys separating them from the coast, the remnant of the republican army and what was left of his Mac-Paps were fleeing, digging in, fighting, fleeing, digging in, dying.

On the third day, the planes appeared, splayed out, searching for their targets. Line after line of them. They soon found the hilltop castle, and the one lightweight Lewis gun and the motley collection of rifles and pistols could do little to stop them. The planes came in so close they could see the pilots, some grim, some smiling, leaning back as they pulled out of their dives. They wheeled and strafed, wheeled and strafed. The little Lewis hammered away, and although a number of German planes went back to base with rows of bulletholes in their fuselages, none fell from the sky.

"Bill, let's get out of here. Get the men together. Fill the water bottles first. Come on. Move. Move." Chuck and Kroker herded the men like sheepdogs, running back and forth behind them, picking up dropped helmets and water bottles that had been left behind. "Go. Go."

They ran down the ancient tunnels, which came out on the far side of the hill. At the entrance to the tunnels, there were four men from another unit, cowering, not knowing what to do. Chuck waved them to follow and pushed the men, one by one, out, to run zigzagging across the open area to the brush and hills behind. As soon as they broke into the open, the planes started in. However, the game of hide-and-seek was not a game planes played very well, and they soon broke and headed back to their base. Chuck and his bedraggled bunch of men made camp beside a small frozen pond about three miles from the hill fort. One of the men had a thermometer in his pack. Who knows why. It read -22°.

The fascist army moved in behind the planes, spreading out and methodically destroying each rearguard action set up to stop them. Chuck's small group of men managed to dig in and hold off the advancing army for awhile, as long as they could, and then they fled further eastward and dug in again. Each time a few more of them were killed or wounded, but they slowed the advance. Dozens of other small groups were doing the same thing. The toll on the men was devastating, their fight desperate. The cry of Madrid was still on their lips: *"Non pasaran."* They shall not pass. They shall not pass. The cry was futile, and each of them knew it, but each of them assured the others that these bloody fascist pigs would not pass. *Tierra y Libertad!*

CHAPTER FORTY-FOUR

Thomas lay against the wall, the stones cold and uncomfortable at his back, but he dared not move. Men ran up and down the tracks, shouting orders, pulling pieces of track into place. He slowly unwrapped the bandage from his head and dropped it in the snow. More blood. He fell forward and vomited. He leaned back again and the scene in front of him began to blur. He wiped his eyes. Who's that? He stared at the train. There between the carriages. It was, it was Margaret. He looked harder. She stepped back and then reappeared, suddenly, at the next opening. She was looking for him. He scrunched down and covered his face with his arm. Waited. He looked again. She was coming toward him. She was at the edge of the embankment. He could see the blood running down her face. He stuffed the bandage into his mouth to stop from crying out. Hide.

The light woke him. He lay where he had the night before. It was day, barely, early morning. No train. He stared around him, at the vomit in the snow. A sound. He looked quickly along the wall. A dog stood at an opening in the wall, looking at him. It had the bloody bandage at its feet. It growled quietly. Thomas tried to move his legs. They were numb. He pulled them out in front of him like puppet sticks. The dog moved toward him, growling, crouched to spring. Thomas cowered down, put his arm up to protect his face. A whistle. The dog stopped, cocked its ears, and ran back to the opening. Thomas tried to get up, but couldn't move the lower half of his body. He closed his eyes, opened them, thought he saw a man standing near the wall. He sighed and reached out, slipped into the darkness again.

The candle moved around the foot of the bed. Thomas watched it carefully until it was right beside him. An old face in the candlelight looked down at him and smiled. *"Está despierto. Vengas. Vengas aquí."* Another old face looked down at him. Uriel. The name of the archangel swirled into Thomas's mind and sounded over and over. Uriel. He said it aloud. "Uriel." Then, again. The two faces looked at each other and repeated the word: "Uriel." They nodded and smiled. "Uriel." They pointed to him. "Uriel." Smiled. He lifted a hand and tried to clench his fist. *"Si. Si."* The old man lifted his hand, clenched his fist in a small salute and said. "Trotsky." The name of what? Thomas thought he knew but he couldn't remember. He said, "Uriel," again. Nodding their heads, the couple intoned, "Uriel. Uriel."

In the morning, Thomas managed to swing his legs out of bed and put his bandaged, well-wrapped feet down onto the floor. The woman rushed in, protesting, but Thomas slowly raised himself to his feet and, leaning on the woman, took a step. The pain stabbed, but he took another. He had to get away.

"Where is Margaret?"

The woman looked at him blankly and shook her head. Thomas shifted over to his limited Spanish, and the woman still looked at him blankly. She called to her husband in the other room and he came to the doorway. Thomas asked him, too, where Margaret was, and he just held up his clenched fist and said, "Trotsky," again. No. Margaret. Margarita. Thomas tried to stumble toward the man but fell onto the end of the bed. The man rushed over and helped him to his feet. The two old people, peasants, smelling strongly of barn and sheep, walked slowly on either side of him and led him out to the other room that served as kitchen and eating room. The windows and door were in ruins and the brisk air filled the room. Thomas smelled the pungent odour of herbs. Mrs. Kruger, across the road, she had picked herbs on the prairie. Wild garlic. There was only one chair and the couple carefully lowered him down onto it. The dog stood in the doorway opening. Now, he was wagging his tail.

In the distance, Thomas could hear the pop, pop of gunfire. So far away. A dream. He looked out at the long, sloping field of snow in front of the hut. Where were the herbs? He searched the room and spotted them hanging in clumps from the ceiling posts. Like hanged angels. The old couple started to talk, taking turns, talking over each other, excited, sad, questioning. Thomas looked from one to the other, understanding some of what they said. They were socialist, but they were not going to let them collectivize their farm. No, that's not right. That's not socialism. That's...That's...They hid their sheep. After they came and took their burro, they hid everything. Thomas nodded off, woke, nodded off. The old man and woman got him some soup with herbs in it and fed him with a tin spoon.

The next morning, the gunfire was closer. The old couple were frightened. They came into the bedroom, distraught. You have to go. You can't stay here. They're coming. Up the valley. They're coming. You can't stay. They pulled on his arms. The old man had brought in his clothes, all washed and dry. Hurry. Hurry. They're coming. Drone of planes. Thomas staggered to his feet and let the couple dress him. They rebound his feet and tied his boots together so he could carry them. Hurry, Uriel.

In the kitchen they handed him his package of bread and cheese and cut off half of a round cheese sitting on the table. Take this. Take it. They ran to the opening where the door had been. They're coming! The sounds of gunfire were louder. The man and his wife huddled by the front door, watching, holding each other. They were old and frightened. Thomas hobbled over to where they were standing and looked. He remembered guns pounding. Before. A long time ago. The booming of artillery pieces was almost comforting. Insistent. You can't resist. Relax. Boom. Boom. And, then, the distant drone of planes.

Far down the slope, filling the road at the bottom of the hill, were refugees. Lines as far as the eye could see. Where were they going? Thomas moved to the back of the house and stuffed the cheese into a leather bag hanging on the end of the bed. As he bent over to pick up his boots, he heard the drone of the planes suddenly closer. He grabbed the bag and boots and thumped into the other room on his bandaged feet. He saw the three lines of planes start down and then strafe the fleeing, terrified people on the road. People fell or rolled into the ditch. One plane veered up and dipped toward the hut. It past over once, low, and then circled, diving down with its engines screaming. The bullets spattered the snowy field like a heavy rainstorm. The dog stood looking up, turned to run and twisted into an arc as the bullets hit him. The old couple stood at the door looking straight into the flashing wings. Thomas fell to the floor, but the bullets strafed the couple huddled at the doorway and ripped holes through the tin roof above his head.

As soon as the plane had wheeled off and disappeared, Thomas pulled himself up. Dead. Everybody died. He put both hands on the table and leaned. Was he dead? He felt his forehead. No. He rushed over to the bodies of the old ones. Bundles of clothes. Dead. But, he wasn't guilty. He hadn't killed them. He...Thomas grabbed his head and stared around the room. They'll say I killed them. They'll kill me. Not yet. A long, sharp knife lay on the table where the old woman had cut the cheese. Thomas picked it up and put the point against his chest. He pushed a little. The point pierced his shirt. No. He stuck the knife into his belt, and, stepping over the bodies of the old couple, started down toward the road, and thought better of it. Poor dog. He ran back to the house, stepping over the bodies. Inside, he pulled the body of the old man onto its back and pulled off the heavy sheepskin coat he wore. He's dead. The old woman stared at him with dead eyes. He pushed her with his foot, pushed her over onto her side. Look out the door. He grabbed the rest of the cheese and, crouching low, stumbling, ran toward the hills behind the farmhouse. His bandaged feet hurt, but the bandages also protected them from the cold of the snow. He travelled as quickly as he could, stumbling, falling by the track he was following, crawling when he slipped trying to get up sudden rises.

One hour. Two. He drove himself. They're coming to get me. He could hear them. Like the rush of wings. He hid. Nothing. Ran again. Fell. Hid. Where were they? The Finns. Where were they? Man the guns, for god's sake. Joey. Thomas fell. He heard a bird. No. Water. He heard water running. A small stream bubbled out of the hill and then froze in the dip at the bottom. Skating rink. He lay there. The sounds of gunfire reached his ears, but he knew he couldn't be killed. Not now. They had had their chance and they missed. They couldn't have another one. That wasn't fair. You only get one chance. Those are the rules. One chance for everyone. He pulled himself laboriously to the top of the hill to see if anyone was coming. Was he all alone? Where was everyone? Come out. Come out, wherever you are. Just as he reached the top, he heard voices. He dropped to the ground and, by belly-sliding to the edge of the hill, he could see a small group of bedraggled men making their way along a path on the other side of the hill. Who were they? He didn't recognize them, but they were speaking English. He ducked down and something cleared in his mind; he could not join up with them. They'd know. They'd remember. He had murdered someone. They'd tell. He would never be forgiven. Never.

CHAPTER FORTY-FIVE

"Shh. I hear something." Chuck held his hand out flat and the five men left in his group ducked down instinctively. They lay, partly concealed by a clump of bushes at the mouth of a small ravine. The extra rifles, taken from their dead companions, clattered. "Okay, I guess it's nothing." Chuck stood up and shoved his revolver back into his jacket pocket.

They started up the ravine, spread out as much as possible, in some places pushing through drifted snow. They knew they were still ahead of the fascists, but how far ahead was another matter. Anyway, the fascists moved slowly, combing every ravine and gully, ransacking every house, rounding up sheep, and shipping prisoners back along their lines. Any they did not kill or rape, or rape and kill. The top of ravines was a good place to dig in. From a simple earthwork, Chuck's men could survey the other hills and, at the same time, wait for the advancing soldiers sweeping up the ravines, and catch them in a pincer movement from above.

At the top of the ravine, Chuck stopped. "We'll stay here tonight. Bill, Walter, scout out along the hillside there and see if there's anything to see." He threw down his pack. Dare they risk a fire? He spotted a part of the hillside that had fallen away, probably in a spring flood of the little creek that ran through the ravine. "Over there. Keep it small and against the wall of the dirt. It'll take some of the frost out."

Bill and Walter scrambled down to the camp that was being set up. "All clear. They're probably checking every one of those empty cans we left along the road, thinking they're booby traps."

"Okay, we'll set a watch and count on their continuing stupidity. But, first something to eat."

"Not much left."

"It'll have to do. I'll take the first watch. Bill, you take charge here. I've got some cheese in my pocket. You go ahead and eat." Chuck got to his feet and started up the hillside. He stopped almost immediately and motioned again for the men to be quiet. Everyone froze. They waited. Chuck listened and then took a few more steps. Listened. He gave them the high sign, first finger touching tip of thumb, and continued up the slope. The men gathered bits and pieces of wood and lit match after match until they had a small flame.

CHAPTER FORTY-SIX

Slowly Thomas eased himself back and lay on his stomach, thinking. How would they know? Anyway, he had to go to them. He was almost out of food. They were Americans or Canadians. From somewhere. From the war. He heard bursts of gunfire every so often, so there was still a war. Once, a plane had flown over, right over him, low. German cross. What were those men doing here? They were his machine-gun unit. Why weren't they back there, fighting? Cowards. He had told them there was nothing to be afraid of. What were they afraid of? Still, he had to be careful. You can't be too careful, his mother had said. What do you want? his mother had said. Nothing, he had said. That's behind the door, she had said. Thomas crept to the ridge again and watched the group of men disappear around the end of the hill. He followed.

He scrambled along the ridge, half crawling, half running, bent over almost to the ground. It was clear of snow on the ridge. When he got close to the end, he stopped and crawled the rest of the way. A stone gave way under him and clattered down the side of the hill that the group of men had come along a short time before. Thomas flattened himself on the ground and didn't move. Where was Margaret? He felt an impatience. He knew she was close. But where? Had she loosed the stone? He gripped the ground. No, Margaret was dead. This thought came to him, often, recently, since he had left the shepherd's hut. He didn't know where it came from. Just, Margaret is dead. Then, he'd sense her near. Especially at night. He'd wake and stare at the skies and think he felt her beside him, still, not even breathing. How he loved her. She couldn't love him just now, not just yet. She was dead. Later, perhaps. Only at night she was free.

He lay there a long time. When he finally crawled to the edge of the hill and looked down, the men were gone. Thomas sat up. Had he seen them? He was sure he had. But how could they disappear? Everyone was disappearing. Margaret. The old man and woman. The dog. The plane disappeared. But they came back. Sometimes. Unexpectedly. Just like Margaret. It was up to him to do something. Soon. Very soon, or it would be too late.

Thomas eased himself down the slope of the hill, being very careful not to kick any more stones free. He still carried his boots, but the bandages on his feet had worn through and unravelled. He sat down and unwrapped his feet. They didn't hurt as much now. He pulled his socks out of his boots and put them on. Then the boots. He had to struggle to get them on. He laced them up and stretched out his legs. He had to get going.

The day had been a dirty grey and now the growing dark greyed it even more. Thomas stood up and saw in front of him tracks. Tracks of the group of men he had seen? They went down the trail a ways and then off into a small ravine. He stood at the end of the ravine and stared into the trees and brush. He thought he heard sounds in the distance. They were trying to get away from him. The half blown-away face of Tiny flashed across his vision. He looked on the ground for blood, but the snow had been crushed around stalks of grass and twigs. He sighed. He climbed the slope and started to walk along the top of the ravine. Smaller gullies cut into the larger ravine and he sometimes had to walk far out from the edge in order to get around them.

There was no peace. Nowhere to lay his head. He sat on a fallen tree trunk and held his head between his hands. He could hear talking quite clearly now. And the sound of scrapings and muffled clangings. He was lonely. At one time they had let him sit with them, drink wine, talk. He remembered the table. Now, they wanted nothing to do with him. It was Chuck's fault. He had taken them away from him and was leading them to someplace where he, Thomas, would never find them. His men.

Thomas got to his feet. It was no use. He kicked at a clump of snow and started to walk away from the ravine. He'd find Joey. Joey wouldn't desert him. Joey was one man Chuck couldn't take away from him. Like he had taken Margaret. Bitterness swelled up in him. He banged one fist into the palm of the other hand. He took the last piece of bread from the package and stuffed it into his mouth. It was hard and dry. He spit it out. I deserve better. I...I...He began to cry quietly as he walked. It was not fair. He remembered that it was not fair. He came to the edge of another, smaller ravine. There was a depression, a sort of cave, at the end and he scrabbled down and crawled into it. He curled up. It was warm there. He pulled up his coat collar and leaned back. Sighed.

CHAPTER FORTY-SEVEN

Chuck was walking carefully south of the ravine when he spotted Thomas's footprints in a patch of snow. Only one man. The footprints wandered back and forth from side to side. At one point there was a clear impression of a knee where the man had tripped or knelt down. Chuck circled to the east and, crouching low, moved slowly forward. The prints led in the direction of a small gully. Chuck crept up to the edge. Nothing. The prints had just disappeared. Then he saw the small cave, and could make out the form of a man lying with his back to the opening. It must be a brigader. Lost. Chuck slid down carefully and knelt at the opening. The figure did not move. Chuck took his shoulder and pulled him over onto his back.

"Tommy."

Thomas shrank back and shielded his face with his arm. "Don't. Don't kill me."

"For Chrissake, Tommy, I'm not going to kill you. It's me. Chuck. How the hell did you get here?"

"I'm not telling."

"Tommy, what's the matter with you? Here, have some water."

Thomas got to his knees and started to crawl out. "Tommy." Chuck grabbed hold of his coat and tried to help him. Thomas started to fight back, swinging wildly at Chuck. Both men, however, were so exhausted, they could only wrestle briefly to a standstill.

"Tommy," Chuck panted, "Hold it. Stop. It's me. Chuck."

Thomas lay still and then put his arms up and covered his head again and turned his face into the ground. "You killed her."

"Who?"

"I'm not telling."

Chuck leaned back on his heels and looked at the figure of Thomas on the ground. "Okay, Tommy, don't worry. I'll be right back."

"Don't leave me."

"Tommy, we're all going through the same thing. Just stay here and I'll get the boys."

"No. No." Thomas sat abruptly. "No. Not the boys." He grabbed Chuck and kneeled in front of him. "Forgive me. Forgive me."

Chuck took hold of Thomas's hands and slowly and gently removed them from his coat. "Now, now, Tommy. Just tell me what's happened."

Thomas turned his face away. "I can't. You'll hate me."

"I'm not going to hate you, Tommy. Tell me. But hurry. We have to get under cover."

Chuck scrambled up the incline to the ridge. He turned and held out a hand to Thomas. Thomas took a step backwards.

"No. No."

"Come on, Tommy. It's okay." He leant down, took Thomas's hand and pulled him up.

Thomas got to his feet. He became suddenly very agitated, looking frantically this way and that. "Yes. We have to. Hide. We'll hide. That's right." Thomas stopped and looked at Chuck. "Chuck, I killed her."

"Who?"

"Margaret."

Silence.

"I had to, Chuck. She was hurt." Thomas bent down and scrabbled at the ground in front of him. "I buried her."

"She was hurt and you killed her?"

"Yes. I shot her. In the head. No. No." He looked up. "That's not true. You. You're the one that killed her. Aren't you?" He looked pleadingly at Chuck, seeming to will him to agree, to understand. "Then I ran. I ran away."

"From your unit?"

"Yes. That's it. I ran away from my unit. That's all. I didn't really shoot her." Thomas pulled himself upright. "You did. You bastard, you killed her. I saw you."

Chuck looked at Thomas. Perhaps because he was trying to understand what Thomas was telling him, he didn't notice Thomas's swift movement, until he felt the knife cut through his trousers and into his thigh. It was a sharp, thin, farm knife, used for gutting butchered animals. It went in deep and cut through muscle and tendon. Chuck grabbed Thomas's arm, but he was already launching a second attack, this time at Chuck's chest. The knife plunged up in between his ribs and Chuck started forward, then looked at Thomas in amazement. Slowly, he fell forward onto the knife which

Thomas had let go of. As he hit the ground the long blade protruded out the back of his leather jacket.

"Chuck, you shouldn't have..." Thomas reached down and gently patted Chuck's head. "Chuck? I didn't mean to, Chuck." Chuck lay still. Thomas stood up. He looked around and breathed in deeply. They were so close to Chuck's men, he could hear their voices. "Chuck, you know you're not really dead, don't you? It's just a game. It's just a game. Margaret is still alive. I know. Actually, I don't think – this I can't quite remember, Chuck – but I don't think she came to Spain. Least, I haven't heard about her being here. And you and I, we're going to go home now, aren't we? Come on. Let's go. My mother and father will be worried about us. Come on, let's go. Get up. Come on, get up. Get up." Thomas tried to lift Chuck's shoulders off the ground. "Well, if you won't come, I don't know what I'm going to do." Thomas squatted down on his haunches and looked intensely at Chuck's back. He reached out and fingered the tip of the knife. "Let me turn you over so you can see the stars." He rolled Chuck's body over. "There, that's better." The knife cut sideways as the weight of the body shifted the blade over. Blood bubbled out of Chuck's mouth. Thomas pulled the cloth from his pocket that had held the cheese and bread, and tried to stop the bleeding.

Quite a ways to the left of the hill they were on, he heard the sound of voices calling quietly for Chuck. He listened and thought about Mrs. Ryan's café. If only...The voices came closer. Thomas looked around and then opened Chuck's jacket. He frantically searched through the pockets. There were only some papers and Chuck's International Brigade passport. A few pesetas. Thomas stuffed the money into his jacket pocket. He sat back on his haunches and looked at Chuck's passport lying beside his body. He picked it up, took out the passport he had taken from the dead man at the train and put Chuck's into his own pocket. He crawled back to the ravine with the dead man's passport. Leaning over the edge, he threw it into the small cave where he had hidden. He went back and, propping up Chuck's body with his foot, pulled the knife out. He wiped it carefully on Chuck's trousers.

"I'll get the ambulance. Don't worry. I'll just be a minute."

Thomas stood up and threw the knife as far as he could down the gully of the ravine. Then, he crouched down, making himself as inconspicuous as possible, and scrabbled down into the gully and away from the voices, away from Chuck.

CHAPTER FORTY-EIGHT

In a little over two weeks, Clara was well enough to move around the ward, and the doctor told Sidney that she could be taken back to Canada. If they travelled first class and if they took it very easy. Did Sidney know her doctor in Canada? Yes. He should be notified.

"How would you like to go home, Clara?"

Clara stared at him.

"Clara, how would you like to go home?"

"I heard you, Sidney. I don't know. I'm thinking about it. I don't know if I want to go home."

"I don't believe this. You don't know if you want to go home? You're thinking about it?"

"Sometimes, Siddie, you just parrot what I say."

"Clara, I spoke with the doctor and he said you could be released."

"Men. You spoke with the doctor. And he spoke with you because you are a man too, and this poor little woman couldn't make up her mind for herself."

"It wasn't that way." Sidney smiled in spite of himself. It was good to see that she was feeling well again.

"Then what are you smiling at?"

"I was just pleased with the thought of taking you home, that's all."

Clara was silent. She shifted her weight on the hard hospital bed. "I still haven't seen Teruel."

"Clara. You're not serious."

"I've come all this way. One more place wouldn't hurt."

"What's at Teruel?"

"Nothing. Nothing, Sidney. Nothing. I still don't know what happened there, but some day I would like to see it. But, now, I think, I think..."

"That's enough thinking. Come on, let's just go home." Sidney bent over and kissed her on the cheek.

Clara looked at him thoughtfully and then smiled, "Well, I guess it would be better than having to put up with this mattress."

Clara settled back in the wheelchair and let the Air Canada attendant roll her onto the plane. Sidney followed, toting the cabin bags and whistling under his breath. It was a glorious day and even Heathrow Airport looked sparkling bright. They were going home.

"Sidney, first class. You are a dear." Clara let the attendant and Sidney help her into the seat.

"You can lean it back afterward and put your foot up."

"God, what a trip this has been! I'll be glad to be home. Away from all this."

"Do you really mean that? Or will you regret that you didn't get to go to Spain and ferret out something more about this Thomas Pennan?"

"No, Sidney. I'm finished with all that. I don't think I need to know anything more about this Thomas Pennan, as you call him. I think I know him very well. Perhaps the details are not important, but I know who he was. He lived with an awful secret, maybe more than one. He must have been haunted. Perhaps, he just needed to be forgiven. And, whether he knew it or not, he was loved, and that's all any of us can hope for. No, Sidney, I'm satisfied."

"That, I never thought I would hear. Well, then I have something that maybe as a basically satisfied woman you might consider."

"This sounds dangerous."

"Well, maybe, but let me ask you a question, Clara. Have you thought about marriage, I mean remarrying?"

"I've thought a lot about marriage recently, Sidney, a lot. And about commitment and dependency and losing your life in someone else's."

"That all sounds rather negative."

"Well, it's negative in one way. In another, it's not. Anyway, marriage is just in your head. It doesn't really exist. I mean, you can't locate it anywhere, can you? It's just a thought."

"I don't know what you mean," Sidney motioned to the flight attendant and pointed to the pile of blankets she was carrying.

"I really meant, well, marrying me."

"You believe something and it's true. Then, you find out it's not true, and really nothing has changed. In reality, I mean. It doesn't matter what you believe."

"I think I'm following you, but does this mean that you will marry me? Or that you won't? I mean, given that it is only a thought."

"No, you're not following me, Siddie, but it doesn't matter." The flight attendant opened a blanket and spread it over Clara's legs.

"Clara, I did ask you a question."

"It doesn't matter anymore." Clara turned her face to the window. The plane was moving slowly out to its runway.

"What doesn't matter? I know it takes time to get over losing your husband, but I was hoping..."

"Maybe it takes less time when you were never married to him."

ACKNOWLEDGEMENTS

There are a number of people and institutions I would like to thank for their support and assistance in writing this novel. I shall mention the following, but there are others, many others, to whom I am also grateful: The staff of the Provincial Archives of Saskatchewan and especially the late Lloyd Rodwell and Doug Bocking, who first directed me to the hundreds of pages of the Royal Commission on the Regina Riot. The staff of the Regina Public Library gave me access to their holdings from the 1930s. At the archives of The Thomas Fisher Library, University of Toronto, I was able to read the personal memoirs of men who had served in Spain during the civil war there. The Royal Canadian Mounted Police Museum in Regina needs to be singled out both because of the exhibition there dedicated to the riot, and its appearance in the story. Lisa Olson took time to go around Regina and photograph key places for me. Thank you. The newspaper files at the Metropolitan Library of Toronto were made available to me, and the staff were helpful in giving me leads to additional materials. A friend in Paris, Evelyne Poret, responded to my requests for help and did research into the situation in Paris in the 1930s. A special thanks has to go to Alfonso Casa Ologaray of Teruel, Spain, who not only gave me access to his remarkable collection of papers and artifacts related to the events that unfolded in that city during the Spanish Civil War, but also took me to the battlefields which lie almost undisturbed near Teruel. And special thanks also to Michael Harris for his invitation to spend a weekend at his country house in Fifehead Neville. During the many times of self-doubt and hesitation, my wife, June Clark, was unfailingly generous with her support and enthusiasm. Also, I wish to thank my immediate family, who read and commented on various drafts. Without the professional expertise of the publisher, editor, and and staff of Coteau Books, I would have missed many points of possible improvement. And last, but far from least, I want to recognize my parents and siblings who told me, when I was a child, stories of the events of national and international importance that shook the little city of Regina in the 1930s.

ABOUT THE AUTHOR

Terrence Heath is the author or co-author of eight other books, including a novel *(The Last Hiding Place)*, a short story collection *(The Truth and Other Stories)*, poetry *(Interstices of Night)*, and a biography *(Uprooted: The Art and Life of Ernest Lindner)*. His notable collaborations with Saskatoon poet Anne Szumigalski include *Wild Man's Butte* and *Journey/Journée*. He has also created numerous exhibition catalogues in his profession as a curator and consultant in the visual arts. Born in Regina, he has lived in Saskatoon, Winnipeg, and, for the past twenty years, in Toronto.